Mourning Doves After the Fire

Mourning Doves After the Fire

November
2012

A Novel

For my friend Octavio M.,
Best wishes xoxo

Charles D. Blanchard

Library of Congress Control Number: 2010913926
ISBN: Hardcover 978-1-4535-7785-1
Softcover 978-1-4535-7784-4
Ebook 978-1-4535-7786-8

This is a work of fiction. Names, characters, places and incidents either are the product of the author's imagination or are used fictitiously, and any resemblance to any actual persons, living or dead, events, or locales is entirely coincidental.

This book was printed in the United States of America.

To order additional copies of this book, contact:
Xlibris Corporation
1-888-795-4274
www.Xlibris.com
Orders@Xlibris.com
79105

Chapter 1

Pennsylvania 1910. It was a February morning. Abigail Whitman blew a fine mist of morning breath on her bedroom window. When she was younger and life held its promise of good fortune, she often drew happy smiles and butterflies on the moistened glass before her artwork evaporated into nothing. That was then. Abigail was now twenty-eight. The fanciful life she read about and dreamed of was only to be found in books and picture postcards at the local drugstore. She could no longer waste time on imagined hopes that were not to be. She wiped the window to the sight of fresh snow. The morning sun showed an immaculate pallor of white surrounding the land around her house.

With this image of pureness, Abigail encountered a new day of varied drunken things called opportunities that were not hers for the taking as they would never materialize into anything special. She sat in front of the tabletop mirror quietly brushing her long brown hair. Her hair was very long indeed, about knee length, when she didn't have it all bound up when going to town. At home, she kept it free, and it swayed back and forth when she moved about. She brushed effortlessly until she noticed a couple of gray hairs gleaming in the sun. She plucked the strands, looked at them, and tossed them in the baseburner. She remembered her aunt, Ruth, who was entirely gray at thirty. Resuming her strokes, Abigail wondered what it was like to grow old. On her bed was the blue dress she would wear that day, if her mother would get around to sewing up the small patch where gypsy moths had attacked the previous fall.

Across the white picket fence, she saw the towering centuries-old oak tree that reached nearly seventy feet high and separated her house from her neighbors, the Kramers. In the summer, Abigail spent many late afternoons sitting beneath its massive trunk that had grown to nearly fifteen feet in circumference. Now the tree had a coating of snow on its menacing limbs. From her window, Abigail could see the two Kramer brothers in their backyard shed. Michael, the elder, was seventeen and just shy of six feet. He towered over the cluster of wood he chopped, some of which was for Abigail and her mother. Michael Kramer was now the head of his family. His father died three years earlier in a fire that burned down their mercantile store. Michael had to quit school and now was earning a living in a lumber camp. He also took care of his mother, Virginia who remained homebound since the tragedy and would not venture outside. Eric, the younger brother, was twelve and seemed always to be wherever Michael was.

Michael chopped the pieces of wood, and Eric divided them for themselves and for the Whitmans into two piles. The Whitman pile was heaped in a wheel cart ready to be delivered next door.

Back at the Whitman house, Margaret Whitman who was called Maggie came in with a tray of hot tea for her daughter and cursed the heavens for spilling the cup of milk in the hall.

"I'm not crazy for tea this morning," Abby said. She preferred Abby to Abigail.

"You drink it," Maggie said firmly. "It'll help take the chill out until Michael comes with more wood." Maggie set the tray on the tabletop and took the napkin to wipe the spilled milk. Abby stopped brushing her hair and turned to face her mother who looked more exhausted each time she saw her. Her mother had single-handedly raised her and managed the household affairs until Abby grew up to help in the struggle to survive another day. Abby was not moved by her mother at all. She didn't know whether she even liked her or not. Chores were assigned around the house, and each woman knew her place within the rigidity of their work habits. Maggie was also a part-time seamstress who mended other people's clothes when they brought them over to the house. Abby was a secretary for the Corrigan Typewriter Company.

Abby took a cup of tea reluctantly but added a teaspoon of sugar that made it drinkable even without the milk. Her mother looked out of the window onto the Kramer property. The curtains on Mrs. Kramer's bedroom window were always closed.

"That poor woman," Maggie said. "She won't answer the door, scared to death of everyone."

"Forget about her," Abby said. "She was never all that pleasant when she had the store."

"Don't talk bad about someone who's in a bad way," Maggie said, although she couldn't deny that Abby had a point. Maggie knew Virginia Kramer's condescending manner when she shopped at their store. Now that the store burned down, Maggie couldn't remember the last time she saw her.

"Do you think you'll be able to get this dress fixed this morning?" Abby asked. "I'm hoping to catch the eight o'clock into town."

"It's too cold to be heading out," Maggie replied. "Wear the red dress for now. I'll mend the blue one tonight. Where are you going?"

"Just going out to get some air," Abby said, deliberately vague. She didn't say where she was going. She had an appointment with the doctor and didn't want her mother to know.

Maggie controlled her intuition where Abby was concerned and didn't delve into matters when common sense suggested otherwise. If Abby needed to catch the eight o'clock car, just to take in the air, that was her business. Abby was after all, of age, well over.

Michael Kramer knocked at the door. The women recognized his soft knock, so inviting and friendly. *As dependable as ever,* Maggie thought, and she went downstairs to greet him.

"I left the wood in a pile by the back porch for you," Michael said. Maggie invited him inside for coffee. But he politely declined since he had to get to his job at the lumber camp. She had watched the two brothers grow. Michael was handsome enough that it was a challenge not to notice. If she were young enough to have a son, she hoped he would be just like him.

The rush of the day was upon Michael, thrust in the position as head of the household. But he always had time to ask about Abby which he did on that visit. He had always been fond of her ever since they went to school together as kids. Abby used to play the piano for him after school. And he grew to love her but was not able to tell her, for he lacked that ability to say his true feelings. When she felt up to it, Abby played the upright piano in the corner of the sitting room, on top of which she organized her favorite pieces of music: Bach's fugues, Beethoven, and Chopin. When she played, it was an invaluable moment she treasured as challenging as the piece she was playing. Maggie told Michael that her daughter was well, and she handed Michael a cold metal container of fresh-churned butter.

"Do you think your mother would mind if I brought over a couple of loaves?" she asked.

"That's up to you, Maggie. I know my mother isn't the easiest person in the world to get along with. I'm sure she'll appreciate it."

Michael gladly accepted the butter and left for work. He did not let on that it was best not to bother his mother. But to himself, he thought perhaps it would be all right.

Maggie shoveled snow for about an hour outside while Abby removed two large bowls of risen dough and three jars of sour milk from the icebox and placed them on the countertop. She went downstairs to the cold cellar where she retrieved another three jars of sour milk. In the kitchen, she poured all the milk into a three-gallon metal churner with a hand crank. Abby changed into the red dress, and passing her mother outside announced her departure and said everything was ready in the kitchen.

After Abby left to see the doctor, Maggie kneaded the dough, shaped it into three loaves, and baked them for two hours. When she finished sweeping the kitchen and sitting room, she cranked the churner on and off for three hours until fresh butter was made. The house was soon perfumed with the smell of fresh-baked bread.

Maggie Whitman was a powerful woman whose fantastic-sized hands never rested. She mended the blue dress for her daughter that morning and sewed the remaining garments for her customers. Later in the afternoon, she hitched up the wagon to go into town to sell her butter and bread. If only her chickens would lay regularly instead of the two eggs that morning, she would be grateful.

There was no Mr. Whitman to speak of. Abby's father left when she was an infant so she never knew him. There were no pictures of him in the house to indicate that he had ever existed. Over the years, Abby would ask her mother about him. Maggie brushed the subject off like an annoying bug. As far as she was concerned, he cheated her out of her share in the joint concerns of life. Tobacco and beer were his keep. Soon Abby stopped asking questions as the years passed, and the memory faded into the past.

Abby quickened her pace along the snow-covered roads. The depot and the streetcar were just ahead. She tightened her coat to keep out the cold and lifted her dress to keep it from getting wet from the snow. Then as if the devil had decided to make her the brunt of his daily torments, he sent along Henry Corrigan to bar her path. Henry was the son of the man she worked for at the typewriter company, and he also worked there as a salesman who sold very little. He was a few years younger than she was. Over the years, his subtle advances for her affection never met with success, but he was not one to give up so easily. Abby was in a great hurry and of all the people in the town, she had to run into him.

"Morning, Abby."

"Henry," she said coldly, not looking at him but at the streetcar approaching her stop. She bounced along toward it. Henry just followed her like an excited dog.

"If you'll permit me?" he said, raising his long hand to carry her bag. Abby ignored the gesture and just kept going.

"My father's been asking for you. You didn't come to work for two days."

"I called in sick," she said.

"Are you heading out to see the doctor? You know how lucky you are to have a job?"

Unbelievable. How did he know where she was going? He couldn't have been so presumptuous as to follow her. Abby knew his condescending arrogance was part of his character, but this was out of line. The sight of his red face and soulless eyes angered Abby and triggered an unfortunate response.

"Stop using your father to get at me this way," she said. "I'm not his property or yours just because I work for him."

Henry's anger was slow in rising but very evident. Abby knew she made a mistake with that remark. He might even tell his father what she said. Henry knew she didn't like him. Even when he was in the office, she would ignore him. But a casual encounter on the street was different. He would get back at her by engulfing her with his presence just to piss her off. Abby remembered hearing of Henry's pranks in school. Once he wrote a fake love letter to their teacher, Mrs. Haversham, who was a relic at the age of fifty. In this unsigned letter, she recognized his sloppy handwriting as he revealed his amorous desires and requested to meet her face-to-face. Following his instructions, she left her response in a note by a well, saying she would meet him there at a certain day and time. On the day of discovery, she had the principal of the school secretly follow her to the well, and they waited and waited behind a tree until they were tired and decided to leave when Henry finally showed his face and he received the surprise of his life, plus one-month detention. He stopped writing those letters.

"When will you be back at the office so I can tell my father?" he asked Abby.

"Tomorrow."

Abby turned away from Henry and waved to the conductor as the streetcar stopped. She knew this conductor for years and disliked him for years as he was not the most accommodating when it came to waiting around for last minute hop-ons. But when he smiled at her for the very first time that morning, Abby was convinced that perhaps on this day he was visited by the spirit of St. Monica, a patron saint, whom Abby prayed to on occasion. Monica was a model of patience at having herself endured a quick-tempered husband and cantankerous mother-in law. Abby smiled back. She placed her money in the farebox and got on board.

Henry's longing eyes watched Abby board the car. She possessed a persuasive charm that was second to none in his eyes. Henry Corrigan was unaware of what kindness was all about. His father, William, was preoccupied with running the typewriter company. His mother, Henrietta, ignored him. He only saw the immediateness of his surroundings and found he could not grasp a way to make his life better. He also realized he had better get to the office and spend some time helping his father before he was kicked out of the house for good.

The streetcar bell rang three times and off they went through the familiar sights of oak and pine houses, in their simplistic and dignified creation, pleasantly dispersed while overhead a sea of telephone poles carried the sound of rushed voices laughing and crying. Abby scanned the crowd, nodding to former playmates from her carefree childhood days that had drifted away so long ago. Riding in the streetcar there remained the casual exchange of friendly glances as the years kept consuming a bit more of their lives. For many of them whose grand plans for the future were an ancient memory, they gradually accepted and even regretted their existence into what had become an increasingly indifferent and changing world.

Abby was no different from anyone of them in this regard. But her world was indeed soon to change on this trip, for it would not be just a routine physical checkup.

Chapter 2

The streetcar stopped at the entrance to the doctor's two-story brick house. Abby got out and stood at the rusted mailbox that bore the name Dr. Raymond Fletcher. The red flag on the mailbox was up, and she decided to bring his mail in to him. There was a single envelope.

She didn't realize that the doctor was watching her from his upstairs bedroom window while he dressed. The street where the doctor had chosen to locate his office was unfrequented for the most part yet near enough to the populated town to be of convenience to his patients, and that's the way he wanted it. This town welcomed him as a member of the family, and he was there to fulfill a common purpose—to help those in time of need. To this goal, he dedicated himself. The doctor was preparing himself as if he were going on a date—plenty of talcum powder, just a hint of cologne, and all the nervousness and excitement that came with meeting someone whose company he had grown to enjoy. Abby let herself in. Her arrival was marked by Stanley, a friendly Labrador retriever. Recognizing her as a previous visitor, he let out a couple of barks and wagged his tail in acceptance. She petted the dog in mutual affection.

"Abby, make yourself comfortable. I won't be a moment." His voice traveled down the stairs and fell around her.

Abby went across the hall, accompanied by Stanley, into the waiting room where a beautifully ornate area rug of rich gold, red, and tea-colored floral design evoked a history of belonging in a castle somewhere centuries ago rather than its present surroundings. The doctor had taste, and she appreciated it. Abby felt the protection and self-assuredness that comes from being in a well-decorated room where live plants adorned the corners and handsome-framed photographs of outdoor landscapes hung on warm tan-colored wallpaper—a homey and professional manifestation of the great male doctor.

She wondered who did the decorating since Dr. Fletcher was not married, and to her knowledge, he was never seen with a companion. There were no other patients in the room, so she removed her coat and anxiously waited for him. She recalled the room and the house. It had been about a year since her last physical examination, and it was well time.

Upstairs, where the doctor lived, was a different matter. There were areas not yet introduced to a dustpan, and things were tossed about. But that did not matter much since no one ever went up there except he and Stanley who never complained. One of the objectives as he grew into his profession was to avoid bad habits that could become a hindrance as he made a name for himself. Not being able to tidy properly was Raymond Fletcher's bad habit. It was something he would work on if he had the time or the inclination. He fumbled around for a tie and knocked over a glass of water.

Raymond Fletcher's reputation was solid. Goodness and fairness in his chosen profession was what mattered, not that he was a helpless creature when it came to housekeeping. It was his New Year's resolution that he would clean up his living quarters. He just didn't have the time.

Abby was not just any other patient, and his influence beyond the deliverance of medicine, beyond the position as one who came into her life five years earlier, was not just as a doctor but as a friend.

He came down the stairs. Raymond Fletcher was a tall man, thirty years old. He wore a full dark blue suit and a light blue shirt. Never for an instant forgetting himself as a public servant where manners of appearance and personal conduct were scrutinized daily, he always made sure he was dressed properly. He remembered Abby played the piano. He went into the parlor and selected a Chopin record that he played on his Victrola. It was a soothing element to have music playing while conducting an examination.

The fiery first movement emerged. Abby recognized the piece as Chopin's Piano Sonata no. 2. Raymond walked into the waiting room and saw a ravishing figure in that red dress. Abby stood up and smiled.

"I'm sorry I kept you waiting," he said.

Abby felt his eyes observing her. She stood up and gave him the letter she had retrieved from his mailbox. He looked at it and saw it was from his mother. He thanked her for the kind gesture. He took her coat and folded it over his arm, and they walked out of the waiting room. Abby, with a hint of nervous laughter, coughed a couple of times, and he detected this as a significant disruption of the flow of things but did not let on how significant it was to him. He knew by the cough something was wrong with her. They walked toward the examination room and exchanged pleasantries as befitting two casual acquaintances.

"How's your mother?"

"She's the same, always worrying about the upkeep of the house. She asks for you."

That was a lie.

She didn't say how Maggie disapproved of the doctor as she never once saw him attend church services. They passed by the family room where an inviting log fire blazed away in the fireplace. Abby would have liked nothing better than to sit by the fire naked, sipping tea with the doctor lying beside her.

"Do you still play the piano?" he asked.

"Yes. It helps pass the time at night. Sometimes, Momma gets upset when I play late in the evening."

There were two examination rooms. Raymond led Abby into the larger room where behind the partition she removed her garments and slipped into a white robe. Meanwhile the first movement ended, and he excused himself to change the record. The calm second movement, the scherzo began. Raymond placed his mother's letter in his office while Abby sat on the examination table waiting. A stethoscope, a reflex hammer, and a blood pressure cuff were on the desk.

He came into the room. She looked like an angel, wrapped in that large white robe, that covered everything except her face, and those large oval eyes were staring back at him. He saw her long hair wrapped up in a bun. He would have liked to see it cascading all over him. She smiled. She turned away. He realized he was making her uncomfortable, so he became uncomfortable and moved toward the table beside her. He placed his stethoscope around his neck. Abby picked up the trumpet end. It aroused him slightly. These thoughts were going to overcome his ability to perform his duty as Abby's doctor. He must concentrate on his work and get rid of such trivial thoughts—lustful, self-serving, and debilitating they were. He asked her how she had been feeling.

"Every now and then it hurts here."

"Whereabouts exactly?"

Abby pointed to the left side of her neck.

"Do you feel any pain when I press down on it?"

"No. My neck gets so swollen sometimes."

"Hard to swallow?"

"No."

The doctor gently placed his hand over her neck, and as she spoke he felt the thyroid was not normal. "Have you had a cold recently?"

"No."

"Headaches?"

"Sometimes."

He checked under her armpits and felt some swelling.

"Does it hurt when I squeeze?"

"No."

He asked her how long she had these symptoms. She said about two weeks. His breath was warm and pleasant. She channeled her own strength and desires as she answered his questions. He felt her head. It was a little warm. He took her temperature. It was a little high but not abnormal. These symptoms led Raymond to the alertness that her condition might be more than just a cold. The word "consumption" came into his mind. He pressed the stethoscope against her chest. He asked her to breathe in and out several times. She was congestive but only slightly. He asked her to cough. He asked her what she felt when she coughed. She told him she felt a slight burning sensation in the chest. What she didn't say was that the previous holidays held no interest for her, and she found it hard to get up in the morning. Her mother had to wake her up so she wouldn't be late for work at the office. She also didn't mention that she looked forward to going to bed by 8:00 p.m. She never went to bed so early. Her vitality was still there when it came to playing the piano, but that didn't change the fact that something of which she apparently had no control over was making her more tired than usual. Raymond produced a needle.

"Where are you going with that?" she asked in panic.

"Abby, I need to get a small blood sample from the area in your neck where you are having the discomfort."

"Trust me. It will be quick. Just think of something pleasant." He aimed for her neck. She did trust him even with her life. But she also knew that the only reason to draw blood is to look for something evil. She attempted to relax. He could feel her quivering as the needle went into her. It wasn't as fast as she thought. He was wiggling the needle around to get enough cells. Whatever the result of the diagnosis, she knew she was in good hands. She hoped there might be something slightly wrong with her so she could pay him another visit. She would not allow herself to become the indifferent object of scrutiny of an impersonal place like a hospital if she could avoid it. She preferred the personal commitment of this fine doctor. This was her pleasant thought. The examination was over. Raymond took a cotton pad and placed it on Abby's neck. He took her hand and held it up to her neck.

"Just press gently for about a minute," he said. He placed a small bandage on her neck and told her to get changed.

While Abby changed, Raymond took the needle into his office. On the worktable, there was a microscope, some vials, and various books and papers.

The record stopped playing, and there was a solemn mood in the house. The music had an effect on the examination. It made it so pleasant. When it stopped, something was missing, abandoned, and buried away in the silence.

He closed the door, sat down, and injected a sample of Abby's blood and placed it between two thin glass plates. He put the plate under the microscope and looked through the lens. Abby walked out of the examination room to the Victrola and removed the Chopin record. Stanley made his way to her, and she greeted him as if he was her own. She felt a part of the place and of this man. She felt a freedom she hadn't known before and took the liberty of looking through his record albums for another record to play when he called her into his office.

She went into his office and saw his framed diplomas and his excellent library behind his desk which took over the entire wall. When she noticed that he averted looking directly at her, she knew something was wrong.

"Sit, please," he said without the casual friendliness.

He went behind his desk while Abby sat in the guest chair in front of him. He looked at his folder on the desk, and he looked into Abby's eyes. She saw that he was uncomfortable so Abby asked him outright.

"Do I have consumption?"

He shook his head. "It's not consumption."

Raymond told her he found traces of cancer cells. It was best to send the blood sample to the laboratory at Pennsylvania Hospital to confirm his diagnosis.

"Let me explain what the word *cancer* means and perhaps that might alleviate some of the concern," he said. Abby was in no mood for a clinical definition of the most feared word in the English language, not even from Raymond Fletcher.

"When cells in our bodies grow and multiply aggressively, it can lead to the cells invading or consuming whatever area of the body they happen to be located in. They call that carcinoma or cancer."

"And I have it?" she asked.

"From the sample I took from your neck, I do see evidence of abnormal cell growth, yes."

"How serious is my condition?" She was direct and knew he would not beat around the bush.

"I don't know. But I want you to go to Pennsylvania Hospital to have X-rays taken of your entire body. I want to make sure there aren't any other areas we should be concerned about."

"I don't like hospitals."

"There's no need to worry. It's the country's first hospital, one of the best, founded by Benjamin Franklin himself," he stated.

"I've never had an X-ray taken. Does it hurt?"

Raymond smiled. "Not at all. They lay you on a large table and take your picture. Just like having a photograph taken only it's your insides that we need to see."

"Can't you do it?"

"I don't have an X-ray machine here. It's important that you do this, Abby, the sooner the better. It'll take the entire day. You decide when, and I'll wire the hospital to expect you."

"Tomorrow," Abby said. Raymond approved.

"When will you get the results from my blood test?"

"I will send them today. It should take about three days. I should have them at the same time as the X-rays."

He looked over his calendar and a time was selected for Abby's second visit, the following week.

"Would you like me to inform your mother?"

"No, thank you," Abby replied. "I'll tell her myself."

He nodded. Raymond Fletcher would employ his own knowledge to grapple with Abby's illness. He knew Abby's diagnosis would have an effect on him personally as well as professionally. He could not afford to compromise his ethical duties and moral beliefs for the sake of his own personal feelings.

The streetcar was approaching. At the front door, he took hold of her hands and told her not too worry. She was ready to place her life in his hands.

Later that night, Raymond opened the letter that Abby had brought to him. It was from his mother who had written saying that his father was very ill having suffered a heart attack, and his glaucoma left him totally blind. She hoped he would be able to come soon. This letter allowed his past to resurface and reminded him once again that everyone including himself suppressed a secret in their past that they never parted with over time.

The present dwindled to recollections of the past. He remembered as a boy when his younger brother was dying of pneumonia. His brother was lying in bed with several of his stuffed animal friends with large soulful eyes that looked as if they were alive themselves. His little brother told Raymond he wanted his stuffed animals buried with him. Raymond asked his brother if he was ready to go to God. His brother was too weak to speak so he nodded. When his brother died, the relationship with the father had died also as he knew his younger brother was the favored one.

Raymond placed the letter on top of the other pile of letters that he would get to at another time. He was not ready to see his father just yet.

It was six o'clock. Raymond usually liked to imbibe at this hour after a long day of seeing patients. He unlocked the liquor cabinet and reached for a bottle of Dewar's White Label Scotch. Stanley made it known to Raymond that he needed to go out. Raymond didn't sleep at all that night. Abby did not sleep all night. She did not mention to her mother about what the doctor found in her blood sample.

Abby called in sick again that morning. William Corrigan was not pleased about her being out again. He wondered what was going on with her. He thought he might have to fire her if it continued, but for now he kept those thoughts to himself. She didn't tell her mother that she was spending the day at the hospital. So Maggie thought she was at work at the office. Abby went to the bank to withdraw the money for the early morning train to the city. She had the X-rays taken at the hospital.

The blood test and X-rays arrived and confirmed that Abby did have a cancer. It appeared to be localized in her neck, and it had metastasized in the lymph nodes in her right armpit.

Raymond wasted no time. He searched the records at Pennsylvania Hospital for any case involving the eradication of cancer. After many hours, he came upon the papers of Dr. Viraj Chandrapore.

Dr. Chandrapore experimented with a bacterial vaccine he injected directly into the cancer of his patients where cancer was localized in the body. The purpose was to deliberately produce an infection that would provoke the immune system to attack not only the infection, but also the cancer itself. Raymond read the file of a young man of twenty-two, terminally ill and bedridden with an abdominal tumor that was found to be cancerous and inoperable due to the proximity to the underlying bones. The tumor progressed, and the young man was deemed a hopeless case. He was given morphine to dull the pain.

As an experiment, Dr. Chandrapore, plunged a syringe of infectious bacteria directly into the tumor mass. He did this over a period of three months, twice a week. The intent was to stimulate the immune system to attack the bacteria as well as the tumor that had been injected, thereby destroying the tumor itself. The challenge was to induce the symptoms of an infection to make the immune system respond. The first five injections failed to produce the symptoms needed to simulate an infection—chills, nausea, and a high fever. But Dr. Chandrapore persevered. Finally, after three months, the young man developed a high fever. He vomited, and his temperature was 105 degrees. The attack lasted for one week. By the time it subsided, the tumor began to shrink, and finally it dissolved completely. This extraordinary effort was not in vain. The patient had no trace of cancer and was up and about within two weeks after the tumor disappeared—a miraculous recovery from certain death. Dr. Chandrapore alleged that somehow the infection was responsible for having cured the young man. Raymond read the report several times. Once finished, he asked the clerk if there were any other files on this Dr. Chandrapore, to whom he had taken a sudden fascination. The clerk researched the library index and found other files on the doctor. Raymond spent the day in the library reading the experiments of this courageous and inventive colleague and found that the success he achieved was by no means limited to tumor type cancer. Dr. Chandrapore was using the toxins for sarcomas, lymphomas, melanomas, and myelomas, all with varying degrees of success and failure. That is what Raymond needed for Abby—to harness the power of her immune system to her benefit. Raymond asked the clerk where he could find Dr. Chandrapore at once.

Raymond sent a telegram to the doctor at his residence in New York City. He explained Abby's condition and if there was a possibility that he could see him in New York. Chandrapore replied that he received many telegrams from doctors all over the country regarding his cancer treatments, the number of cases he proudly mentioned as around three hundred. Chandrapore mentioned he was no longer practicing but was always available to speak with a fellow colleague. Raymond booked a seat on the first available train to New York and canceled his appointments for the next three days.

When he arrived at Dr. Chandrapore's apartment, Raymond felt like he was at the start of a long journey. He had second thoughts about the trip while on the way to the train station, while sitting in his compartment, and still when riding in the coach over to the doctor's apartment. He did have concerns that if it were exposed that he sought a consultation with a professional colleague, that it would leave an impression of incompetence on his part to meet the urgency himself. Raymond never claimed to know it all. What doctor could? There would always be moments when he looked to his colleagues, be they miles away, for consultation. Would the doctor be of the disposition to invoke all of the necessary information about his toxins that were needed for Abby to have a successful treatment? Would Chandrapore add to his efforts in curing Abby by imparting his knowledge and skill? Would there be harmony between himself and the doctor? He hoped. He knocked. The door opened.

Chapter 3

The man who appeared at the door was small with a mane of thick graying hair that accentuated his dark skin to the point that he was rather imposing despite his short stature. His dark eyes under his spectacles could bring back the dead with one look.

"Dr. Chandrapore, I'm Dr. Fletcher." Chandrapore bowed his head.

"Come in please. My bird is sick."

"Should I come another time?"

"No, of course not. You made the trip. By all means, come in. The hallway is cold." Chandrapore looked frail. His wrinkled host jacket and pants seemed too big for him.

Inside the apartment, the foyer was lit by several candles placed on two hall tables on either side of the foyer. It provided a comfortable orange hue like a sunset.

"Please. You can hang your coat here and your shoes also," he said, pointing to the hall closet. Chandrapore had a syringe in his hand and showed Raymond into the living room.

First impressions are never really what they seem. In that instant when two strangers meet, the thoughts of what questions to ask and how to approach are momentarily put on hold until the passage of time can allow things to take their proper course. The telegrams provided a link between the two men. Now that they have met, the bond that Raymond hoped existed would be put to the test. Raymond hoped that this doctor would find not only a solution to Abby's illness, but also contribute to Raymond's understanding of himself. Raymond drifted after him into the living room. Speechless. He looked around. A roaring fire in the fireplace made the apartment very warm. The walls were painted deep red, and the windows were draped in equally impressive tones. There were low wooden three-legged stools, handcarved chairs, and a sofa. Paintings adorned the walls everywhere. The north wall had paintings of the ocean; the east wall contained paintings of sunsets. The south and west walls had paintings of mountains, deep valleys, and animal life—horses and elephants. Plants adorned the corners of the room. Its effect brought images of an ancient time where a nobleman lying on a couch could do nothing but think how his every wish could be granted as he was fed grapes by a servant. Raymond felt easily serene within this symphony of color like no other place he had been before.

Chandrapore walked over to a birdcage, depressed at the sight of a yellow—feathered parakeet at the bottom of the towel-covered cage, its head down and breathing heavily.

"This morning she was fit as a fiddle." Chandrapore said. "She was eating and singing. Now I must feed her myself."

He thought about letting Raymond assist in the delicate matter of administering to his sick bird.

"Would you help me?" he asked.

"Of course, what can I do?" Chandrapore handed the syringe to Raymond. He opened the cage door and carefully took the bird into his hands.

"Dr. Fletcher if you please, I will open her beak and if you would place the needle gently in her beak."

Chandrapore gently extended the bird's neck. The bird bit his finger and wouldn't let go. Finally, the doctor placed his mouth over the bird's head pretending to bite the bird himself. The bird released her painful grip on Chandrapore's bleeding finger.

"Strong little devil. She hasn't the strength to eat, but she can still bite something fierce," Chandrapore joked. His tired eyes, so pained were all-knowing, all seeing, and all feeling, and as he looked down at his dying companion, he realized that there wasn't much hope. Fletcher slid the needle into her beak.

"Now inject twice. When you see her tongue move, she has had enough."

"What is in the needle?" asked Raymond.

"Water and a teaspoon of honey."

Once the bird had swallowed her dosage, Raymond removed the syringe. Chandrapore massaged her back and returned her to the cage, where she rested.

"There now. She will rest for the night." Chandrapore placed his handkerchief on his bleeding finger. Raymond loosened his tie.

"I'm sorry is so warm in here," Chandrapore said, noticing his guest's discomfort. "I assure you it's not to remind me of the scorching summers in India," he smiled. "But she needs to be in a warm environment until this passes, I hope." He knew he was deluding himself into thinking she would survive, but he had to remain positive.

"What ails her?" Raymond asked, genuinely interested.

"I'm not sure actually. She has had some eating difficulties recently."

"She probably needs a vet," Raymond suggested. He thought how stupid it was for him to suggest what the doctor already knew.

"I have been reluctant to take her to one as the stress might kill her. Also, I don't want to risk her getting worse by catching something else from other sick birds."

"Perhaps the vet can come here," Raymond suggested.

"Perhaps. We shall see tomorrow depending on how she is."

Chandrapore noticed Raymond was rather parched. "Please sit down. Would you like a cold drink?"

"Thank you, yes."

"I'll be right back," he said and excused himself into the kitchen. Raymond waited until the doctor left the living room before sitting on the sofa. After the sounds of glass and pouring liquid, Chandrapore emerged with a tray of some fried hors d'oeuvres and a side dish of chutney, neither of which Raymond recognized.

"Help yourself."

Raymond looked at the plate. Chandrapore eased his guest's indecisiveness by taking a sample for himself and dipping it in the chutney and biting into it.

"It's called samosa." Seeing Chandrapore devour the morsel made his own mouth water as he imitated how his host ate it. The exterior was delightfully crispy, and the chutney just added to the pleasure. After a brief moment discussing the doctor's impressive apartment, Raymond knew it was time to banish all else from his mind. He was there to make Abby the central focus of the visit. And he felt ashamed for the digressions that he succumbed to. From now on, the conversation pertained to Abby's health. Raymond presented Chandrapore with her test results.

"Is Abigail in pain?" he asked.

"She is experiencing chest burns when she coughs."

Chandrapore studied the results and continued to talk to Raymond without looking up from the pages.

"The cancer could be eroding into her nerves, which might explain the burning," Chandrapore suggested.

Chandrapore insisted, "The lymph nodes under her right arm will need to be removed immediately." Raymond concurred, "What most concerns me is . . ."

"I know," Chandrapore interrupted, "her neck." He looked up at Raymond and removed his spectacles. "Ultimately the true remedy for a disease of this kind is to turn to our own physical resources and make them work harder," he said.

"How did you come upon this manner of treatment?" Raymond asked.

"Oh, purely by accident." Chandrapore became enlivened. "There was a teenager who was admitted to my office with a massive wound to his side. He had been involved in a knife fight—blood all over the place. Terrible. I treated and closed the wound as best I could, but the boy developed an infection that turned into gangrene. I didn't know what else to do. Then the boy developed a high fever and was unconscious. The only hope to stop the spread was to remove the infected tissue which left a massive hole in his side. The fever persisted, and the patient improved a little each day. The infection gradually healed. Nevertheless, he was left with unpleasant looking side. But he lived."

"You thought the high fever was responsible for the miraculous cure?" Raymond asked.

"I am certain that was the case. A postoperative infection was key to the boy's survival. In this case, a high fever was the main element crucial to achieve success. I needed to imitate a naturally acute infection. So I decided to test it on various cancer patients who were in different stages where it was inoperable." Chandrapore was feeling better as was always the case when he spoke about his accomplishments.

"Why did you switch from live bacteria to killed bacteria?"

"Much too dangerous. I had successfully infected two patients with live, and the tumors did shrink considerably. It was most encouraging. However, both patients unfortunately died, not from cancer but from a severe biochemical reaction to the infection. As a result of this adverse symptom, I needed to alter my strategy."

"What happened to them?"

Chandrapore explained that in his research to find an infection to imitate, he discovered, isolated, and cultured the bacteria responsible for erysipelas to be injected in the patients.

Raymond had had his fill of samosa and was riveted once hearing about the fatal skin disease.

"The unfortunate result was that they died from the developed erysipelas which was supposed to provoke the immune system to attack it as well as the cancer."

After numerous tries with some success in tumor regression, he came to the conclusion that an intentional infection might have better healing effects not from the injected simulated disease but from an unknown component of the bacteria that was lethal to the cancer itself.

"Without creating another disease that might be as harmful to the patient as the cancer itself?" Raymond was following Chandrapore's thinking.

"Exactly," said Chandrapore. "That led me to the use of killed bacteria."

"Streptococcus pyogenes and Serratia marcescens?" Raymond said.

"That's right. I needed two toxins of killed bacteria to generate the reaction that I was able to get with one live bacteria."

Raymond took a sip of refreshment, relaxed his thoughts before asking the one question that he knew he needed to ask to a very fine doctor, "Do you think Abby is a good candidate for this treatment?"

"Yes. Her cancer is isolated. Remove the lymph nodes under the right arm and concentrate on her neck."

"I'm concerned about the pain she will suffer," Raymond said.

"It depends. Some of my patients were far down the line, and their pain disappeared after the first several injections. Tumor regression can begin within hours after injection. However, significant immune response is delayed for about one week. It is important that you keep up the injections twice a day, if Abby can handle it."

"How may I obtain the doses I need? Can you teach me how to make them?" Raymond asked.

"I'm not a microbiologist. I relied on those scrupulous technicians at Pennsylvania Hospital to make the preparations for me."

"What are Abby's chances?" Raymond asked, fearing the response from such an intelligent and experienced doctor.

"My friend, I can only tell you that as each of us has different responses to the daily insults in this life, so does our own metabolism to what attacks our bodies. Patients respond individually. Some will be cured. Some will not."

The two doctors went through the steps on how much to inject and how often.

"I have the confidence that you will manage it properly," Chandrapore said, bringing the meeting to a satisfactory conclusion.

Raymond had done it. He had visited this case onto another doctor and would leave with the knowledge that something could be done. Raymond thanked Chandrapore.

"I know I don't have to tell you that you are not to speak of anything you are doing for Abby as an experiment," Chandrapore said, offering his hand to his new friend.

"Of course, I won't." Raymond knew the opposition to doctors for trying something experimental; for the same reason it was not advised to give certain patients trial bottles of some experimental medicine from the pharmacy. But this was about as good a remedy for Abby's illness as he had ever seen.

"I hope your bird is well again," Raymond said to the doctor as he walked into the cold hallway to the street outside.

Back home, it was night. Raymond put on his hat and coat and walked into the woods. The ground was brown and dry under his feet and the bliss of the stars over his head was as transparent as a cloudless evening sky could be. The trees bristled in a gentle breeze. In this tranquil solitude that was akin to his nature, he thought long and hard about Dr. Chandrapore and how impressed he was with his medical achievements and his good nature. He thought of the natural order of things as he ideally envisioned them. He would inherit the special talents and good fortune of having met Dr.

Chandrapore which would translate to Abby's complete recovery. Then he will congratulate himself on a job well done. If he allowed such infantile thoughts to run amok, he might endanger the well-being of a dear patient. This reason was enough to call on another doctor. He was wrong to think such a thing. He could not escape the fact that he loved her. She came to him seeking his knowledge, and he owed it to her to do everything humanly possible to make her better, if not cure her.

Chapter 4

William Corrigan sat behind his desk in his fitted brown suit, drenched in perspiration. He fumbled for his bottle of whiskey which he kept hidden in the back of his desk drawer. He wasn't normally the nervous type, but he needed the drink most of all. The batch of memos and sales reports on his desk were beyond his concentration. All he could think about were Lydia Ramon, his former personal secretary, his wife Henrietta, and Abby.

He knew Abby had seen him with Lydia coming out of the hotel that night. He was unable to gather his thoughts as the peril that threatened all he had worked for could be shattered if Abby or Lydia spoke. Perhaps if Abby hadn't seen Corrigan and Lydia kissing, he might have been able to conjure up some story to explain to his wife if she ever found out.

Upon Abby's recent discovery, Lydia resigned from her position through mutual financial discussions with Corrigan, but he could not guarantee that it would end there. He poured himself a whiskey and sat back in his chair rethinking the events that led him to this point where his position as a well-respected member of the community could at any moment be in jeopardy. Lydia was unmarried; she had no children and young. He on the other hand was married, had a son who hated working at the company, no respectable heir and was stout and balding, but with lots of money. He made subtle advances to Lydia over time. She responded. They needed a place. The office? No, too risky, even having her stay late was taking a chance. It was decided the hotel outside of town served their purpose, for a few carefully chosen hours to spend time together. When Abby spotted them walking out of the hotel, Corrigan made eye contact with her, and everything came to an end. The first day he saw Lydia for her interview, he looked past her white and gray blouse, imagining her lingerie. He was taken by her simple "good morning." These things were as distant a memory as the day Henry, his son, was born. He knew it happened, but the recollection of it was not that important anymore. What went through his mind was the ambition Lydia had for a potential managerial position in the company.

"I don't like starting at the bottom," Lydia said after several months on the job.

"That's the only way to learn a business. Any business," he said.

Lydia was keen on getting into a position beyond secretarial, but at what price, she wondered. She began to suspect his stalled nurturing of her ambitions. This cheapened her. This was the prejudice against women, who had to fuck in order to climb to a responsible position. In making the decision to have an affair with Corrigan, Lydia also knew that success or failure rested not with him but within her. If things got ugly and either of them called it quits, eventually, he would regard her as a dangerous interloper whose very existence threatened his own identity and distinction, and she would be discarded like an old rag.

As it stood, there was nothing he could say to justify it. Now all he had to do was figure out what to do about Abby. She was an assistant secretary which meant she was expected to provide administrative tasks for anyone in the company who needed help.

Corrigan made certain no one watched him through the large windows that surrounded his office before he gulped down his drink. If he fired Abby, for whatever reason, she would surely be filled with enough venom to strike back at him by telling his wife or his son about his infidelities. Anyone if provoked by an unfair act of betrayal could resort to making it their goal to seek revenge on the perpetrator. He was a successful businessman who had grown accustomed to the convenience of having his own personal secretary. From his desk, he only had to look up to see Abby faithfully sitting at her desk typing on one of his front strike typewriters. The best thing he could do was to offer Abby the job recently vacated by Lydia.

William Corrigan was a self-made man who through hard work and determination proved himself capable of managing and succeeding in the very competitive world of typewriter manufacturing. His headquarters filled five floors, employing over two hundred people. In the administrative offices, stenographers worked alongside their male colleagues. His corner office had glass window panels all around so he could see the activity that he was responsible for. It still left a good feeling of accomplishment to see all of his people working and growing with the company.

Abby sat by her Dictaphone transcribing a letter to a customer regarding a faulty typewriter they received. Her concentration was not on her work. Her life had only just begun, and it seemed that through design by Providence she was contemplating her own mortality for the first time. She wasn't sure how she would deal with knowing if her time was short.

Corrigan settled his thoughts, had one final drink, adjusted his tie, wiped his forehead, and walked past a large mahogany table displaying the eight Corrigan typewriters currently on the market. He opened his office door, surveyed the terrain he created, and called Abby into his office.

Abby stopped the transcribing, picked up her pad and pencil, and as she went into Corrigan's office, his smile was noticeably disconcerting. He stepped back to allow her to go inside first. She noticed his water glass was empty. She went to the pitcher and filled his glass before she sat down. Corrigan took a sip of the water and let it cool his throat before speaking. His half-smile suggested absolutely nothing except that he was the boss, and his word was law. Abby sat with her hands clasped on her notepad awaiting something mostly likely unpleasant.

"How long have you been with us?"

"Three years," she replied.

"Really that long? Seems like just yesterday." He paused and played with the glass on his desk. He was hesitating—something he was not used to doing ever since he became successful with his first large order for typewriters from a business school. He always looked ahead not backward.

"I'm so preoccupied with running the place that I sometimes forget to let a worker know how much they're appreciated. That doesn't mean that I fail to notice, you understand." He occasionally glanced out the windows to see who was walking by.

"I know you take an interest in your work here, which is more than I can say for some people, including my own son. All that boy does is shrug his shoulders, and take his anger out at the world. He'll never amount to anything." He was getting personal, and it bothered Abby.

"I've got people working here who would rather get a red hot poker in their eyes than work overtime. Shit, some of them don't even know what day it is," he excused himself for the profanity.

"You're not like that," he said. His words reached Abby's ears with unemotional clarity. Her potentially life-threatening illness was not the main focus of her attention right now.

"Abby, as you know, Lydia is no longer with us."

She nodded.

"I need a dependable secretary that will be there for me without question. I'm interested in growing the company, and to do that I need experienced people who know how things run so I won't have to go through the hassle of training someone new. There is an unprecedented industrial buildup taking place not just here in the US but all over the world. You name it, it's growing, steel, coal, medicine, the fucking government!" he excused himself again.

"Just go and visit any city, and you'll see architecturally how they are changing. It's going to be a very different world. Well, all of these growing industries require more and more office management to help run things smoothly, which is where we come into play. Pretty soon, anyone in your position will no longer be viewed of as a secretary but as operatives because of the service you provide in helping companies produce more as we become more organized. We're getting more and more orders for typewriters to meet that need."

"I'm offering the job to you, Abby. I'm not sure where your heart lies regarding your continued employment here. Regardless if your ambitions are here or elsewhere, let me tell you that given your excellent performance, good things are almost certainly to happen to you if you continue with us."

"Is that your personal guarantee?" she asked.

"It is. I wouldn't say it if I didn't believe in your potential."

He mentioned the salary would increase to ninety dollars a month. These words of encouragement echoed a strange familiarity given the fact that he said the same thing to Lydia. When things fell apart, he and Lydia met a final time to discuss the financial arrangements necessary for her comfort and the well-being of their child as she paid a visit to Dr. Fletcher who confirmed that she was pregnant. She told Corrigan the child was his.

Abby not only considered the increased salary which was welcomed in light of her health problems, but she also considered the man who sat across the desk. The fact that he offered her a better job at more money was against the grain of the time when women were not expected to remain long in the workforce. They got married and raised a family, and therefore, it made no sense to train them for a more responsible position. He, on the other hand, enjoyed taking advantage of younger women. Corrigan never spoke of that night at the hotel to Abby, and she never mentioned it either. To do so would invite mistrust and possible threats of blackmail. There might come a day when Corrigan would have to admit to his wife on how he let things get so out of hand. He knew this, and Abby did also. What she didn't understand was the real reason he chose her. Once she took the position and enjoyed the responsibility and privilege of being his personal secretary, he knew she was smart enough not to jeopardize it by talking out of turn about one slight glance at the hotel that didn't concern her in the first place.

Corrigan poured himself a glass of water and asked Abby if she wanted some.

"Yes, please," she said, amid the amplified sounds of the office outside. She told him she would think about it. That night, Abby told Maggie of Corrigan's offer and the prospect of more money coming into the house. Maggie was pleased with the news and told her to grab the opportunity. She still didn't know how sick her daughter was.

Maggie stood on the porch watching Michael Kramer, handsomely dressed in overalls that seemed tailored as they fit him so precisely, leave for work as Eric followed him out the door to go to school. It had been years since the last time she paid Virginia Kramer a personal call to her home. She remembered the day when Michael was Eric's age wandering in the woods, and he accidentally stepped on a hornet's nest. Maggie had been in town one day to sell her eggs and to pick up some cornmeal when on her way home, she saw Michael running down the street screaming for his life. As he got closer, she saw the bees fly about him, sticking to his legs, his arms, and his face. Maggie pulled on the reigns of her horse and climbed on the back of the wagon where she grabbed a large blanket and ran toward Michael who was screaming in agony—his body on fire from the stings. Maggie thrashed the towel against him as hard she could. She felt a burning sting under her skirt and grabbed Michael pushing him onto the wagon. They dashed off until they were certain they had gotten far enough, and they both jumped out and went to the lake's edge where they both made mudpacks and put mud all over themselves to take all the fire out of those stings. Dirty and smelling like two wet dogs, it didn't take long before things calmed down, and Maggie and Michael began to laugh about it all. *This is what neighbors are for,* Maggie always thought, *to help each other in a crisis.* She decided that it was time to act as neighbors do with regard to Virginia Kramer. She went into the kitchen and wrapped a freshly baked loaf of bread in brown paper.

Maggie knocked on Virginia Kramer's door, loaf in hand and waited for a response. Assuming Virginia answered, she realized it would be the first time she would see her face-to-face in years. Maggie thought she was wasting her time standing there trying to communicate with a person who never appreciated her patronage and who harbored what seemed to be an unjustified resentment. Maggie knocked on the door again and called, "Giny!"

Maggie caught some movement of the curtain in the front window. She turned toward the window and saw the ghost of Virginia Kramer standing behind the curtain in the same clothing she wore in her mercantile store. Virginia peered through the window suspiciously and recognized Maggie Whitman.

"What it is, Margaret?"

Maggie did not recognize the voice behind the door. The voice was without the strength that characterized the contentious self-important proprietor of what was the town's main mercantile store. The voice was that of a person who had lost her way and could not regain that fortitude to reenter the world she once occupied.

"I brought some fresh bread, just baked. I thought we could have a chat. I promise not to take up too much time."

Taking up too much of Virginia Kramer's time was not something Maggie had to worry about. Virginia was the recipient of valuable time that she wasted every day. When Maggie shopped in their mercantile store, she would notice Virginia's unfriendly gaze from the back room, a mouth that never quivered and only the briefest most condescending responses to inquires as if to say she was not a desirable customer.

Maggie avoided any direct contact with her if possible and dealt with the husband who was always very obliging and Michael whom she saw grow up into the fine young man he had become. When she thought about it, it made her very angry how a person could behave so badly. Neighbors! Virginia Kramer never thought much of neighbors. They were the secondary figures that were subject to her discerning eye by reason of their proximity and nothing more. She held that belief in her work at the store and at home.

Before long, she watched others through the kitchen window milling about the ruins of their homes looking to salvage what they could of their pitiful existence like going through old clothes and trying to pick out what could still be worn—victims of bad luck too exhausted to recognize the intensity of their distress. But what Virginia failed to realize hidden deep within the confines of her own pitiful existence was that everybody else had that same problem.

Like a bad dream, Maggie put it out of her mind. What couldn't be dismissed was that this woman was her neighbor for almost fifteen years, and she was a loyal customer for all that time. When the store burned, and the husband died in the fire, she retreated, lost her way, and would not face people again.

After a time in silence, Maggie felt foolish standing at the door.

"I'll leave the bread by the door," she said, angered by Giny's refusal to even engage in a proper greeting.

"Thank you, Margaret," was all Maggie got as she walked back to her place in anger at having wasted her time on someone who didn't appreciate a friendly gesture and didn't deserve it.

Fuck her, Maggie thought as she slammed the kitchen door. *I hope she chokes on the bread.*

The sun warmed the morning sky. Droplets of water poised to fall from crackling icicles indicated that winter was soon to end, but the chill was still there. The milkman greeted Maggie at the back door and gave her three bottles of fresh milk and took the empty bottles.

For Maggie, the fire within her at being treated with scorn once again by that woman, even years later to that present morning, burned as clear as the ice crystals melting around her. She decided it was best not to bother with Virginia Kramer anymore.

Chapter 5

One hour later, there was a knock at the front door. Maggie opened the door to a bearded man of about sixty years of age. His eyes were that of an early riser who looked forward to when he could shut them again. He removed his hat and addressed himself by name. The manner in which he spoke had the trace of a confidence that at one time blossomed during the exploration of new possibilities that no longer existed. The call to travel and the freedom of being on the road away from the trappings of domestic life were as ancient as his soiled worn-out overcoat and ragged shoes that tread through miles of hostile reactions, at times at the point of a gun in his face. The lines traveled around his reddish eyes like lakes, and when he bowed his head in submission to Maggie's presence, she saw his ugly baldhead littered with scars perhaps obtained from having fallen prey to drinks during many an unfulfilled evening. He had with him a small wooden crate that he placed on the ground in front of Maggie. The crate had several holes in it from which the unmistakable sounds of meowing could be heard. In making his trade going door-to-door, he often sold packaged food products. He didn't care if he never saw another can of pork and beans again. He tried his hand at selling clothing and hardware until he found the physical problems of handling massive sample trunks too cumbersome for the daily struggle of traveling the expansive commercial landscape. He had come to realize that it didn't matter what he sold; he had to stand firm and pray that he would get someone to buy his kittens.

"What I have here, ma'am will melt your heart." He opened the crate, and when Maggie saw the four kittens at play she was truly reinforced in the belief that if God didn't exist, there was no way that such creatures could have been created. The salesman noticed her interest.

"They're just two weeks old," he said, slowly feeding her inborn desire to touch them. "Go ahead, you can hold one." Maggie held one kitten close to her face and felt the fragility and tenderness as a newborn baby and thought how unfortunate for the kittens to be cooped up in a crate.

"They are five dollars for the lot," said the salesman, confident that it was money in the bag. Maggie sensed his eagerness and was almost reluctant to spoil it for him.

"We can't have cats in this house, I'm afraid," she said regretfully "My daughter, you see, she's allergic to cats' hair. I'm sorry."

"I knew someone who also suffered from cats' hair, couldn't get close to one without his eyes turning red like tomatoes," he said. Maggie took note of his eyes and kept her thoughts to herself.

"I have that problem myself," he joked, pointing to his own eyes.

"Your daughter would just need to wash her hands with some soap and warm water and remember to tell her not to touch her eyes after she plays with the kittens." The kitten's meowing left Maggie guilt ridden.

"We raise chickens, and when the kittens grow they'll be after them," she said. "I've seen cats around the coop at night. The chickens are locked in so I'm not as concerned as during the day when I let 'em out for a while to roam the yard."

Maggie placed the kitten back in the crate with the others. She was definitely not going to take them. The salesman knew it was not to be. "Well, everyone knows their business best," he said as another unfortunate encounter went to the heart of his identity.

"Would you like something to drink before you go?" she asked, not wanting him to leave so offended.

"No, thank you," he said firmly. The morning chill passed through him as he prepared to leave. He paused to ask, "Do you know of a store in town where I might pick up a few articles for my travels?"

"You're sure to find whatever you are looking for at Mrs. Clark's store." Maggie pointed in the direction to the town.

He thanked her, his dark eyes filled with sadness, picked up the crate and bowed with grotesque politeness. Maggie pointed to the Kramer house. She mentioned that perhaps he should try next door. *Perhaps,* she thought, *Virginia would condescend to take the darlings off his hands.* He thanked Maggie for her time. The kittens continued to meow as Maggie extended her hand to the salesman for a final good-bye. She watched him carry the crate back to his wagon. His feet were heavy on the ground as if he had lead in his shoes. He placed the crate in the back of the wagon and bundled it with a heavy blanket. He stood there in the cold for about a minute. The salesman did not go to the Kramer house. He tapped the reigns on his horse and slowly moved on. Maggie listened to the grinding sound of the wagon's wheels. It was a broken and painful sound against the dirt road that was paved with the transgressions of the salesman's wasted life that he was flattening over as he decided to leave his battered existence behind.

Later that afternoon, Maggie watched in astonishment from her kitchen window as Virginia Kramer emerged out of her house as a beast from hibernation dressed in a bathrobe and walking barefoot on the unanimated ground of melting snow and mud that unleashed its silent ascent into spring, carrying the loaf of bread Maggie had brought to her. She stood under the oak tree, nibbling on the bread and tossing an occasional morsel to the birds from the tree gathering around her.

The traveling salesman went into town and visited the animal clinic to see if there was anyone who might want to buy the kittens and offer them for adoption. The clinic was already full, and they had no room. He wandered into the eatery and devoured a plate of ham and eggs and drank three cups of coffee before entering Mrs. Clark's store to purchase a rope and a large sack with the last money he had.

Ella Horn had risen early in the morning. Her grandfather, Zachariah, with whom she lived in a dilapidated house outside of town, said he craved for a good stew that evening, and that meant hunting for a snake. At twelve years of age, Ella did most of the chores around the house. She also did the hunting.

That morning, she made Zachariah's breakfast as usual, put on her overalls and her sweater, got her knife, slung her rifle and lance over her shoulder, and carried a bag to put her kill in. Zachariah was unable to accompany his granddaughter on hunting trips in recent months. He had arthritis in both legs, and he confined himself to their place.

Ella walked down the familiar narrow trail of the forest that led to the lake. The storm that moved through just before dawn left the trail one long stretch of mud and a morning mist bleeding through the dense woods, which made everything gray and aching for the sun to light up the day. She listened to the sounds of the squelching mud under her bare feet. The bird chatter filled the air. There were still patches of snow an inch or two alongside the trail. She reached the lake and walked along the reeds. She saw a section of reeds expanding as if coming to life on their own. It was an unnatural occurrence, and she knew it must be a snake. She poked her lance into the bushes several times. The snake revealed itself through the reeds. It had an indentation on the sides of its head. Ella looked at its catlike eyes and knew it to be very dangerous. She stepped back a bit and ascertained the snake's size to be longer than her. Ella remembered Zachariah's advice when on the hunt.

"You must have self-control," he said. "If you lose your head, you might very well pay for it by giving the beast cause to defend itself by attacking you, and this you will regret most surely."

His confidence in her abilities as a shooter was solid since that first day he put a rifle into her hands and taught her to aim and fire. He knew she had a talent for shooting, and he didn't worry too much when she ventured off alone. Besides, they rarely shopped for things in town and only when it was absolutely necessary.

The snake sensed it was in danger and slithered away in the protection of the reeds. Ella thought to shoot it in the back of the head, if she could provoke it into coming out again. She followed the snake, occasionally jabbing at it with her lance, hoping it wouldn't escape into the water. She kept poking it until it became annoyed and lunged at her this time exposing all its twisted body before her. She dropped her lance and grabbed her rifle. She aimed. The snake raised its head and hissed at her. She cocked her rifle and got ready to put an end to the confrontation when all was disrupted by the meek wailing cries in the distance up ahead. It sounded like a child crying but it wasn't. She listened carefully to the thin frail squeaking sound of that innocence in whose peril all present considerations were tossed to the wind. Ella left the snake behind, following the cries through a canopy of green where time stood still to guard against the unseen.

Ella reached an opening in the forest and saw the salesman removing a bulging burlap sack from the back of his wagon and also a large rock. She remained hidden behind a tree. The man took one of the kittens out for a second while he put the rock in the bag and the kitten back inside and tied the bag with a rope. With this added provision, he was confident the kittens would drown.

Ella watched the man walk toward the edge of a pier, the sounds of kittens crying for help from within the sack. When he reached the end of the pier, he threw the bag as far into the lake as he could. He waited for a moment to make sure the bag did not surface. When he felt satisfied the job was done, he walked back to his wagon and drove off.

Ella watched the wagon until it was far enough. She dropped her weapons, ran to the end of the pier, and jumped into the lake. Ella swam in the direction where she thought she saw the bag sink. Her arms and legs were stinging from the frigid waters. It was difficult to breathe but she pressed on. She dove down several times for what seemed an eternity. Each time she came up for air, she thought of the kittens dying a horrible death as they still lurked beneath the murky depths. Ella absorbed the cold, painful as it was, and she went down again. A black mass on the weedy disarray of the bottom caught her eye. It appeared to distinguish itself from just another big rock. She swam toward it thinking; it had to be. Ella pulled the bag with all her might. She was losing air. Panic set in. A savage pain ravaged her chest. She was drowning, and there was no one to help her. Ella's resolve was secure. She did not let go of the bag. Her arms were strong, and all thoughts vanished from her mind apart from getting both the kittens and herself out of that water. She gave a final pull to the bag as the last bubbles of air escaped from her mouth until she broke through the surface. With each gasp of air, she was losing strength, and she was not able to keep the bag out of the water. It was just too heavy to swim with that damn rock in it. She maneuvered the bag onto her back, and with one hand, she held the rope to secure that the bag didn't fall back into the lake, and she used her free arm to swim back to the pier and free herself from the lake's relentless enormity.

Once out of the water, Ella trembled in the cold; her chattering lips muttered curses to God for permitting such an evil act. She fumbled to untie the rope. Her fingers were numb. She remembered her knife was still in her pocket. She took it out and cut the rope, trembling with the fear of finding all the kittens dead. She removed the blasted rock from the bag, and with an anger directed at the most obnoxious townsfolk when they looked at her and her grandfather with disdain, she hauled the rock into the lake as if aiming for their heads. She picked up one kitten and held it upside down to drain out any remaining water. She carefully placed it on its side and began to gently rub its chest. She blew into its mouth. The kitten did not respond. She tried this with two more kittens, and when they didn't respond either, her anger rose at the thought of the man who was responsible. If she ever saw him, she would make him pay. There was just one kitten left. Ella began to rub its chest and blew into its tiny mouth just as she had done with the others.

"C'mon," she said. "Dear God, if you even exist, don't let this one die." She stopped and looked for movement. Any movement at all from its tiny chest would prove that God, who exercised kindness, justice, and righteousness in unseen forms, did on the rarest occasions, speak to preserve the existence of some of his living creatures. The kitten's chest rose and dropped slowly. Ella believed she was witnessing a miracle. She picked up the living kitten and carried it with its dead siblings back to the location where she left her rifle and lance. She worked in silence digging a small grave and buried the other three kittens in the sack they drowned in. As Ella knelt down beside the grave, the kitten was by her side, poking around the dirt when she heard that unmistakable hissing sound again, and the snake was just behind her demanding unfinished business. Its head emerged between the first and second coils of its body and was flat on the ground. Ella picked up the kitten from the ground before the snake decided to make it its main meal of the day, and she rose slowly placing the kitten on a high branch where it cried in terrified observance.

The snake opened its mouth and hissed again—its impulse making it known that it didn't approve of Ella's presence in its territory. Ella stepped back to get her lance on the ground and slowly bent down to pick it up, careful not to move her arms too much for fear that the snake might lunge at her again and get a bite. She held the lance upright, with the point about a foot off the ground. The snake held its ground. Ella took the advantage, and with lightning speed, she raised her lance way up and speared the snake with just behind the neck, through its hard skin, pinning it to the ground. It gave a tremendous loud hiss and twisted violently. Ella had the snake where she wanted, but it was so long and strong that she wasn't able to hold it for long. She wasted no time and picked up her rifle and blew its head off.

She grabbed hold of its tail and straightened it out. It was a whopping six feet long.

"It's quite a catch, isn't it?" she said proudly to the kitten in the tree. She took out her knife and cut a good chunk of the snake's midsection and used the sack she brought to carry it back home. She carried the kitten in her arms. The sack with the remains of the snake, her rifle and lance, were all slung over her shoulder. Her grandfather would have his snake stew afterall.

At home, Ella saw her grandfather in bed taking a nap. On the floor next to his bed was an empty bottle of rum. She knew he would be asleep for the rest of the afternoon, and that would give her the time to see where she could hide the kitten where it would be safe, and there would be no danger of it escaping and surprising her grandfather. She could try to keep it in her room, but if her grandfather wandered in and found it, then he would make her get rid of it.

Later in the evening, Zachariah sat on the front porch. It was a fine stew. He enjoyed smoking his pipe and reading the paper unaware that in the kitchen, Ella was mixing a tiny helping of snake and potatoes into a paste for the kitten that she hid in the woodshed. The night air was cold. His arthritis was starting to act up, and soon he wouldn't be able to get up from the chair without asking Ella to help him. *Dammit,* he thought. All he wanted was to get some air. He reluctantly got up to retire for the evening inside the house. His long legs felt weighted with iron. He heard what sounded like a child crying. He ignored it until the cries began to take hold of his short attention span and take his mind off his ailments. His curiosity at least was not impaired. He listened again, tossed the newspaper on the chair, and grabbed the lantern to venture toward the shed. The closer he got to the shed, the more defined the sound became. He realized that whatever was crying behind the shed was small and defenseless. He opened the shed, and in the dark, the kitten jumped up with its silent paws onto Zachariah's leg. Startled, he thought it was a big rat attacking him. He held the lantern still for a moment, and the light captured the tiny kitten below walking between his legs.

"How did you get in here?" Zachariah asked his new friend, watching the kitten climb up his leg without fear. He picked up the kitten and saw it was a male with a large head and large ears that seemed too big for its body. One glimpse into its young green eyes brought memories of his youth to Zachariah when he was yearning for whatever the world offered to him. Even an animal just in the throes of life had this instinctive curiosity. As inquisitive as the little kitten was, the warmth and delicate essence became contagious upon Zachariah, who was as taken aback as only a seventy-five-year-old ailing useless son of a bitch could be. *The kitten must have sought out the shed for protection,* he thought. He wasn't about to send him off into the merciless world right away.

"Ella!" he called.

She readied the plate to feed the kitten but left it on the countertop when she heard her grandfather calling. From the back door, she saw him with the kitten. She grabbed her shawl and went outside.

"We've got a visitor," he said.

Ella walked toward the shed, and the little kitten raced toward her and jumped up. He knew something was up. "He's taken a shine to you already. Any idea where he came from?" he asked.

She avoided looking up at her giant of a grandfather and picked up the kitten. Zachariah placed his hand gently under her chin to raise her head so their eyes could meet. At six feet four inches, he was a challenge for Ella to look at when standing right in front of him. Her eyes illuminated by the lantern's orange hue conveyed guilt. She admitted that she found the kitten and brought it home. They went into the shed and closed the door to keep out some of the cold. She recalled for Zachariah how she came upon the man who threw the kittens into the lake and how she dove in and rescued the one kitten before him, the others having drowned. She told him how she also nearly drowned.

Zachariah convinced that his granddaughter was speaking the truth complimented her courage for risking her life in this way and for killing the snake just so he could have the meal he wanted. He was filled with shame.

"Ella, I know I'm not much use to you," he said. It was the first time he ever admitted his own worthlessness to his granddaughter, his only living relative.

"No. You're not," she replied with well-intentioned humor. At least, he wasn't angry about her hiding the kitten.

"You do know you can depend on me," he said. "The day will come when you will leave."

"I'll never leave, Grandpa. Where would I go anyway?" The kitten cried persistently.

"He's hungry," he said. "It's a he. I looked."

They walked back to the house, and in the kitchen the kitten ate the snake stew and potatoes voraciously.

"I guess we won't have to worry about his appetite," she said.

"How are we going to afford to feed a growing cat?"

"I don't think it'll be a problem," she replied. "You see how he's gobbling up that snake. If he can eat snake, he'll eat anything."

"So we can keep him?" she asked.

"Why not," he said. "Keeping a pet might be a blessing around here. I'll even help you take care of it."

"You'll probably spend more time playin' with him more than help me clean up after him," Ella said.

Zachariah thought about it and she had a point. "They leave a lot of hair around and raise a fuss all night," he said.

CHAPTER 6

On the day of the next appointment, Raymond told Abby of the confirmed diagnosis. There was no error in the results, he stated. It would have been easy for Abby to take a dim view of her outlook but she never even thought to ask why her. Hearing this news and all the black in the thunderclouds and the deafening sound of the rain outside made for an arduous way to spend an afternoon. Remaining positive was the challenge.

"Have you told your mother yet?"

"Not yet."

"She needs to know now."

"I will tell her tonight." Abby's willful determination prompted her asking, "How do we fight it?"

"We'll need to remove the lymph nodes under your right armpit. There's no need to worry. You'll be in and out of the hospital in a few days." Abby suppressed her emotions.

"I have to go back to the hospital?"

"You have to have the procedure done at Pennsylvania Hospital."

"Will you do the surgery?"

He conveyed the fact that he was not a surgeon but to ease her mind, he personally guaranteed she would have the best of care, which he meant.

"Cancer cells travel through the lymph nodes and can spread. Once we remove the node, we will have more X-rays taken to see if we have removed all the cancer from that part of your body."

"What about my neck?"

Raymond told Abby about his treatment for possibly getting rid of the cancer that was inside her.

"My approach is to inject killed bacteria into your neck and have your antibodies attack it and the cancer at the same time."

"Inject me with bacteria? Sounds dangerous."

The challenge to inspire his most beloved patient was ahead of him as he tempered his wisdom with humility. He went about describing how he came to discover Dr. Chandrapore and his cancer-killing creation. Abby trusted him when he spoke, but she was disturbed by this procedure. He spoke with eloquence and as much conviction as he could muster.

"So you are going to give me headaches and chills?"

"Have you ever had the flu?" he asked.

"Yes. When I was about six years old, Momma gave me a hot water bath. I mean it was almost scalding. The steam was so thick. I remember I sat on her knee in the bathroom for almost three hours before she finally took me out of there." Abby paused. "How long will this treatment last?"

"That depends on your response. We will start with a small dose twice a week, gradually increasing it for about a month and see how it goes. Keep it in mind, Abby that it's best to start with these injections when you are home and not planning on going out so there are no complications with the fever, once it comes about."

"You will be at our house?" she asked, perfectly satisfied at this one prospect.

"Yes."

"How long will the fever last?"

"About two hours with each injection if all goes as planned."

"I'm not looking forward to this at all."

"Please understand the fever and nausea you will experience is the whole point of the treatment. And we have to make sure your body doesn't become tolerant to the bacteria."

"How much will all this cost?"

"Money isn't the important factor here," he stated sincerely. Raymond told Abby he will not charge her for the visits only two dollars each week for the injections.

"That's it?" Abby was surprised beyond belief.

"For my part, yes." He explained to her that there would be charges relating to the room, medicines, and naturally the surgery itself. He gave a rough estimate.

"The main thing is to get you well."

"Have you diagnosed this cancer in other patients?" she asked.

"A few, yes."

"How many of them are still alive?"

Raymond hesitated. "None."

"When will I have the operation?"

"I'd like to have you at the hospital by the end of the week."

This was not an uncommon practice as those patients who could afford to pay more were billed more and vice versa. There would also be the inevitable appeals to the doctor to reduce fee of the visits. It was an accepted form of negotiation if a patient who is under lesser circumstances as many in the town were, to "request" for a slight reduction in fees to accommodate a limited income. Some sought not a reduction but a restraint on increasing the fees. There were those in the community who tried to get away with not paying the full amount, but the doctor could always tell whenever someone who could afford it was trying to pull a fast one.

Raymond ran into William and Henrietta Corrigan on the street. These two in particular were not among Raymond's favorite people. When the fussy Henrietta Corrigan had an appointment, she presented a complicated story of ailments that never materialized except in her mind. He sent the bill, and she hadn't paid for those appointments for almost eight months. For those who took advantage of his generosity, they were mistaken in thinking that he knew nothing about business. As honest as Raymond was with himself and his patients, on occasion he encountered those persons whose economic standing masked a sense of gratitude so dead that it would never occur to them to pay on a timely basis. Among his patients were many who could not pay. He provided the same treatment for them as to those who were of means. But clearly, he was being taken advantage of by these two. It didn't matter. It was his obligation to pursue a thorough examination, and he would opt to discover some trifle that would make her feel better. But he had to be careful what he said as Henrietta might become more anxious about her health under this supposed scrutiny and keep coming back. All he wanted was to see the last of her.

On the corner even before saying hello to him, she vented her latest ailment in his face.

"Dr. Fletcher. I'm so glad to see you. I have been getting the most dreadful headaches lately. It feels like someone is drilling a hole in my head and won't stop."

She kept on. He said nothing to her but took note of the shopping bag from the local dress shop. Ignoring her, he turned toward the husband.

"Mr. Corrigan, can we talk for a moment?" he said, leaving Henrietta cold in her tracks.

William sensed a problem. He excused himself from his wife, and the two men took several steps until they were satisfied a somewhat private conversation could be had.

"Fletcher, what's the idea, ignoring my wife like she doesn't exist."

"Personally, I don't give a damn about your wife or you," Raymond replied.

"You know, you're a very popular person in town. I came very near to having a fight about you the other night."

"Really. How's that?" Corrigan asked.

"I was in the drugstore, and some of the neighbors were talking about how tough it is to make ends meet. I mentioned how tough times can also impact those of us in the medical profession when patients don't pay their bills. Somehow your name came up."

"If my name came up in the context of that conversation, Fletcher, I have no doubt it was you who mentioned my name first."

This was true; however, Raymond stuck to the issue at hand. He would not be so impulsive to say what was on his mind that Corrigan was a cheap profiteer womanizer whose one constant thought was for more money and to sing the praises of that one true love.

"I've wanted to ask if you have ever allowed any of your customers to buy on credit."

"Sure. We also have an installment plan, provided they are trustworthy and pay on time. Are you looking for a typewriter?"

"I'm looking to you as an honest businessman to pay me what you owe me for your wife's visits."

It made Raymond sick to think he was just another cog in the wheel that churned according to the mocking will of William Corrigan.

"My wife comes to you when she is not well. Don't forget that."

"I find nothing wrong with her," Raymond said. "She has gotten into the habit of arranging appointments when there is no cause."

What Raymond did not say was that it wasn't his fault for being overly attentive to a woman who complained about headaches after she had spent the morning at home alone on a drunken binge because she was married to you, Mr. Corrigan.

"I want you to pay the outstanding bills that you owe me and then find another doctor."

"Now. Let's not be too hasty," Corrigan said. "We're both respected men in the community. And like all men of refinement, we are imperfect."

"In your case, that's putting mildly."

"Fletcher, I'm sure you have more important things to do than throw insults so let me put this to you, I'll arrange to have my secretary call your office tomorrow and get the final amount, and I will handle it personally."

"Let's hope so. Good afternoon," he said and quietly walked away. Abby called Raymond that afternoon, and as soon as he recognized her voice, he was no longer troubled about the fifty dollars Corrigan owed him.

Evening came. Abby was in a deep sleep. The images of a man had infiltrated her dreams with the utmost clarity. He was in his late thirties, tall, dressed in an overcoat with closely clipped hair. His shoulders hunched forward making him look older. His long tired eyes drooped on either side of his thin face. Under his eyes the skin puffed out, and the lines stretched like veins to his cheeks. His mouth was firm and long, extending outward a good portion of his lower face. His mouth never moved to express anything but the unhappiness he must have been feeling inside. When she awoke, she knew she would never forget his face.

The aroma of fresh-stewed meat and potatoes made its way upstairs to Abby's bedroom. Maggie was preparing their dinner downstairs. A pain suddenly gripped Abby's heart, not a physical pain but one that extended itself to her mind and soul. It was the same pain she felt when leaving Raymond Fletcher's office after he confirmed the diagnosis. It was time to finally tell her mother about her condition. Once that was done, she thought, her pain would be lessened. If there was ever a time not to be self-critical, this was it. She realized that she did not have control over how quickly her life could be destroyed. Abby's legs stiffened as she got out of bed. She hadn't recalled such a feeling in her legs before. Maybe she was starting to get old. The comfort of being at home on a cold night with the prospect of beef stew had no effect on her as she walked down the stairs following the aroma.

She and her mother ate their meals in the kitchen. The dining room was rarely used as it was just the two of them, and they didn't' entertain much. Maggie couldn't resist sampling the stew over and over with the wooden spoon she had been cooking with. She stopped stirring when she heard Abby coming down the stairs. Satisfied that it was as perfect a stew as she could make, she reached for the plates. Abby sat at the table, her immensely long hair down to her ankles. Maggie began to plate large helpings for themselves. The activity of cooking and serving made Maggie very active with the tongue. Abby wasn't paying attention to Maggie's gossip about how the traveling salesman she encountered was found dead, having drowned at the bottom of a lake.

"No one claimed the body. Poor man," Maggie said, quite condescendingly. "It's a shame to see someone struggle and work all their life only to go their reward alone, nobody caring."

"Isn't that the same for all of us?" Abby asked, gently ironical and disillusioned.

"You're not alone. You have me."

The lake water had flooded the salesman's nose and mouth and throat. He probably deserved it after what he did to the kittens. At death's door, he could no longer fight the rush of water that filled his lungs. And he didn't want to. As he neared the closure of his earthly existence, his fear subsided at last. Forgotten were the daily disappointments and betrayals that led to his sinful actions. The eternal emptiness he once felt no longer pressed against him, dragging him down to the bottom of the lake. What he found instead was a cleansing that finally gave him the courage to stand once again. This time he stood before his Maker, who welcomed him with open arms. The man realized that his life did not belong to him but was a gift. He finally achieved the freedom in death that he sought in life; someone to hold on to him and tell him, it's all right.

"Maybe I shouldda bought the cats. Oh well. What's the sense of making a big to do over it?" Maggie served the stew to Abby and noticed her daughter's lack of enthusiasm.

"What's come over you, girl? Didn't you sleep well?" Maggie asked.

"I slept fine," Abby replied. It was almost too much to consider on how to fake having an appetite as Maggie was so proud of the dinner. Abby sipped her glass of water and stared at the steaming stew in front of her in mute curiosity. Maggie sat down and broke off a piece of crunchy bread and passed it to her daughter.

"I didn't see you all day."

Abby took the piece of bread and placed it next to her plate. Maggie sensed something was wrong.

"Why aren't you eating? I made it especially for you."

"I went to see Dr. Fletcher today. He took a blood sample from me, and I had X-rays taken at Pennsylvania Hospital."

Maggie stopped eating, placed the spoon on the table, and stared at her daughter.

"They found a cancer."

"How certain is he that it's cancer?" Maggie asked.

"He's very certain. The test results confirmed it."

"Where is the cancer?"

Abby pointed to her neck and lymph nodes.

"Luckily, the cancer is localized in these areas; otherwise it would be much worse," she said.

Maggie got up from the table. "I'm going to telephone Raymond right now," she said defiantly.

"Momma, don't disturb him. He's busy enough all day. Let him alone."

"How can you just accept it?" Maggie asked.

"I've known about it for a while. But I wasn't sure until today."

"When?" Maggie insisted.

"I went to see Raymond last week for my physical examination. I didn't tell you where I was going that day. It was then that he told me what he suspected."

"You've known all this time and didn't tell me?"

Abby slammed her hand on the table. "What's the point in worrying you about it if he wasn't sure?"

Maggie sat back down at the table.

"What do we do now?" she asked.

Abby told her about the surgical procedure she was scheduled to have at Pennsylvania Hospital at the end of the week to remove the diseased lymph nodes. That would be the first step. She proceeded to explain to her mother of Raymond Fletcher's proposed treatment.

At the conclusion of this, Maggie was beside herself. Not only was her daughter seriously ill, but she agreed to the risky injections of bacteria that may compound the problem. The stew, untouched, grew cold. They sat at the table for two hours, drinking water to fill their shared pain.

"You're going to have to quit your job working for Corrigan."

"I can't quit," Abby said. "We need money, now more than ever. Quittin' is the last thing on my mind right now."

"What did you say to Corrigan when you needed the time to have the X-rays taken?"

"I called in sick. It's not far from the truth, Momma."

"Does he know how sick you are?"

"No. I don't want him to find out."

"You don't need to be afraid to explain to your boss that . . ."

"I'm not afraid," she said in defense. "I'm trying to avoid other people from finding out. It's no one's business."

"You're going to be out for at least a week. It'll be better if you're up front with him. He'll understand."

"No, he won't."

"What will you tell him?"

"I haven't the slightest idea. Maybe I'll tell him I'm taking some time off."

"You know there's nothing to say except tell him the truth. They'll be days when you're too sick to work. And if you try fighting it in the office, you won't be able to concentrate."

"Are you afraid to tell him because you think he'll fire you?"

"It isn't about that, Momma," Abby said. "If he finds out, he'll tell his son and everyone in the town will know."

"He won't tell," Maggie insisted. "I promise you he won't."

Abby couldn't see eye to eye with her mother. If she could cope with fighting cancer, working at the typewriter company was not such a burden despite loathing William Corrigan and his good-for-nothing son Henry. She remained as stubborn as Maggie was to help her daughter.

Chapter 7

Maggie thought about it all night. She couldn't have cared less about what Abby might think of her meddling in what was the most difficult part of her life. Even if Abby found out and vowed never to speak to her again, it had to be done.

Maggie knew she couldn't telephone William Corrigan at the office since Abby was sure to answer his calls first and would instantly recognize her voice. So she prepared a note and folded it in an envelope and sealed it. On the front she wrote, William Corrigan, URGENT. She sent for a messenger and firmly instructed him to hand-deliver the note to Corrigan personally and not to allow anyone else to take the note away from him. If Corrigan was not available, he should return the note to Maggie.

Corrigan sat down at his desk and opened the note. Maggie asked if she could meet with him outside the office regarding Abby as soon as possible. It was a very private matter and Abby was not to find out about the note. Maggie had written her telephone number at the bottom. Corrigan immediately telephoned. Maggie asked if he knew of a place where they could meet where neither of them would be recognized. He said yes and he offered to have his driver pick her up at home. Maggie refused the offer. She would meet him at the place.

At 1:00 p.m. that day, Maggie entered an eatery at the outskirts of town. She saw Corrigan sitting at a table and hadn't recognized him at first since she hardly ever ran into him in the past and had virtually no contact with the Corrigan family other than the fact that her daughter worked for him. They exchanged pleasantries, and Corrigan told Maggie how pleased he was with her daughter's performance in the office.

"You should be very proud of your daughter, Margaret."

"I am, William."

The waitress arrived. Maggie wasn't that hungry so she ordered coffee.

Corrigan ordered coffee and a tuna sandwich. Maggie went through the words in her mind on how she would tell Corrigan but as always, it is the immediacy of the moment that confuses and discards all prepared thoughts and ideas out the window, and the best thing to do is be up front and direct.

The waitress served the lunch, and Corrigan took a bite of the sandwich and washed it down with the coffee. After a couple of sips of coffee, Maggie relaxed herself a bit.

"William, I wanted to speak with you in private about a delicate matter concerning Abby." Corrigan was all ears.

"You see, she has just told me that she has a cancer. We are not sure how serious it is, but Dr. Fletcher wants her to have an operation this week."

William Corrigan never lacked empathy. In business, he learned through experience never to overreact to terrible news as any action taken in response would set the path for the future. That was the way his mind worked.

"Margaret, how can I help you?" he asked calmly and with sincerity.

"Just so you know that she will be out for at least two weeks, maybe more."

"I don't understand why she didn't tell me herself?"

"She didn't want you to know. She doesn't want anyone to know."

"Margaret, you have nothing to worry about. I won't breathe a word. I will pray for Abby's speedy recovery." Maggie was relieved.

"There's another problem," Maggie said. "She wanted to tell you that she was taking time off without any other explanation. She's never to know that we spoke."

"When she comes to me, I'll say fine. I might give some resistance so she won't get suspicious, but I won't ask her for specifics. So she'll be at ease with it. She has enough to think about."

"I can't thank you enough, William. You don't know how upset she was when I suggested my telling you about it. I'm sure you can understand how difficult it was for me to go behind her back and betray her."

"You're not betraying her, Margaret. Don't you upset yourself with such thoughts," he said, taking her hand. "Your daughter is a courageous principled woman who doesn't want anyone to fight her battles for her. And she's right to keep it private. We'll see to it that no one finds out. Did they tell you how much it's going to cost?"

Maggie mentioned an amount and added that when they arrive at the hospital, the full expenses would be disclosed to them.

William Corrigan studied the situation in his mind and heart. He didn't know why Abby's young life was being tested in this way, but he did know that she couldn't afford to pay for the operation once it came time to collect. And whatever the outcome, it was in her nature and in her best interests to fight even the cruelest and most unfair trials of life. As he had many times in his life, Corrigan stepped up to the plate.

"Don't worry, I will have the hospital send the bills to me," he said.

Maggie thought she was going to drop dead. Never before in her life had she known such generosity.

"And don't tell Abby I'm involved financially. She'll think she's indebted to me for life."

"So many secrets to keep," Maggie said as her spirits lifted. "I feel like we're doing something dishonest." The tears rolled down her face. She quickly wiped them.

"When I get to the office, I'll send a telegram authorizing the hospital to send the bills to my attention at the office."

"If there's any problem, you contact me directly."

Corrigan gave Maggie one of his business cards.

"What happens if Abby comes across a bill?" Maggie asked, placing the card in her purse.

"She won't know what it's for. It'll be addressed to me, and no one opens my mail in the office but me."

Maggie saw the waitress come out with a tray of hot beef barley soup for some customers. Her hunger had returned, and she relaxed over soup and the realization that for the present, the world was not crashing around her.

Maggie was at Abby's bedside at the hospital when the head surgeon returned to the room after having examined Abby. Maggie greeted the doctor nervously. He carried all the charm and intellect that one would expect as the head of surgery at one of the most highly respected hospitals in the country.

"Don't be so nervous, Momma."

Maggie excused herself. "I'm sorry, Doctor," she said. "I guess I'm not used being in a hospital. I seem to get nervous meeting anyone here."

"It's a normal reaction, Mrs. Whitman," he said, conscious of his power without being egocentric. He told them that Dr. Fletcher was to be commended for having Abby brought to the hospital so quickly to have the operation.

"Has the cancer progressed at all?" Maggie asked.

"The X-rays show no further progression."

"You'll still need to operate?" Maggie asked.

"It's essential we remove the lymph node and any of the surrounding tissue that could have a trace of cancer cells just to be safe. I will be honest with you both. When dealing with the presence of cancer, no operation is 100 percent foolproof. Abigail will require lots of rest, and she must not exert herself by doing things around the house for at least a couple of weeks."

"Doctor, what about the cancer in her neck?"

"I'm afraid that is inoperable. Dr. Fletcher has informed me of the treatment he is proposing, and while personally I am rather skeptical about it, I know that Dr. Fletcher would not take unnecessary risks if he wasn't certain that Abby would benefit from it."

"I have advised her to get a second opinion, but she refuses," Maggie said. At this point, Abby became indignant.

"I don't need a second opinion!" she lashed out.

"I firmly believe Abigail is in good hands with Dr. Fletcher."

"When will you operate?" Maggie asked.

"Tomorrow morning."

"Before we proceed, Mrs. Whitman, you will need to visit our accounts department to arrange for financial payments."

"Of course, I'll take care of it right away."

"Fine, I will see you later, Abigail."

"Abby. I prefer to be called Abby."

"Abby, I will see you later. Get some rest." He left the room.

"How are we going to pay for this?" Abby asked.

"I have it all worked out. Don't worry about that."

Abby was confused at what her mother meant, but she was too tired to discuss it.

Maggie apologized for the second opinion business and while Abby slept, she went to see the hospital accountant. She entered his private office, which was rather small with a large secretarial desk with numerous little compartments and filing cabinets along the wall. He was a slender odd sort of man with spectacles that came down his nose that made him look neither young nor old. He typified the single-minded person whose purpose was to make anyone who crossed his path be they patient or physician, understand that there was a business side to running a hospital, and he was prepared to respond to any complaint regarding charges. Maggie was no exception. He folded her receipt with professional delicacy and promptly gave it to her and explained in a salty thin exacting voice that the rent for Abby's room was due in advance of each week. Maggie unfolded and was surprised at the amounts. He recognized her expression immediately. He explained the additional costs of the operating room, the nurse care, and medicines were common enough.

"This is a private institution, Mrs. Whitman. As our costs increase, we have no alternative but to pass them onto the patient. But as I'm sure you already know we have been instructed by Mr. William Corrigan to send the bills to his attention. This copy is just for your records."

As she prepared to leave, he added, "Your daughter is getting the best care possible."

"I understand," Maggie said, fumbling with the receipt. She wanted to shatter his glasses until the glass fragments wedged deep in his horrid face to bleed profusely for as along as her daughter stayed at the hospital. She thanked him instead and returned to be with her daughter who was fast asleep.

On his way home from school, Eric Kramer accompanied by two other boys succumbed to their curiosity as they changed their route and ran toward the house where they knew Ella Horn lived with her grandfather. The boys darted past a well and hid behind a tree. The problem was it was too far away to see Ella through her small bedroom window. Eric looked to make sure the grandfather wasn't around, and they quietly stepped closer to the house. They ducked underneath her bedroom windowsill and slowly raised their heads to see that she was changing her undergarments.

The boys had their secrets collectively satisfied and bonded in achieving their goal, the sight of her young naked body. Ella knew she was being spied on. She turned toward them to make sure they got more than what they thought of. She allowed all of her front to be displayed for their pleasure. If that wasn't enough, she commented on how silly it was for them to be spying on her when they could get a feel inside her room. She dared them to come in through the window. As soon as one of the boys tried to climb, a massive force instantly pulled him back and rolled over like a wheelbarrow. Zachariah surprised the boys with curses and threats if he ever caught any of them on his property again. He warned them to stay away from his granddaughter. They ran into the weed-choked ground to avoid the giant grandfather who shot his rifle into the air to make them run even faster. He chuckled to himself watching them go like scared rabbits.

"You know those boys?" Zachariah demanded.

"Never saw them before," Ella replied.

"It's not proper for a young lady to tease boys like that. They'll take it as an invite to come around again."

"It was only a joke," she replied. "I don't think they'll be comin' back."

"That's not the point. If they think you enjoy their company and parade yourself half naked, they'll think you're a whore and chase you around like one."

"I'm not a whore!" Ella shouted back and lashed out at him, but he just walked past her and she kept clinging to him like a little dog that wouldn't let go.

A month later, Eric cut school and loitered around the railroad yard, throwing rocks at the passing trains. Police officer, Paul Hannay, recognized Eric and called out to him. Eric dropped the rock he was carrying and jumped over the many rails, quickly disappearing in the movement of sound and smoke of passing trains going back and forth. Hannay attempted to run after him, but there was too much activity on the yard to run after him, and he wasn't in the mood to chase after him on foot. He stood by the operations tower and observed Eric heading toward the woods. Hannay got into his police car, and since it was a boring day, he drove after him just to see where the boy was heading. Eric knew the path that led to Ella's house from the previous adventure there. He found the cabin and hid inside the woodshed. He saw the chopped wood piled neatly about four feet high. He walked around the woodpile to a little area in the corner where there was an old blanket. The area was comfortably hidden behind the woodpile so he decided to sleep there for a while.

Eric's sleep was short lived when Ella, who had just returned from rabbit hunting, noticed the shed door ajar. She went inside, and she threw two dead rabbits on top of the woodpile, startling Eric that sent him like a lightning bolt into the present. Ella spotted him in the back corner, and the little kitten now one month old was with her. Eric eyed her rifle by her side.

"I remember you from the last time you were here," she said.

"I'm sorry. I fell asleep here."

She leaned the rifle by the woodpile and joined Eric. This was the first time he had seen her up close. She wore trousers and a cap, and her face seemed permanently soiled. Her beauty showed through. She looked like a discarded plucked sunflower that had been rained on, trampled on, with gaps where some petals had fallen off. Ella wiped the streaks of dirty sweat that had made lines down her face. Eric's inexperienced mind imagined what Michael told him secretly of acts performed between a man and woman. Had he only been a little older, Eric satisfied himself to think, he would as Michael joked, "have her on the floor" of this shed. Eric embraced her with a glance.

"You killed those rabbits by yourself?" he asked, very impressed and somewhat embarrassed as the young man he was, that neither his father nor Michael took the time to teach him to shoot.

"I did. My grandfather's got arthritis. I do most of the work around here and the hunting. Why did you come back here?" she asked.

"I don't know. I wanted to see you."

"Oh yeah? My grandfather gave me hell cuz he doesn't want boys hanging around here." The kitten rested his body on Eric's leg. He stroked the kitten.

"He likes you," she said. "What's your name?"

"Eric Kramer."

"I'm Ella Horn."

"Why aren't you in school?" she asked.

"I'm playing hooky. A cop was chasing me by the railyard, and I ran into the woods. I knew where you lived so I came here. Do you go to school?" he asked.

"No. We have no money for that."

"Where's your grandfather now?" he asked, with some trepidation.

"He's inside, probably taking a nap. He never goes away from the house. I take the wagon into town to get groceries once in awhile."

"It's just you and your grandfather here?"

"That's it."

"Where are your mother and father?"

"They're dead." Ella got up, and Eric did also. "As long as you're hiding from the police, why don't you come inside?"

"What about your grandfather?"

"Don't worry about him. His bark is worse than his bite."

"He sure is big."

"That he is."

"I don't want to cause any trouble."

"It's no trouble. Besides, I have to feed the cat and clean up the place." He followed her into the cabin.

"Go ahead." Eric went inside slowly. He saw the grandfather sitting at the table nibbling on a cookie. Eric stopped in his tracks, awaiting the giant to give a loud roar and chase him out again.

"He won't remember you," she said.

Ella introduced Eric to Zachariah whose attributes Eric couldn't help but respect. The old man got up with some difficulty. He was as Eric remembered a giant with taut legs, the substance of teakwood and stretched as roman columns. His broad head was covered by long stringy white hair that flapped over his forehead. Zachariah aware that his presence was disturbing to his guest, extended his hand and Eric's hand quickly disappeared in the massive palm of his host. There were no false illusions in this place. Zachariah invited Eric to sit at the table with him and help himself to milk and the plate of sugar cookies. "Ella baked them," he said proudly. Eric shyly bit into a cookie. Ella skinned the rabbit for dinner, and fed the cat while the two men chewed the fat a little.

Zachariah relaxed with his pipe and saw himself exactly fifty years earlier. He spoke to Eric of his service as an enlisted volunteer in the civil war, a position he chose of pure patriotism and the youthful want for experience.

Eric sat and listened. Zachariah worked in a cook's tent, cooking and washing dishes for one hundred men within two miles of the enemy camp.

At night, the Confederate campfires were clearly visible. Zachariah laughed when he recalled how some of the men in his camp got bored and threw some shells over into the enemy camp to see what the enemy would do. He recalled how the white smoke from a burst shell curled up in the dusk like a ghost.

"We had some deserters from our camp. It was terrible weather, raining and snowing every day. Sometimes the mud was up to my knees. I was on picket guard, and I saw mere boys being captured not much older than you," he told Eric. He didn't blame the deserters for wanting to escape. "There were deserters on both sides," he explained. "They were drawn into it, ya see. They had no sympathy with slavery and no interest in a struggle they didn't understand. They knew the penalty if they was captured."

"What was that?" asked Eric, anticipating the answer he knew to come.

"They were shot." Zachariah couldn't resist showing his war trophy. He pulled up his trouser leg for Eric to admire the bullet hole in his knee.

"I still have my old uniform," he boasted. They went into Zachariah's bedroom, and in the closet was the battle-scarred uniform consisting of a soiled dark blue coat and light blue pants. There was also the high-crowned hat he wore when drilling with a fastened brass eagle on the front.

Officer Hannay found his way to the Horn house. Ella received him at the door.

"Do you know a boy named Eric Kramer?"

"Never heard of him," she said.

"He may have passed this way. He's about your age, short dark hair, white shirt, dark pants."

"I haven't seen anyone."

"Is your grandfather home?"

Eric overheard the conversation while in Zachariah's room. He told Zachariah that he was supposed to be in school, but he was playing hooky. Zachariah told Eric to stay in the room. Zachariah went outside and met with Hannay. Ella retreated back into the house and joined Eric in the bedroom. They were silent as mice.

"Haven't seen anyone here," Zachariah said.

"Would you mind if I take a look inside the house?"

"Do I have a choice?" Zachariah asked.

"No, you don't," replied Hannay.

Zachariah let the officer pass. Ella came out to see what was going on.

"It's all right. He's just having a look for himself," Zachariah said.

Ella didn't seem too concerned. Hannay passed by the kitchen and the dining table. He saw two plates of partially eaten cookies and two half-empty glasses of milk. Ella even went as far as offering to show him both bedrooms. After Hannay saw the bedrooms, he was convinced that it was just the two of them in the place. He was frustrated that somehow he was outwitted and that these two knew Eric's whereabouts but weren't saying anything. There was no point in pursuing him there so he didn't make a fuss.

"How long you have lived in the area?"

"About one year," Ella said.

"You don't go to school?"

"I stay home to take care of my grandfather."

Hannay knew of them only by the occasional gossip from the townsfolk who saw Ella in town once in a while. These two kept to themselves and clearly didn't invite trouble.

Zachariah felt the weight of his legs get the better of him, and he wanted the cop out of the house. "You've seen everything," he said. Hannay was suitably impressed with the older man's size and firm approach. There was no point in lingering around. He left them alone. Eric escaped through the bedroom window and hid in the woods until he saw the police officer's car drive away. He went back to Ella.

"You best get back to school now," she said.

"It's too late. School's lettin' out now."

"That cop might go to your place, since he knows you. You best get home."

"Can we meet again?"

"Sure."

It was a fine afternoon. On the way back home, Eric passed by some of the neighbors who were sitting on their porches taking in the air. They exchanged greetings and a question or two about the police car in front of his house. These chance encounters at inopportune moments were always inevitable with nosy neighbors. When he got home, Eric thought he would have no choice but to admit to his mother his guilt and face the consequences. He never did anything like this before so it would be something new. When he got home, he saw Michael and Officer Hannay waiting for him on the sidewalk.

"Mr. Kramer. Nice to see you again," Hannay said with a feeling of selfish superiority and eager to get payback.

Eric walked up to them. "Where were you?" Michael asked. "You didn't go to school today."

"Didn't he tell you?" Eric said, referring to Hannay standing next to him, "I was at the railyard."

"I know."

"Momma's waiting for you."

Eric dreaded going inside and staying out. The sight of a police escort meant something bad in the eyes of the people. Giny was sitting at the table with half-empty cups of coffee. The cop had obviously been there for a while.

"The school called. You weren't there today," Giny said.

"I didn't go."

"What the hell were you doing at the railyard? You had us worried."

"Just hanging around."

"I'm not paying good money to send you to school so you can make an ass of yourself and embarrass me by throwing it back in my face."

Hannay sought to suppress the situation. "Giny, since this is his first offense, I'll overlook it. I won't write a report," he said and facing Eric, he continued, "just be at school tomorrow." Eric said nothing.

"He'll be there," Michael said.

"Thank you for the coffee." Hannay left the family to handle the situation.

Giny began cleaning up the table.

"What's come over you, Eric? Is there a problem with one of the kids at school or the teacher?"

"No, ma'am."

"Why did you take the day?"

"Just had to."

She turned to Michael for some support, "Tell your brother what the officer said to us."

"He said if you keep missing days, then Momma is subject to a fine of up to twenty-five dollars," Michael told Eric.

"It won't happen again," Eric said.

"I know it won't," Giny replied. "Michael. I think its time you showed your brother to respect our household. Take him out to the shed."

"No!" Eric shouted back. He wasn't going to take that type of medicine. "If you whip me, I'll do it again."

"I don't think so," Michael said confidently.

Michael went into his parents' room and took his father's strap that hung behind the closet door. Eric ran out the back door, but Michael was too fast for him. They went into the work shed and closed the door.

"What are you going to tell the teacher?"

"I'll tell him to go to hell."

"Suppose you tell me what you were up to before I give you the whippin' of your life."

"You know Ella Horn?"

"The girl who lives with her sickly grandpa? I've seen her around."

"When that cop was chasing me, I knew she was close by so I hid in their shed. Ella caught me there, and we got to talking. They're not as bad as everyone makes them out to be."

"You saw the grandfather?"

"I did."

"What's he like?"

"His name is Zachariah. He's big and well built, and he fought in the war."

"Is he as big as me?"

"He's taller than you. Let's get on with it." Eric pulled down his draws and bent over the workbench. Michael was impressed by his little brother's spirit of adventure and told him to put his pants back on.

"Momma's disappointed in you. You can't keep creating problems for her by cutting class."

Eric offered a suggestion. "Do you think Momma would mind if I invited Ella over to the house?"

"I think she'll get a heart attack."

"I like her, and I think she likes me."

"If you're going to continue to see her, the best advice I can give you is to plan ahead. See her later before it gets dark and not too late either."

"That doesn't leave time to spit," Eric said, annoyed that his brother was meddling in his business.

"Then see her on the weekends. Just make sure Mom doesn't find out, and don't miss school again," Michael said. "Keep your head down, and go straight to your room. She'll think you got whipped."

Giny pumped half a bucket full of water and got a bar of soap and bent down to scrub the kitchen floor. She couldn't remember the last time she cleaned the floor herself.

Eric went to his room unnoticed by his mother. *The weekend was not a bad idea,* he thought about his brother's suggestion. Why not even this weekend?

Chapter 8

Eric woke up in the middle of the night. He looked to see that Michael was asleep. Quietly, he got out of his pajamas and threw on the shirt and pants he kept under his bed to avoid opening the dresser and making unnecessary noise. He went out the door and into the night. It was so quiet; the only sound was his footsteps. He rationalized the consequences of sneaking out at night should he be caught again. The only thing he could be accused of was just being himself. He met Ella at her house. It was the first time he saw her in a skirt, and she looked more girlish which intrigued him. She carried a picnic basket and a lantern in her hands, and he offered to carry them for her.

"You take the basket," she said. Pointing the lantern straight ahead, she led the way into the woods.

Ella saw the desired spot to set up their picnic by the remnants of a fallen tree, its trunk lying on the ground, where they were safe from any prying eyes, at least from human eyes. Inside the basket was a blanket and a jug of applejack.

Ella liked Eric, but she was an untamed sort with a secret interest in housebreaking. She pondered about getting Eric involved as the effect of applejack took its hilarious toll on both of them, and in their youthful exalted state, Ella introduced another side of herself.

"I get bored sometimes, especially, at night when the dishes are washed, and my grandfather reads the paper and dozes off. Not even the stir of a mountain can wake him."

"I know how you feel." "This," Eric said, referring to the applejack, "helps the time go by faster."

"Sometimes, I go into town late at night like tonight when everyone is asleep and look around," Ella said.

"You don't like folks in town, do ya?"

"They look at me like I have leprosy."

"So why go there at night?"

"Where else is there to go? Besides I . . ." She paused and struggled to see into his eyes as the world revolved carelessly around her. "If I tell you something, will you promise not to say anything to anyone? I mean anyone."

"Scout's honor," he said, raising his hand, followed by a hiccup.

Ella explained how she easily entered other people's homes through the icebox door late in the evening when the owners were asleep. She emphasized that she never disturbed anything, never took anything, but just for the satisfaction of having done it and gotten away with it. That was the accomplishment.

"Why are you telling me this?" he asked.

"Maybe you can go with me one night."

Eric finished the last of the applejack and lay back on the ground as Ella's words rolled, flew, and spoke to his wandering mind. She got close to him on the ground and propped herself with her elbow. Their faces were only inches apart.

"You're not kidding about this?" he said, looking up at her in the moonlight.

"No."

"How many times have you done this?"

"A few times."

"Always alone?"

"Always alone."

"What if we get caught?"

"We won't."

"You don't know that." He was sobering faster than he wanted. He thought of that cop, Hannay, and other cops at his house, a criminal record, jailed, and more shame on the family.

Ella wanted a companion, someone to share things with. He wanted the same. She wiped a fly off his forehead. He was warm, and he took off his shirt and rested on his back facing Ella. She placed her hand on his chest, feeling its smoothness. Eric liked it and didn't want her to stop. This was the first time he ever knew such feelings, and it was the same for her. Ella grew bolder and slid her hand underneath his pants between his legs and finally felt what it was like, never having felt one before. It was like a dead fish, at first, but quickly firmed up. He liked having her hand down there and didn't want her to stop. She moved the lantern closer and attempted to undo his pants so she could see it better. He helped to remove his pants in the most hurried manner. His nerves thrashed and jumped and crashed within. She went down to him and kissed him on the mouth. He placed his hands around her head and shoulders and pressed his mouth against hers. Slowly he found his way to her breast, and she began to remove her blouse and skirt so there would be no obstruction between them. They started to know each other, and for the next hour before they both crashed they unleashed sounds, smelled and tasted from the well.

After it was over, she produced a cigarette and introduced Eric to smoking. He took a couple of puffs and couldn't keep his eyes open.

"Remember . . . to waake . . . mee . . . uup . . . eaarlyyy toommmorroww . . ." he said, yawning and went out like a light, and she did soon after. Sleeping, gently sleeping, the two of them in each other's arms.

When they awoke, it was already light. "What time is it?" she asked.

"I don't have a watch," he said rather embarrassed. They rushed to get dressed so they could get back before anyone woke up. Ella offered to give him a ride back into town in her wagon, which he gladly accepted as it would save time. She checked on Zachariah, and he was asleep.

They were quiet during the early morning ride. Through unspoken words, Ella's heart yearned to continue to share with Eric. She felt fragile and true to herself; immersed in shapeless patterns of strength and shades of light from which she could call upon now and then to take revenge upon the heartless town she had come to know.

"Have you thought about what we talked about last night?" she asked.

"I've thought of nothing else."

"I promise it won't be a way of life. Come with me one time."

"If your grandfather finds out, he'll kill me for sure."

"He won't find out. He's never found out cuz I don't get caught."

"And you won't take anything?"

"We'll leave the place as we find it. In and out right quick."

"On one condition," Eric replied, feeling he had the upper hand. "You teach me to shoot."

"It's a deal," she said. "I think my grandfather would like to go shooting some time."

"I meant you and me," he said.

Chapter 9

A female mourning dove perched herself atop a telephone pole. Her eyes blinked steadily as the first crow swooped down on her mate and pecked at his eyes and neck. This attack was in retaliation for the doves foraging for food in the following manner.

The doves tossed some hard-shell nuts earlier from a tree onto the street and waited patiently for passing wagons to crush the nuts and expose the tender flesh inside. After a wagon successfully crushed the nuts, they flew down to feed on the tasty morsels, when a group of crows, at their opportunistic best, spread their black-crested feathers in the sunlight. As constant scavengers and aggressive predators, they followed with a loud "caw-aw-ah!" indicating the pair of doves as the intended target. The surprised couple looked up toward the ominous gathering. The crows made it clear that the nuts were for them.

"No matter what, we will not let you escape from this place," cried the crow leader.

The mate told his companion to fly away immediately. She needed to live, for inside her she carried two eggs. She knew this to be the order of things as he would not survive what was about to happen. He realized that as many of his own brethren had fallen to the slaughter by the crow so he knew this also to be his fate.

"You must be strong, my love," he said to her. "You will have to fend for yourself and our squabs. Raise them to be strong, and trust no other birds, not even our own kind."

"I will find a safe place. I promise," she replied in anguish, as this was the last time they would see each other.

They kissed, and she flew upward out of harm's way onto a telephone pole. The mate stared at the crows, ruffling his feathers. The crows did likewise. He knew them to be among the wisest and most calculating of creatures. To say they did not have an affectionate disposition was merely a trifle. Larger in size and strength, they were killers who widely deserved to be hunted even more so than his own kind. Soon there were many crows perched in the trees and on windowsills, watching and cawing eagerly for a bloodbath. A mourning dove that is mobbed is unable to turn the tables on its attackers. This the crows knew all too well.

"What merit will you gain by my death?" the dove asked in vain.

"It's not for you to question why we do this," replied the crow leader, before proceeding to peck at the dove's eyes. It didn't take long for the dove to lose one eye and fall onto his back. The dove flapped his wings in futile defense. His wings rose and fell in a dissonance of jagged movements as his life ebbed away even as the will to fight remained against an assault of deadly energy. The female dove watched helplessly as they pecked at his neck and head with great vigor, gouging out the other eye. His chest sank to the ground. He could no longer see. He could only hear the cheers of the odious mass of crows around the darkness that surrounded him. He was soon dead. Most of the crows flew away after the excitement was over. Some joined in to get a few nibbles on what remained of the carcass. The female dove followed the crow and watched as he took the remains of her beloved mate and buried him in a backyard, taking great care to cover it with some leaves and twigs until satisfied the carcass was well hidden.

For reasons that she was not yet aware of, but would be in time, she would not forget the crow leader who planned and carried out the attack that killed her mate.

Abby was in pain, but it felt good to be outdoors again. Abby entered Mrs. Clark's General Store to the pleasant mixture of scented candles and fresh-ground coffee—an indication of the improvements Mrs. Clark had made to her establishment. There were shelves filled with new items Abby hadn't seen before: ceramic tea sets, purses, quilts, dolls, and imported tea and coffee.

Mrs. Clark emerged from behind the shelves where she had been organizing canned jams and jellies. She greeted Abby enthusiastically as if welcoming her for the first time as a successful businesswoman in her own right. Mrs. Clark had won the war with the Kramers. Her store was no longer playing second fiddle to the Kramers' much larger and more popular store, and she wanted the town to know it.

"I'm looking for a gift for someone," Abby said, anticipating Mrs. Clark's probing questions.

Mrs. Clark sensed an opportunity for discovery here but her instincts fell back to discretion not to offend a well-liked customer by asking too many questions. Abby, by the same token, did not want to reveal that it was for Raymond Fletcher. If that bit of news found its way out of the store, it would surely spread quicker than a plague.

Mrs. Clark directed Abby to the display cases. The many choices among the handsome nickel-and-silver-plated watches and charms were gratifying if not practical since they were priced too high. Farther down, along the wall were the overpriced men's and women's hats. Abby turned toward one of the windows and saw a music box displayed in the corner almost hidden away. She picked it up. Its walnut burl finish, rosewood border, and hand-painted roses in the middle of the lid only added to her desire to have it. But again the price tag caused her heart to break. Mrs. Clark noticed how impressed Abby was and offered to wind up the box. It played Beethoven's Fur Elise. Abby knew somehow she had to have it. Mrs. Clark offered to hold it for her. With reserve not to display her disappointment, Abby thanked her but ultimately declined.

Even her illness was not justification for overspending on items of frivolity.

Mrs. Clark continued to follow Abby around and suggested items as they moved into the men's section. "Perhaps a man's comb and brush set or this gray felt homburg hat."

Abby was indifferent to but well aware of Mrs. Clark's presumption that she was buying a gift for a man. She was right of course, but it was still none of her damn business. She turned away from Mrs. Clark to look for herself. She began to carefully select a pair of gloves that would fit the doctor's large hands. She wasn't sure about the size so she put the gloves back and went to the jewelry case where a pair of brass cuff links with a high polished violet stone in each caught her eye. The price was a little high but manageable. She decided the cuff links were more suitable without being too intimate a gift. Oh, hell! Who was she kidding? Of course, it was an intimate gift, and perhaps she wanted it to be so.

At this point, Ella Horn entered the store surreptitiously. The ringing bell signaled her appearance. Mrs. Clark's rigid acknowledgment of Ella's presence was not masked very well for the cold greeting it was. For Ella, to be on the receiving end of such savageness was business as usual, and it was of no consequence to her. She was there to obtain what she needed and not to make friends or so she thought.

"I'm looking for a new pair of shoes for my grandfather. His is comin' apart," Ella said.

"Our shoe selection is right this way. What's his shoe size?" Mrs. Clark asked hastily as her time was too busy to deal with those who were not up to her standards, particularly when there were regulars like Abby to take care of.

"He's got big feet." Ella held up her hands to indicate the size.

"A twelve inch," Mrs. Clark said. Mrs. Clark found a bargain at $1.50, but it was a ten inch.

"He'll like this pair," she said, noting the wool lining.

Ella noted the wool lining and also that it was not the right size.

"Do you have this one in a twelve inch?" she asked.

"Unfortunately, that's the only size in that particular style." Mrs. Clark grew impatient and fished for the larger size. Ella casually walked over to the tonic section. Her grandfather needed some liniment for his arthritis and a new razor. When she saw Mrs. Clark was occupied, Ella quickly stuffed a razor in her skirt pocket and a small bottle of liniment in the other pocket. Ella calmly walked back to Mrs. Clark confident that her task was partially complete. What Ella didn't notice was Abby behind the doll section who witnessed her brazen act. Abby was slightly disturbed by what she saw not so much for the items that this young girl whom she didn't know had pocketed but for the reasons she imagined why the girl was compelled to steal. Abby said nothing as she pondered whether to leave and just order the damn cuff links from the Sears Catalog.

Meanwhile, Mrs. Clark was hands deep in boots when she picked up a twelve inch in a more expensive style. Mrs. Clark walked over to Ella somewhat weary and proclaimed, "It's the latest—a crack proof rubber boot guaranteed not to crack or puncture." She handed one of the boots to Ella to admire the quality for herself.

"It's five dollars for the pair."

Abby watched the calculating nature of an overconfident adult trying to manipulate a young girl so shamelessly. Apart from the fact that Ella was not so innocent herself, secretly Abby was in Ella's corner.

"They're very nice, but I'm afraid we can't afford it." Ella handed the boots back to Mrs. Clark. "I'll take that shoe repair kit instead for one dollar." Mrs. Clark was unable to exert her persuasiveness over this little person who as far as she knew probably never had two coins to rub together most of the time.

"That will be one dollar." Ella could feel the air as it rushed out of Mrs. Clark's nose. She abruptly placed the repair kit in a bag. As Ella pulled out the dollar from her pocket, the stolen razor fell on the floor. Mrs. Clark picked it up and realizing it was one of her stocked razors, grabbed Ella's arm and fumbled inside her pockets to fish out whatever else she had stolen. The bottle of liniment was quickly discovered.

"You little thief, you stay right where you are!" Mrs. Clark shouted. She went for the telephone behind the register.

Abby walked over to try and diffuse the situation in view of the fact that the only customers in the place were herself and Ella. Abby thought she might have a better chance to talk Mrs. Clark out of calling the police.

"Mrs. Clark, perhaps we can resolve this without the police."

"Abby, please keep out of this. I'm not killing myself in this place only to be victimized by this trash."

Abby faced Ella and felt a strange partiality toward her situation. "Your grandfather needs the shoes, and I am only too happy to oblige," Abby told Ella.

To Mrs. Clark she said, "That way you can get the sale and hopefully you will overlook this incident." The seconds passed amid an internal test of wills and friendly persuasion for the two women. Ella remembered her grandfather's advice when confronting the goodwill of people, "they will have you by the throat if you allow them to." Ella reluctantly gave in. So did Mrs. Clark, who reconsidered calling the police but vowed, "she is never to enter my store again."

"Fair enough." Abby held up the pair of brass cuff links. "I've decided to take these please. How much for this jar of red cherries?"

"Forty-five cents."

"And please allow me to pay for the razor and the bottle of liniment." Mrs. Clark added the up total. Abby paid her for everything. Mrs. Clark's disappointment evaporated. Abby was decidedly gleeful at being the savior. Ella tugged at her arm. Abby bent down to get closer. Ella gave her a soft kiss and gave her the single dollar she had.

"What is your name?" Abby asked.

"Ella Horn. Thank you for my grandfather."

"I'm Abigail Whitman, but you may call me Abby." She gave the dollar back to Ella, and they both left the store and went their own way.

Ella gathered the proportions of this encounter with a stranger who made her feel special. A moment before she didn't know Abby at all, and the likelihood of opening her heart to another person as Abby did so generously with her filled her thoughts incessantly, over and over discharging fragments of hope of how she might change her view of a world where love was out of reach.

Mrs. Clark removed the music box from the window and put it behind the counter, confident Abby would be back for it.

Chapter 10

It was 5:00 p.m. Raymond Fletcher made the first house call to the Whitman home. He was going to give Abby the first injection that day. Maggie was there, and Abby was upstairs in her bedroom drinking orange juice. There was nothing that compared to being in her own bed after spending time in a hospital. The usual activities around the house would be altered. Until the soreness where the lymph nodes were removed wore off, Abby would not be doing any lifting or arm raising of any kind, which meant that she was not useful for anything at the moment. The soreness reminded her when she had her tonsils taken out as a kid. She couldn't swallow for a week.

"Come in, Doctor," Maggie said. "She's upstairs." Maggie accompanied Raymond to Abby's bedroom. "She's been quite anxious for your visit this afternoon."

Maggie knocked on Abby's bedroom door, and they entered. Abby looked quite fit as he examined her arm. She could do with a fresh dressing. He would take care of that after the injection. He placed his medical bag on the night table and removed a sanitized towel carefully placing it on the table first and then laid out the instruments he needed—a needle kit which contained the vial with the bacteria inside and a bottle of iodine.

"Where is your bathroom?" he asked.

Maggie directed him down the hall. Both women commented secretly on the needle which was a silver metallic object with a circular handle that Maggie found rather alarming. Abby had now become somewhat familiar with it and was less apprehensive.

"Momma, would you open the dresser draw and bring me the small package inside?"

Maggie retrieved the package, handsomely wrapped in blue and red tissue paper. "What's this?" she asked with a mother's curiosity.

"It's nothing, Momma. Just hand it to me. And when he comes back, please leave us alone, OK?"

"Are you giving him presents? You must be joking."

"There's going to be a lot of these visits, Momma. I'm a big girl. Please."

Raymond washed up and returned to Abby's bedroom. Maggie very annoyed, respected her daughter's wishes. "I'll be downstairs, Abigail," she said, nodding to the doctor.

"Are you ready to do battle?" he said, standing by the night table.

"First things first," Abby replied. "I want you to close your eyes for a moment."

"Why?"

"I have something I want to give you." This was the little girl inside her that planned to surprise Raymond, and she looked forward to seeing his reaction, but not in front of her mother, thank God.

Raymond, somewhat surprised by her childish mood, found it awkward and endearing.

"A gift for me?" he said playfully, but not forgetting his ethical position as doctor and protector. Hands folded in front, not even he could resist the anticipation of receiving a gift.

"Give me your hand," she said, placing the box in his hands.

"Open your eyes."

He undid the wrapping most carefully and opened the box to admire the brass cuff links. A profound sense of pleasure invaded them both at that moment. It was something tangible yet elusive. He took her hand and thanked her. It was time to get to the reason for his visit.

"I know it will be quick and painless. I'm ready for it," she said.

Raymond injected the bacteria.

"It's hot," she said, visibly nervous as a warm flush passed through her cervical region. And so the war was waged, and there could be but one victor.

"You need to start eating soup, mostly liquids right now."

Abby spent the night drinking water and orange juice and a bit of Ready Relief. She couldn't hold a thing in her stomach so she threw up a lot and just rested.

The days passed and Abby had no visitors, only Raymond who came twice a week to administer the injections. Abby was with each visit, less intimidated by the needle.

As Raymond indicated previously, the administering of the injections was timed to occur around when she arrived home from work or had the day off so she could be relaxed at home as the effect of the bacteria began to take hold. She slept mostly. Her fear subsided. And what was the point of worrying? There was no point.

"How are we feeling today?" was Raymond's habitual greeting. Inwardly, Abby would have liked to throw her arms around him and kiss him. Sometimes, depending on how she felt, she would have liked to punch him right in the nose. It was this that she found so terribly funny that on occasion she would laugh to herself.

"Have you been eating?"

"No, she hasn't, Doctor," her mother intervened as mothers do much to the frustration of Abby and her pride.

"It's time to start eating regularly," he told Abby. "Your body can only fight if it's strong. A weak body won't do any good." He injected her.

"When you are feeling better," he said, "perhaps you might care to listen to some of my records sometime?" Abby's world lit up a bit with that invitation to spend some time with him. At last, maybe she had found someone in that town who appreciated music and could share it with. She had a piano but didn't have a Victrola. He had a Victrola but didn't have a piano.

"Yes. I would like that," she said. Later that night, she vomited something fierce and the chills and headaches came as he said it would.

Abby read the daily papers most nights while the treatment did its work inside her. She noticed a particular advertisement for summer camp counselors.

The Best Summer of Your Life!

Camp Shallow Lake seeks college-aged men and women who have a passion for working with young people to work as camp counselors and want to challenge themselves with new adventures. Coed environment. Separate Camps for boys and girls. Located in southern Berks County, Pennsylvania, approximately ten miles south of Reading. Over hundred acres of athletic fields, meadows, and woodland. All land and water sports. Swimming and hiking.

Abby never gave a thought about this type of work before. She did like the idea of being in the outdoors, and she had absolutely nothing to lose by applying for a position. She went to her desk and wrote a letter of interest to the camp director, whose name and address were at the bottom of the ad.

Eric walked over to the Whitman property. Maggie was in the coop collecting the eggs that her chickens thankfully were laying regularly. The coop was raised on legs above the ground to protect it from flooding rains and fenced in so her chickens could graze comfortably. But there was no roof in the grazing area only in the coop so the chickens were not entirely safe from cats or hawks. Maggie saw Eric come over through the tiny window in the coop. Eric offered to help her. Pleasantly surprised, Maggie said she was nearly finished and invited Eric inside the house.

Over two glasses of lemonade and the prospect of a fine spring that came with the change in the weather, and notwithstanding that things were going well with Abby, which Maggie kept to herself, they talked about plans for the summer. Eric mentioned camp, but he wasn't sure. Maggie mentioned Abby was also interested in going to camp as a counselor.

Eric knew through the neighborhood gossip train of Maggie's fine workmanship as a seamstress when neighbors brought their garments over for her to mend. And he needed her help.

"Do you know Ella Horn?" he asked.

"The name doesn't ring a bell," she replied.

"She's the girl who lives with her grandfather outside of town."

"Oh yes. Abby mentioned her to me before. She bought some liniment for her to give to her grandfather."

"Zachariah, that's her grandfather. He's homebound on account of his arthritis so he can't work much."

"I'm beginning to know what that's like myself," Maggie said, referring to her own hands which hurt and were cracked all over. Not withstanding William Corrigan's generous assistance, Maggie saved made every bit of money possible, and she worked harder with the dress mending and selling the eggs and bread in town.

"I asked Ella to the church banquet," Eric said.

"Good for you. Did she accept?" Maggie saw Eric's eyes light up when he mentioned the girl.

"She'll go only with something suitable to wear. She doesn't have a proper dress, and she's not allowed back into Mrs. Clark's store on account of what happened before. And I can't go and buy a girl's dress."

Maggie knew what was coming. She saw the pile of dresses near the sewing machine that required her attention. *Oh god,* she thought, *another damn dress to make when she had so much work to do.*

"What does your mother have to say about you going out with her?"

"She doesn't know. Why get her all riled up."

"If she's going to steal whenever she gets the chance, it's more than likely she will end up in jail or shot. And if you keep hanging around her, you might get into trouble yourself."

"No one in town wants to help 'em."

"I know. Very well, have her come here tomorrow after school. I'll take the measurements and see what I can do," Maggie said, thinking how fine it must be for this boy to have someone to fill his eyes so that he would make such a request.

"Oh, she doesn't go to school," he said, knowing that it was no one's business and that he should never have said it.

"Thank you so much," Eric said with excitement. "Please don't say anything to my mother about it just yet."

"You're going to have to tell your mother about her before the banquet, you know."

"I will."

Eric left content, and Maggie sorted through her fabric pile to collect several patterns for Ella to see the next day.

Chapter 11

Ella showed up at Maggie's doorstep. Maggie noticed her bare feet and soiled skirt. She was a young pitiful sight. Maggie, aware of Ella's discomfort, invited her in and assured her that she had nothing to worry about. Ella wouldn't budge. Maggie went back inside the house and stood by the pile of wrinkled garments on the table.

"I'll need your help in selecting the right patterns," she said.

Ella wondered how on earth a dress could be made from a scattered pile of cloth. But Eric told her that Maggie was a talented seamstress and just as gracious as Abby, whom Ella hadn't seen since that day at Mrs. Clark's store.

Ella finally entered the house.

"We're only going to select the right colors today," Maggie said. "Then you'll come back for a fitting." Once Ella was happy with the pattern selection, Maggie saw a glimpse of the little girl within the little girl. Maggie spread the material on the floor and held it in place with the use of jelly glasses. Then she cut away.

Ella returned the next day for a fitting. Ella was visibly uncomfortable during the boring process of being handled by Maggie turning her, this way and that way, sticking pins into her until they were both satisfied. Maggie made her judgments on "taking it up a little here and letting it down a little there." Ella felt the dress was a little long. Maggie told her that it was proper to allow for shrinkage as she was still a growing girl.

On the final visit, the coronation was complete. Eric arrived to see how Ella looked in her new dress. The pink, white, and yellow patterns on her dress merged into one another spreading out like a flower bed ingratiating Ella's expression of relief that it was over. Eric praised Maggie for the fine work and he asked Ella if she could meet his mother. Ella was hesitant at first, but the sight of herself in the mirror with just a slight touch of lipstick at Maggie's suggestion brought about an acquired strength, and she stood out fearlessly in the room. She agreed to meet Giny.

As she walked with Eric across the lawn to the Kramer property, the bright green of the grass receded under her feet. In the warmish air, they passed under the dark leaf laden branches of the oak tree half obliterating the sun's indirect rays.

Giny was in the living room working on her framed collection of family photos when Eric came in with Ella. Giny noticed the girl's attractive dress and her critical eye passed from her son to the girl and from the girl to her son.

"Momma, this is my friend, Ella Horn."

Giny put the dustrag down on the table and sat on the sofa, anticipating the worst.

"Come here, sit please," she said.

Ella maintained her confidence for Eric's sake, walked over and sat next to Giny, anticipating the worst.

"We haven't met before, have we?" Giny asked, unimpressed with no unique expectations of this girl whom Eric called a friend.

"No, ma'am."

"So what has my son told you about me? Anything pleasant at all?"

"Eric has told me that you stay at home and don't go out much and we have that in common."

"You don't have friends here?"

"Just Eric, my grandfather, and Mischu, my cat."

"What about friends in town?"

"No one. I'm not interested."

"I know what you mean. I used to run a mercantile store with Eric's father for many years."

"Eric told me."

"Sometimes when you've spent your entire life serving a small community and in truth they don't appreciate it, it is better just to withdraw."

"Don't let her get you down, Ella. She's always putting herself down," Eric said.

"My dear, you're so young to be feeling that way. What about friends in school?"

"I can't afford school."

"There's no price too high for a good education."

"My grandfather taught me everything I need to know. He taught me how to use a rifle and how to hunt. He taught me to chop wood and take care of the house and how to ignore folks in town when I go shoppin' for stuff."

"What does your grandfather think about where your life's heading?"

Ella didn't like the ill-timed comment, and Eric sensed a problem. "My grandfather raised me. He's the reason I'm still alive," she said. "I'm home to take care of him like he took care of me."

"And your parents?"

"Dead."

"I'm taking Ella to the church banquet. This is her dress for it."

"It's very nice."

"Thank you. Maggie made it for me."

"Maggie Whitman? Indeed. Will wonders never cease?" Giny got up.

"I'm going to take a nap. I'm tired. It was nice meeting you, Ella. Eric, I'm sure you'll act like a gentleman should at the banquet. Remember, poise, grace, a little levity, and be attentive to Ella. She is, afterall, your significant other, at least for the duration of the banquet."

Chapter 12

Raymond Fletcher entered the gate to what was his childhood home. It had been so long since he had returned. The place no longer looked the same as the vivid memories languished in his mind. He walked along the path and saw the lawn needed to be cut. His fears and suspicions of the past were rekindled. If it hadn't been for his mother's letter on his father's deteriorating condition, he wouldn't be there. He knocked on the door, and a paint chip fell off. The entire house needed a good coat of paint. His mother opened the door, and he didn't recognize her from the last time he saw her. Her hair that used to be red and down to her shoulders was silver and up in a bun. Her skin resembled the paint peeling off the cracked ceiling, ready to be stripped clean. They embraced, and she felt so small and frail. When she smiled, he was able to see a trace of her former self through her many lines. She took his hat and coat as a courtesy offered to a guest visiting for the first time, not like a son who hadn't visited for fifteen years. The carpeting was faded. Everything in that house seemed to offer the hopelessness that comes from neglect. Correspondence from his mother kept him updated on his father's health.

"No one comes to visit anymore," she said.

"Where is he?" Raymond asked.

His father sat in the living room in a rocking chair by the window so he could see the light from the sun that he distinguished from total darkness. His hands were raw boned and lifeless, mangled twists of flesh. Raymond remembered his father's massive soiled hands that held the reigns to the horses when plowing the field. These were the hands that never hugged him, but when his temper flared, when the frustration of an unfulfilled life became too much, the hands were a heavy and useful tool for beating with a closed fist or to hurl large rocks at his remaining son.

Raymond approached his father whose eyes no longer saw. He was now homebound for good. His eyes always nervously searched the barren darkness to an earlier time when he could see the sunlit fields that were just outside the window, where gophers popped their heads through the mounds, where the clouds that grew darker and thicker and threatened to drench him with rain when he was out in the field—of his team of horses without which he never would have gotten a day's work done, the golden fields of majestic cornstalks, row after row, spearing toward the heavens, of chasing bluebirds and squirrels out of the corncribs and the sound of the cattle in the barn.

Raymond sat next to his father. He sensed movement. There was someone else in the room, not his wife.

"Who is it?" he asked. The mother standing in the back told him that his son Raymond was in the room.

The sound of his son's name caused a stir in the father who sat attentive to the fact that although he was blind, his son was seeing him at his most vulnerable moment, and it was pissing him off.

"Well, you finally had the nerve to show after all this time," he said, grabbing his cane. "You came to see me off, did ya?"

"I asked Raymond to come," the mother said.

"Why?"

"I thought it was time you had a doctor look at you," she replied. "You don't trust any doctor around here, why not your own son?"

"You try and talk some sense into him," she said to Raymond. "I can't anymore." She left to go into the kitchen.

Raymond wished she hadn't left so soon. He was ill at ease. He recalled as a boy walking toward the horse-drawn riding plow his father used and the sound of the grass as he stepped across the hot sunbaked grounds. His father held the reigns and at the sun's mercy sweated to plow for fresh corn to be planted. He had his back to Raymond so he didn't see him coming and neither did the horses until it was too late. Raymond spooked the horses by lurking silently and suddenly coming out of nowhere. The horses galloped at all speed, and the father pulled on the reigns unwilling to give up a losing battle against an assault of flying wind and dirt. He held the reigns for an eternity until he managed to subdue the horses.

After that storm was over, Raymond felt another had just begun. He was going to meet the hangman when his father dragged him out of the house and gave him the strap in front of the passing neighbors.

That was the end of his life with his parents. Raymond was approaching fifteen, and he decided he had enough. He gathered his clothes and spent the next two years at a friend's house and vowed never to return home. He never did. He occasionally saw his mother but refused to speak to his father. The father couldn't have cared less.

Raymond not wanting to wear out his welcome thanked his host family and began a new chapter in his life. He left for the city to study medicine. Raymond did so well on the entrance exam that he received a full scholarship based on merit and need since the family he stayed with had no obligation to continue to support him, and he would never ask anything of his parents.

Raymond was no longer a struggling medical student but a respected member of the medical community. Now was the time for him and his father to find common ground.

"Did your mother tell you I had a heart attack?" his father asked.

"Yes, she did."

"Maybe it's all for the best. Can't see a fuckin' thing. I'm not scared to go, ya know."

"I'm sure you're not," Raymond said, very certain.

"In fact, I'll be glad when it comes. I cheated you, your mother, and your brother out of a lifetime."

"You were busy working."

"That's the problem. I spent all day out in the field, too tired to spend time with you and your brother. But not too tired to go to the bars and play gin rummy with the guys."

"And other things," Raymond added, sarcastically.

The other things involved the father visiting his lady friends. His wife knew about this other form of relaxation, and so did Raymond when one day a young woman came to the house looking for the father. The mother was in town, and the father told Raymond to go outside and tell the woman he wasn't at home. She became furious and made a spectacle of herself vowing to tell the wife of his infidelities if he ignored her. This proved to be the case that very day when she found the mother and told her everything.

"You've got two men here, dyin' of thirst!" he shouted in a typical bullheaded fashion when he wanted something and expected it immediately. His blindness only gave him the appetite for throwing his weight around with a vengeance upon a world he no longer was a part of. Raymond's mother was the long suffering wife still within the range of his voice.

"I'm making some ice tea," she replied, placing the glasses on the tray and thinking if he shouted any louder, perhaps he might drop dead and allow her to live the remainder of her life in peace.

"I only thought of you as a not-so-good farmhand."

"You're right about that. I wasn't."

"Are you married now?"

"No. I haven't found the right girl."

"You keep waiting much longer. You'll be passed wanting to look."

The mother came in with the tea and asked Raymond if he could stay the night. Raymond said he couldn't as he had to get back to the office.

"Do you want me to examine you?" he asked his father.

"No," he replied most definitely.

"What harm could it do?" asked the mother.

"Because I said so, that's why," he said loudly. "I'll be wrapping up my time here soon enough."

There was a rainstorm that happened years before, and the result was the destruction of the Fletcher family.

Raymond's little brother had a paper route, but it was very burdensome for just himself to manage. So Raymond took over part of the route to help his brother out. They were both on bicycles, and they separated the delivery route between them carrying the newspapers on the back of their bicycles. Each brother had a large pouch on their shoulders, filled with folded papers from which they either threw or put in the mailboxes.

While the brothers diligently went about their route, the rains began as a drizzle. They used the cloth under the papers on the bicycles to keep the papers from getting wet. In a matter of a few minutes, the rains drenched the brothers and everything in sight. The brothers took shelter where they could, under a tree or on a porch. The rains didn't let up. The boys continued delivering to the last paper before going home. Getting caught in the rain was more of a nuisance really, not deserving of a second thought until the little brother wasn't himself after a few days. He coughed and began to have a fever. The mother thought maybe a doctor should be called. The father didn't trust doctors. He felt all they wanted was to keep you coming back to them and pay them forever. The best thing was hot tea and honey.

Raymond, however, saw his brother through caring eyes each night he was up with him. The mother decided to call the doctor in the morning regardless of what her husband thought. He was too sick to go to school, and Raymond took over the entire paper route. He was getting weak, and she telephoned the doctor to ask if he could come to the house to see him and not risk exposing him to the elements.

The doctor arrived. The boy was in bed with a wet pad on his head. The doctor took his temperature. It was high. The boy asked what his temperature was, but the doctor smiled and said, "Smart doctors never give out information. If they did, then the patients wouldn't come back." He turned to the father, "Isn't that right?"

"That's the truth," the father said.

The doctor asked the boy if he had any pains. The boy said his chest hurt.

"It hurts when you cough?" The doctor examined his pulse.

"Most of the day," the boy replied.

"How long has he had the cough?" the doctor asked.

"A couple of days," said the mother.

"We got caught in the rain, delivering papers," Raymond said.

"Is it contagious?" the father asked. The doctor's eyes fired up as a bubbling cauldron of invisible flames and burned into the face of Mr. Fletcher. He turned to the mother and explained that she should get a fire going in the fireplace and have the boy sleep there all night. He also explained to use damp cloths of cold water on his head and wipe his face at all times to bring the fever down. He faced the father from whom he sensed not an ounce of compassion for his own son and asked to speak with him privately.

"Is that all you're concerned about? Whether you can catch anything? He has pneumonia."

"Will he get better?"

"I don't know. And to answer your previous question, only those who have been close to an infected person are at risk. My guess is that your elder son and wife are the only two people in this house who might catch anything."

The boy slept all night in front of the fire. His mother and brother were with him for that last night. The father slept in the bedroom.

In the morning, the boy died. The father held his son's body until the casket came. The father did not speak. It was Raymond and his mother who made the unfortunate arrangements for the burial.

The father was left for the rest of his life wandering in the eternal darkness celebrating his dead son's birthday each year by visiting the grave and going into town to drink himself into a stupor.

When Raymond saw his brother lying in an open-faced casket, it was a turning point in his life. It was the menacing grasp of his brother's illness that took hold of Raymond's mind and through the hurt of the present and the promise of the future, lodged within him the desire to become a doctor.

The female mourning dove was tired. She had been flying around looking for a suitable place to build her nest away from predators. She barely escaped the bullet of a hunter.

Without her mate, she braved a world that each day tried to destroy her. She needed to lay her eggs very soon and time was running out. She was hungry. She paused, fluffing her feathers soaking the sunshine and rested beneath a honeysuckle shrub. She looked around the houses and around the trees. She saw something that lured her curiosity and flew closer to inspect. It was an open feeder that hung off a tree. There were seeds there, not much as other birds had gotten to it but enough to satisfy for the day. There were no other birds around so she flew onto the feeder which had a roof and floor. It was comfortable, and she ate to her fill. She looked about and thought to build her nest there, but it would be difficult as other birds were sure to come and chase her away. So to spend the time and effort to build a nest there was not going to work despite the room. She napped in the feeder until two sparrows flew by to chase her out.

They told her that this was their place to feed and she was an unwelcomed intruder who had to leave. The dove explained that she was carrying eggs, and the sparrows paused to take pity on her and they directed her to the path of houses just around the corner where an abundance of trees might provide the shelter she needed. They saw she was in no condition to fly endlessly for very long and wished her luck.

She came to a house where she saw a basket full of colored eggs by the front porch. She flew around the basket to see how it looked, and she rested on top of one of the eggs to familiarize herself on how it felt to protect an egg. It was too large, and she wasn't able to sit properly so she went between the eggs. It was still uncomfortable so she gave up and flew away when it began to rain. She flew for a bit when as luck would have it she saw an open shed, where Michael Kramer was fixing a chair. She flew past him landing unnoticed on a dusty table behind a toolbox and some paint cans. Soon after, Eric and Ella's cat entered the shed. The cat sprinted about featherweight as if walking on air, moving his whiskers from side to side in order to detect what he apparently smelled. His senses sharply alive to everything, he looked around.

"Why do you have to bring that cat here?" asked Michael, very annoyed.

"That's Ella's cat, Mischu," replied Eric. "He shows up when he feels like it."

"You mean he walks all that way over here from her place?"

"He's gettin' used to being here."

"You might want to tell Ella to keep the cat at her place. Maggie has chickens next door."

"He won't hurt 'em."

"He's following you back after your visit with Ella. That's why he knows where we are."

Michael smelled cigarette breath coming from Eric.

"Has that girl been teachin' you smoking?"

Eric put his hand to his mouth to check his breath.

"Drink this soda pop to get out the smell before Momma finds out."

The rains came down hard, and the shed was vibrating with sound. Mischu looked up, and he didn't know if he could make the jump onto the shelf. It was quite high. But as he moved his ears back, he could hear something stirring up there. He looked at the chair that Michael was working on and saw he could make that jump. He jumped on the chair. Michael tried to grab the cat by the tail, but his hands just glided on his soft fur. Mischu jumped from the chair to the shelf where he and the female dove made eye contact. She flew out of the shed with Mischu in pursuit, once again jumping on the chair which Michael had just finished painting.

The rains mercilessly attacked, reducing the dove's sense of direction. She came to the limbs of the massive oak. In the midst of an abundance of green leaves and large branches, she found an easier footing. She decided this would be her sanctuary from the elements and predators for now. She decided to build her nest here. It wasn't long before a pair of robins, three starlings, and a pair of finches approached, ready to thwart her homely desires.

"Can we help you?" asked the female robin, not out of kindness but a direct inquiry as to the dove's presence there. The dove mentioned that she didn't mean to intrude but a cat had chased her out of the garage next door and she wound up in the tree. The robin told her she had nothing to worry about. The cat was harmless and had been adopted by a girl who lived a distance outside of town and was in the vicinity on occasion when she came to visit the younger boy.

"I'm looking for a place to build a nest."

"Where is your mate?" asked the female robin.

"He is dead," said the dove.

They did not take kindly to a stranger invading their territory. However, this disclosure lent itself to a collective understanding among the residents of the massive oak toward this newcomer, before telling her she was not welcome.

"How did he die?" asked a starling.

The birds listened intently. The female dove explained how she and her mate were ambushed by a gang of crows as they mistakenly searched for food in their territory. She escaped, and he did not.

"The crows are without mercy in their killings and do not deserve any sympathy as they cry for being slaughtered in abundance themselves," said the male robin. The other birds concurred on how hated the crows were.

"They should all be shot, their nests burned, their food poisoned," said one of the finches, eager to get his opinion in. The robins spoke of a blue jay they once knew who lost one of his young to a crow.

The birds saw the dove was due to lay her eggs soon. The starlings were adamant that she go find another place. The finches were in agreement but less vocal about it. The robins, however, had a strain of understanding in their character. They had just given birth to two babies themselves the previous week. They took pity on the dove, and the birds talked among themselves whether they should let her build her nest in the tree or not. The dove rested on a branch, and the rain quietly ended. Time passed, and through the leaves she saw Abby feeding two stray dogs.

"Is she a good neighbor?" asked the dove.

"Yes. She is mindful of her own business and will leave us food from time to time," replied a finch.

"She works with her mother around the house," said the female robin.

Fat pigeons were not ignored as they lingered about waiting for any leftover scraps. They found an ally with their human counterparts in the sharing of morsels. Hope finally arrived when the female robin flew over and told the dove that an agreement had been reached to let her stay.

"As my mate and I have our wings full with our young, we may not be able to grant too much of our time to your needs," the robin said freely. The dove understood this.

"However," one of the starlings graciously interjected. "All of us will do our utmost to ensure that your squabs are born in a safe environment. Neither you nor your squabs will be in danger of any serious want as is within our means to provide for you."

"Welcome," said the female robin who with her mate presented their two babies to the dove. It was a welcoming gesture, and the dove began her new journey.

Chapter 13

One day, Abby became acquainted with the mourning dove when hanging the clothes to dry, and the dove perched herself on the clothesline. Abby greeted the dove whenever she saw her. She noticed that the dove was always alone and asked playfully as if the dove could understand what she was saying, "Don't you have a mate?"

Abby went inside the house and came back with a dish of water and some stale bread crumbs put through the mill and left it for the dove by the base of the tree. The other birds commented to the dove on how she was receiving preferential treatment from the woman. The dove argued that after all she had been through, she deserved it. The dove ate all the bread crumbs heartily by herself.

As the time to lay her eggs drew near, the dove attempted to gather twigs in her beak, but the weight of the eggs inside her made it difficult to fly back and forth. The few she was able to gather were tossed in a disorderly fashion in a little nook in the tree where the nest would be built. One of the starlings brought two French Fries in its beak so everyone in the tree could take a piece. The birds organized themselves and took over the function of building the dove's nest. And so it was that friendship was extended to the lonely dove that had the task of rearing her two young squabs, but she would not be alone.

After a time, Abby missed seeing the dove. She knew she was there in the tree as she often heard the dove's call in the morning and at dusk.

Abby went into the garden to check on her flower beds, carrying a bag of morsels for the birds. The stems were bent in some places, and there was a litter of petals amid a foul odor. She looked closer and saw that some animal had been using it as a litter box. Angry, she walked to the base of the massive oak where there was an unusual amount of twigs and broken stems on the ground. She thought the birds were not capable of leaving such a deposit in her flower beds. She looked into the tree to see if she could see the mourning dove. She could not but saw hidden in a crevice of a large branch, the edge of stems and twigs sticking out. *It must be a nest,* she thought. She couldn't see the dove, but she could hear movement in the nest. The dove was probably sitting on her eggs. Abby did ask the birds in the tree as if she were talking to another person if they knew who vandalized her flower beds. She listened to the chirping and wondered what birds talked about.

The birds did in fact know that it was Mischu, the frisky cat who was responsible. The birds chuckled among themselves as to Abby's problem.

Abby tossed the mixture of bread crumbs and sesame seeds she had in the bag on the ground enough for all the birds in the tree. "Let's not waste time," said one of the starlings. "Those pain-in-the-neck pigeons are waiting on the roof. You see them, ready to grab our food. There's no stopping them with the appetites they have. C'mon."

All the birds flew down and began to eat to their fill with the exception of the male robin that guarded their young and of course the dove that was occupied incubating her two eggs. With each week, the dove began to feel at ease in the company of her neighbors and the woman who offered food and kindness for which all in the tree were grateful.

The dove sat on her eggs for two weeks mostly at night and during the first half of the day. During part of the day, one of her neighbors would stand guard and protect the eggs from predators while the dove left the nest to defecate and look for food since Abby didn't leave food every day. The dove thought about when the eggs would hatch. She thought about her mate, the crows that killed him, and the hawks and other crows who knew no boundaries to speak of when it came to their acts of cruelty.

Abby asked Michael if he could build her a small bird feeder that she can place by the tree. He was only too happy to oblige. The feeder was erected, and Abby left some food for the birds when she looked up and saw two little heads popping out from the nest. Protecting the hatchlings became the primary focus of the birds.

"We in this tree have been blessed with your presence, it seems," said the female robin to the dove. "We have food provided for us by this gracious host," referring to Abby. "And it's because of you. When the days come when there is no food, I will watch over your young while you go out to exercise."

"And if they are occupied," said one of the finches, "we will take over." There were no objections, and there was no time to waste. They gathered at the feeder to eat. One of the pigeons made an attempt to land onto the feeder and pushed the smaller birds out of the way, but the feeder was too small to accommodate all of the birds so they succeeded in harassing the pigeon out of the feeder. The pigeon knew he wasn't welcomed. But he was bigger, and his disposition dictated that he would try again for food another time.

Chapter 14

Morning. It was time for breakfast, and that meant apple picking. The ground below was damp, and squirrels quickly unearthed their buried acorns for breakfast. It was bewildering to Lydia Ramon how the squirrels could remember the precise location where they buried them. Now and then, a lush wind of fragrant wildflower passed her way, and she felt her stomach drawing upon her unborn child silenced against whatever predetermined measure of time would allow her baby to be born.

Lydia experienced another contraction. It wouldn't have been such a shock if only she hadn't climbed up that ladder to pick an apple. Her body seemed to twist and tighten, and she found it difficult to breathe. She had to get down. The ladder made a cracking sound. She looked down at the squirrels, and they emerged with increased clarity until she could see their large eyes looking up at her dropping their acorns and dashing out of the way. Soon the ground below rushed toward her, and the world was stilled. Some time passed before Lydia opened her eyes. She wasn't sure how much time had passed. Against a bright morning sun on her face, Lydia felt the wet muddied ground on her back. The apple she picked for herself to enjoy was being enjoyed by the squirrels. She laughed to herself at the ridiculous stupidity of risking the life of her unborn child for an apple. Her father John Ramon knelt beside her.

Meanwhile, Beatrice Kirscheimer, an aging madam, known as Bibi to everyone including the handful of her remaining clients, sat in her oval shaped sumptuously adorned parlor with gold and silver souvenirs, her treasured gifts from long gone callers. It was here where she took her meals, and due to her failing eyesight she had one of the girls read the most interesting parts of the daily papers to her. The parlor also served as the place where she conducted her interviews for new girls.

The morning sun penetrated the parlor's large bay windows and lent a desired comfort that enhanced the informality of the madam's existence to the extent that she buried the self-imposed restrictions in her younger days as a struggling prostitute. Spread out in a red flannel robe, Bibi carefully balanced herself with the aid of her cane and settled her nearly three hundred pounds into every inch of her large mahogany chair. She looked out the window, and her eyes diminished the beauty of her beloved rose garden to an undistinguished blur of muddled pink and red colors. She kept a calendar on the side table and noted the days when it rained, when the sun shone, and how long it had been since the gardener had visited to prune her rosebushes. Next to the calendar was a ledger book stuffed with that week's unpaid bills. She lit her cigarette in a solid gold-foot-long holder and grasped it firmly between her lips. She hated doing the accounts, in part because it bored her, and as she was unable to see the numbers clearly, she would have to hire an accountant soon.

After thirty-five years as the head of prostitution house, Bibi could only shake her head in mock disappointment at her vocation for she remembered all the trials she overcame to succeed, and at this point in her life she was marked by despair and cynicism but she was too proud to show the vulnerability.

In the beginning, she took advantage of people's instinctive desire to be loved starting out with a small crowd of "little tricksters" of every conceivable type from millionaires to freeloaders to the sincere man-about-town with silk suits, the smooth touch, and not a cent to their name. It wasn't long before she realized her talent for extracting favors of a kind. Soon, she was earning a decent livelihood, at times equaling that of some of her clients. And with some hired girls, she built a small fortune that established her position as a successful businesswoman. Striving for independence if not respect wasn't without risk. Her judgment was tested all the time. Many unsavory clients that she thought were trustworthy passed through her doors on credit only to never be seen again. It wasn't long before she was being exploited by the very same that she exploited for her own personal enrichment. But that's the way it went in life. As the sole administrator of her client's interests, if a client complained, career adjustments had to be made. Regina quietly slipped through the purple satin curtains carrying a tray.

"Coffee, Bibi," Regina said softly, well aware of the onslaught of verbal lashings when her approach was too disruptive. Regina was once a prostitute in the house. Nearing thirty and tired of catering to the diplomatic routine of providing sex, she asked Bibi if she could quit and stay on as the housekeeper. Bibi accepted and never regretted it as she knew Regina as a responsible and trusted person to run things properly. Regina placed the tray on the table in front of Bibi and poured her a cup, adding just the right quantity of milk and sugar, as Bibi liked it.

"Your eight o'clock is here," she said.

"You need to dust off the bookcases in here once in a while," Bibi said, taking the cup and sipping very slowly until the first drops of coffee settled into her, miraculously calming the swell of waves inside her into a lull of raindrops until at last she found it easier to breathe in her hulking mass.

"Who did you say was here?" Bibi asked.

"Your interview to replace Melinda."

The large grandfather clock sounded eight chimes. The telephone on the table rang. "There goes my peace and quiet," Bibi said most annoyed. "Answer that."

"It's Melinda," Regina said, handing the phone over to Bibi, certain the conversation was not going to be pleasant.

"Where were you yesterday afternoon?" demanded Bibi. "Apparently, you forgot your date with Mr. Hoffenberg. You were to meet him at the track. He came by the house looking for you, very upset."

"I wasn't feeling well so I stayed home," said the unconvincing voice on the other end of the line.

"Mr. Hoffenberg is one of our best clients," Bibi said.

"Bibi, I told you before that I can't stand him. When he takes his clothes off, he sweats terribly."

"You made the decision to cancel with one of the few respected members of our clientele without telling me!" her voice thundered. "If you didn't want to go with him, we could've gotten a replacement. But to have a client come looking for you is unforgivable! Come and pick up your pay!" Bibi slammed the phone.

"Give me a moment," she said, dabbing her forehead with a silk cloth, "and then show her in."

Regina knew that Bibi had planned to get rid of Melinda even before the phone call. It was difficult enough to maintain order and satisfaction to the clients without having to worry about an employee who thought more of herself than the client to whom she owed everything. Business was business.

Marceline Alexander heard the entire conversation in the waiting room just outside the parlor. Her polished layers of makeup were beginning to run from the perspiration. Regina peered through the curtains and told her to come in. The sun found its way into Bibi's eyes that were sensitive to sunlight, and she quickly retrieved her sunshades, an old habit of also wearing them during talks with strangers.

Upon entering, Marceline matched the great barrel of the woman with the voice who just minutes before exercised her authority with great fervor. She sat down opposite her interviewer. She looked the part of an aging duchess with overly painted rouge on her cheeks. Her hair was not her own but a wig that burst like a firecracker of waves and curls extending all over her head like a big brimmed hat. As Marceline digested this stout figure of unshakable rectitude with whom she was to spend the next several minutes, she sensed an uneasiness about the whole situation as her half-smile to Bibi confirmed. Regina left the parlor while Bibi shouted several instructions in her direction.

"Regina! Make sure Yvette doesn't burn the toast. Tell her, it's her turn to wash everybody's undies thoroughly. Don't let her get them all mixed up this time! You know how particular everybody is about wearing someone else's!"

Yvette's voice echoed a faint reply from the kitchen. "I don't think the neighbors would like seeing all that underwear hanging out on the lawn again. They've been complaining."

"Never mind, just do what I tell you!" Bibi's wind of words roared vigorously past Marceline, who stared at Bibi's chair that seemed to grow out of her.

"Getting the laundry done right is very important here, Ms . . . ."

"Marceline Alexander."

"I'm Beatrice Kirscheimer. Call me Bibi. May I interest you in some coffee before we start?" Marceline declined. Her apprehension slightly vanished at the sight of the many handsome adornments around her. Bibi took note of her admiring curiosity.

"Everything in this room is a gift from satisfied clients, Marceline. I've had this old cigarette holder for over thirty years." Bibi implemented her instincts for capturing the misguided who desperately sought a place where they didn't belong, especially when they tried in vain to look younger. She thought again and decided to at the very least get to know what made this woman tick.

"Well then, let's start off with you telling me how old you are or how old I think you are."

"Old enough for the job," replied Marceline.

Bibi wasn't impressed. In a tone clearly suggestive of a warning, she said, "Young lady, at my age and at this time of the morning, I can't be bothered with a smart aleck. So do us both a favor, and leave your impudence elsewhere."

Marceline's vanity was short lived and reduced to a level befitting her present situation of someone who needed a job. Bibi continued, "Since you've placed me in the embarrassing position of having to answer my own question, I'd say you're . . ."

"I'm twenty-seven, and I don't think it's too old."

"My clients don't pay for overly expressive older women with sass. They want girls, preferably still in their teens. So you see, I need 'em young, pretty and without opinions. You aren't any of these things, my dear."

Marceline listened on to the insults as her hopes for getting the job all but disappeared.

"You didn't come here to hear insults from me, did you?" Bibi asked rather proudly. "As I see it I'm accommodating you, not the other way around."

"I'm a responsible person and well versed in courtesy," Marceline said.

"I have no doubt. But you're too sensitive when you're challenged. I don't think you'd fit in this line of work. I often wonder, what makes an intelligent person like you choose prostitution as an option?"

"I don't have any other prospects."

"Ridiculous. You have brains. Get a job in an office," Bibi said.

"I've had jobs from time to time, but nothing long standing. I have two boys so I can't allow myself to become destitute for their sake if not my own."

Between the questioning, the madam's cigarette smoke found its way right under Marceline's nose. She tried not to cough. It just wouldn't seem right to gesture negatively to the personal habits of a potential employer, no matter how unpleasant they were.

"Two boys?"

"Yes, David and Brian."

"Still married, or did he dump you?"

"We're divorced."

"Same thing. I must say that's not what I usually hear from other hopefuls looking for work. Then again, the girls are usually a lot younger. Some are runaways who've gotten pregnant or they can't live with their folks anymore and have to leave. If you can raise two boys on your own without a man, I salute you. I never had any real kids of my own. I have my girls here. We look out for each other, like a real family."

Bibi's smile etched new lines in her face. Marceline wasn't interested in false praise. She wanted to shorten the lapses into family life and get right to the point.

"How would you rate my chances of landing a job?" she asked without enthusiasm.

"If you're looking to enhance your standing economically, it won't pay for the sacrifice that you'll have to make if you work for me. You'll hate yourself later on, and it won't take very much time for you to communicate it to clients. And that's not good for business." Bibi knew what she was talking about. She had spent a lifetime in a profession where self-loathing fades away into pity and submission. She knew after the first meeting whether a candidate could survive the long-term effects of such a life of degradation.

Bibi was certain that Marceline lacked confidence in herself and was simply resorting to prostitution out of a desperation she could overcome if she wanted to.

John Ramon drove his Model T as fast as he could. His daughter, Lydia sat next to him, her hands on her stomach.

"You don't think you're going too fast," she cried. It was her first child, his first grandchild. John knew he was a distance from Raymond Fletcher's office. He floored the gas pedal, nearing the car's top speed of forty miles per hour.

"Don't worry, we'll get there," he said, his eyes running left and right at stop signs, traffic lights, and people coming at him dangerously close.

In her maternal heart, Lydia dreamed of lullabies, of watching the little chest going up and down when breathing, of sleepless nights, of the person her child would become. Now she only thought how much longer before the baby arrived.

Just before turning, John noticed Abby Whitman walking on the side walk, heading to work. A moment later, he turned the corner when he was caught by surprise by a big truckload of mill wood that had just tipped over onto the road. John swerved to miss hitting the wood, and before he could even think, his eyes were blinded by the bright morning sun. He didn't even see the lamppost until it was too late. John's head hit the windshield but luckily did not go through. Lydia was shaken but all right. She looked at her father.

"Your head is bleeding," she said calmly. The blood slowly ran a single red line down his face. He didn't even know he was hurt.

"Are you hurt?" he asked.

"I don't think so."

John grabbed the door handle on his side, and with his weight, he pushed the door open. He staggered for a moment to get his surroundings. The steam hissed steady out of the punctured radiator leaving a white cloud on the front of the car. John went to Lydia's side to get her out. The unmistakable sound of a car crash had disturbed the usual formalities of an early workday and got the attention of people who gathered around the car to see what had happened. The men stopped reloading the wood back onto the truck and rushed over to the car.

Among the curious, Abby rushed over to see if there was anything she could do. She recognized the woman as Lydia, the former secretary to her boss and whose job she currently had. But there were so many others around the car, Abby stood as close as possible and observed. Police officer Paul Hannay ran toward the car that was partially on the side of the road and part on the curb. He made his way through the crowd and asked both John and the other man to move out of the way.

"My daughter's in there! She's going to have a baby, right now!" yelled John.

Hannay gently lifted Lydia out of the car and felt that she was all wet. He carried her onto the sidewalk.

"I don't think we have time to get to the hospital," she said. Hannay smiled and looked toward the madam's house.Abby watched as the policeman carried her up the stairs and pounded on the madam's front door.

With the excitement over, the crowd dispersed, and Abby continued on her way to work.After having seen a father and daughter comfort each other in an unexpected situation, she thought about what her father was like and if he would ever worry about her in the same manner.

"Well, this is a first," Bibi said. "We've had plenty of kids conceived in this house, but we never had a baby born here."

Regina said, "You're in luck. I think Dr. Milstein's still here," she said.

"At least I think so. Didn't see him leave last night."

"We'll go upstairs and check, fast. Hopefully he's not passed out," Bibi ordered.

They took Lydia into the madam's spacious bedroom on the ground floor with a large brass bed.

Yvette placed a hot towel on Lydia's head. Upstairs, there were five bedrooms. All had the doors open except one. Regina burst through the door and found the unconscious doctor lying naked in bed.

"Dr. Milstein!" she screamed at him. "We got a lady downstairs whose gonna have a baby, right now! You better put your clothes on, quickly."

Alan Milstein was a doctor in Lancaster who occasionally traveled by train to visit his girls. Milstein dragged himself downstairs. He had just finished putting on his shirt and was about to head for the door like a thief trying to escape when Hannay stepped in front of him.

"Where exactly do you think you're going?"

"I promise you, I'll get someone to come here, but I need to leave," said Milstein.

An angered Hannay replied, "Listen, Doc. Just 'cause you sneak in and out of here for a good time doesn't give you the right to skip out in an emergency 'cause you're afraid of someone recognizing you." Regina applied her own pressure on Milstein.

"You're gonna help that young lady or believe me I'll call your wife right now and tell her where you've been."

"All right, all right! I won't charge for a house call," said Milstein, smiling nervously. "Where is she?" Before they went into Bibi's room, Regina placed her hand on his groin.

"Your zipper's open," she said.

Lydia lay on the bed breathing heavily.

Milstein entered the bedroom. "Good morning, everyone. I see you have the hot water and . . ."

"And fresh linen, yes we know the basics, Alan. Now all you have to do is help out with the delivery," Bibi said.

Marceline convinced the doctor to let her stay and help Regina as she was a mother of two boys and knew a thing or two about giving birth. She stayed throughout the delivery and spoke to Lydia on the joys of motherhood while her father nervously waited with Bibi in the parlor. Whenever Bibi popped her head into her bedroom, the birthing room, she was struck by the look of concern and total strength on Marceline's face and to see her in bed with Lydia comforting her and rubbing her back as the hours passed, and it was getting tough for Lydia to relax. It was the kind of strength that doesn't permit another soul to perish in lonely frustration, the kind of strength that knows great enthusiasms and in time of trouble consciously shares those enthusiasms with others. Lydia cursed and felt the need to push, but Milstein said to wait and not push too soon, in a patronizing irritated sort of way, being forced to assist in Lydia's childbirth and hating her and everyone in the room for it.

When the excitement was over, a handsome boy, Corrigan's boy was being cleaned up and brought to his exhausted mother. Bibi took Marceline aside.

"You've got guts and a good heart, lady. I'll give you that," Bibi said.

"I told you I have two boys of my own so I know something about delivering babies," Marceline replied.

Bibi changed her mind about hiring Marceline and making her a part of her life. This admiration could not be kept secret. Through it all, it was Marceline's presence that liberated Lydia's anguish and turned it into elation.

Bibi could not contrive a sufficient reason not to hire Marceline, nor did she want to.

Abby went to work thinking about what she had witnessed, a father and daughter overcoming what could have been a tragedy by being there for each other and making the bond even stronger than before.

At her desk, Abby imagined what breakfast in the morning would have been like if her father and mother were at the same table. Perhaps it would have been a symphony of arguments that would eventually lead to his leaving, perhaps not. What would the talks about boys have been like with a father? Would the warnings against the tendencies of boys have been as swift as her mother's? Abby was in her own world searching for a man whose face she never saw. She didn't even know if he was still alive.

She also recalled the face of the man in her dreams with the long face and overcoat and close cropped hair. Was he someone whose path she was destined to cross?

Chapter 15

Spring. Easter Sunday. The church banquet. Sunshine always prevailed on this day as if it came with the Lords' blessing, a day to enrich and make splendid all that is good, at least in the imaginary sense of things.

On this day, Abby turned a blind eye from her illness as an unavoidable occurrence of nature that did not belong to the present. Instead, mother and daughter focused on baked molasses cookies, buttermilk custard, and a strawberry shortcake. Abby enjoyed baking as it became an added element to her resilience against fatigue. In this sense, she compared herself to Beethoven when confronting the inevitable loss of his hearing; he counterattacked by remaining active and writing his best work even when he couldn't hear a single note.

The church was a white gabled erection standing alone in a vast meadow. Huge sequoia trees claimed the vista. The faithful began to gather around ten o'clock. Parked carriages were cluttered to one side and blankets, parasols, and a sea of wicker baskets came together on the grassland. A large elongated table was set up for all the baked goods.

Soon enough, all thoughts and worries were let loose like dried leaves blowing about, swapping the latest gossip and renewing a tether here and there between sips of lemonade. Abby and Maggie were pleased with the positive response to their baked goods. The strawberry shortcake was the winner as many shamelessly came back for a second piece only to discover that it was all gone too soon. An outing would not be complete without the musical accompaniment of three trumpeters, a pianist, and two violinists. The dance floor was a wooden platform where shoes clicked to the song, "Blood Lilies" just for starters. Maggie ran into Michael and asked where his brother and Ella were. She wanted to see Ella showing off her new dress. Michael regretted telling her that Ella became despondent and frightened when they got into the carriage, and without a reason she refused to go. She ran home. As a result, Eric didn't come to the banquet either but went to her place.

"I'm sorry for all the hard work you did on her dress," he said.

After a time, it was Henry Corrigan who wandered by the outing, drunk and displaced. He spotted Abby dancing with Michael Kramer, and he readied himself to do what he did best to disrupt the merriment of others as just cause for his own troubled existence. He walked past the crowd. Some looked at him at length, formulating their opinions, others only veered for the occasional glance in his direction and quickly looked away. His father and mother did not attend the festivities.

"Look who's here," Michael whispered to Abby. They continued to dance, but their concentration was on Henry walking up to the stage, tripping as he stepped onto the platform. He motioned the orchestra to stop playing, and only the wind echoed.

"Ladies and Gentlemen, how about giving a hand to this great orchestra?"

"Henry Corrigan, you get your tail outta here!" shouted one annoyed townsperson, and then another voice echoed the same sentiment.

"Oh, c'mon, show your appreciation." Henry began to applaud by himself and seeing no one else joining him he stopped.

"You wouldn't know good music if your life depended on it!" a voice shouted.

"I know more than you think. We have a star among us." His eyes fixed on Abby who wore her favorite blue dress.

"Abby, play something for us," he said.

She was embarrassed and angered at Henry's audacity. Henry began to applaud again. Michael Kramer suddenly joined in the applause. Soon other hands clapped at random upon recognizing her presence. What else could Abby do but submit to this sign of approval. She bowed her head and smiled.

"You said you always wanted to play before an audience," Maggie said.

Michael kissed Abby on the cheek and led her to the piano. She thought about what to play, an ensemble piece perhaps. What better way to boost her self-esteem than to play before an audience of mostly familiar faces.

"Does anyone know the Brahms trio no. 1?" she asked the musicians.

Their heads shook.

"Beethoven, Mozart?"

Their heads shook again, not to her surprise. Abby opted to play alone, the Chopin ballade no. 1 in G minor.

All were quiet in anticipation. Abby sat at the piano bench and waited for a moment. She was now experiencing what it felt to be the center of attention, a concert pianist. No one else mattered but her. Nervously, she began to play the piece. Its opening, an unsettling harmony of darkness and hesitation was reminiscent of how precious her life was and how she must never waste another minute. Soon her hands relaxed as the poetic sound of each scale made her feel distinct and dreamlike. Anything her soul desired could be fulfilled as long as she kept playing as if Chopin's spirit was guiding her through his masterful scales and passages.

Raymond Fletcher arrived at the banquet. He recognized the Chopin piece and followed the music to the platform where Abby played. The tempo changed into a romantic melody from which a climax of strength and heroism emerged to find its way into the hearts of the people there. For an encore, Abby played the third movement of Beethoven's Appassionata.

After the recital, the crowd applauded enthusiastically. Abby began to shake inside so overcome from the response. Michael walked her off the stage, holding her hand and congratulated her with a kiss for all to see. Maggie was all smiles for the first time in many years.

"Could we talk in private for a moment?" Michael asked. She noticed a small package in his hand. Raymond Fletcher wanted to offer his personal congratulations to Abby, but Michael had taken her inside the church before he had the chance.

They went into the empty foyer. Michael checked inside the church, while Abby waited. There was no one inside but for the invisible spirit of God, they were all alone. Michael presented her with the small box. Abby unwrapped the colored tissue paper, and to her surprise it was the small music box she saw in Mrs. Clark's store that chimed the theme from Beethoven's Fur Elise.

"How did you know I wanted this?"

"Mrs. Clark said you had your eye on it for sometime."

"How did she come to tell you that?"

"I went to shop for an Easter present for you and . . . and in her own way."

"The subject came up," Abby said.

"That, it did."

"I'll keep this always." She thanked him and kissed him on the cheek.

Henry Corrigan stood at the church entrance, heard everything, and directed his anger at both of them. He entered the foyer, grabbed the music box from Abby's hand, and with rage threw it on the floor, and then to finalize the deed, not satisfied that it wasn't broken enough, he stomped on it, breaking it into pieces. Abby saw his red eyes filled with hate and his body a quivering mass.

"Ungrateful bitch!" he shouted. "After all my father's done for you!"

Michael grabbed Henry by the collar and punched his face, knocking him to the ground. They began to fight. When the orchestra stopped playing, the scuffle carried outside disrupting the festivities.

Abby ran outside. Michael took Henry by the collar and pushed him out and sent him tumbling down the steps to the ground where he landed at Maggie's feet.

She took him by the neck and pulled him up until he stood on his feet. Mrs. Clark and the church pastor were with her. Michael came outside with the remnants of the music box.

"Gotten off on the wrong foot again, Henry?" Maggie asked. "What is he up to now?"

"I gave this music box to Abby. He grabbed it from her and smashed it." Michael showed the crushed box for all to see.

"Yes, that's the box I sold to Michael." Mrs. Clark said.

"You're going to pay for breaking that box," Michael said, and warned him to stay away from Abby.

Henry didn't respond. He spit out blood in Michael's face and left humiliated, disappearing into the sequoia trees. So much for Abby's attempt to win the respect of the people. Michael apologized to Abby and Maggie and to the church pastor for interrupting the banquet.

"You don't need to apologize for that vermin," the pastor said. "It wasn't your fault."

Michael stayed at the banquet for a little while longer, and by midday he headed home walking down a path lined with early blossoms of blue indigos and the chirps of swallows, herons, and jays gave harmony to the natural order of things, forever changing, forever growing. Possessed by this charm he thought of Abby, the music box, and of course Henry Corrigan, who suddenly stood before him with hands clenched and an expression that could only mean he was filled with the same anger as Michael ready to fight and finish what he started.

Michael couldn't have wanted it more. They were alone in the woods, and they came alive with all they had hurling themselves against each other, crushing the blue indigos beneath their feet. They buried their fists in each other until their faces bled and even afterwards they kept up the fight until their mutual seething hatred subsided out of the need to rest. Michael regained his senses. He felt something soft on his face, something tickling his nose. He opened his eyes to blades of grass. His body was a block of stone unable to move. Henry was gone.

Maggie and Abby rode home in their carriage. They talked about the picnic, the remarks made about the food, the piece Abby played, Michael, the music box, the doctor, and of course Henry Corrigan.

"You're a lucky woman to have men fight over you," Maggie said.

"I'm not so lucky, Momma," she said, dismissing the remark.

"Michael thinks the world of you to buy you a present like that. It shows you're special to him."

"Henry Corrigan thinks I'm special too. He winds up breaking the thing."

"That young man will never amount to anything. He's no good, and his father knows it. I feel sorry for him."

Abby didn't hear her mother's words. In the depths of her thoughts, she asked herself if death was kind. "Momma, what are you going to do after I'm gone?"

"Don't speak that way again." She didn't like hearing her daughter resign herself so easily. She raised her better than that.

"We'll have to talk about it sooner or later."

"No."

Abby took in the air, and with a sense of finality, she said, "It's in God's hands anyway."

Maggie refused to argue so she kept quiet. The only sounds were the horses' hooves gracefully caressing the dirt road. The women spotted a man lying off the road. He looked like a beggar in tattered clothes, but as their horse drew closer, Abby recognized Michael Kramer. Michael heard a woman's voice call his name. His eyes opened to the sight of a woman's skirt, a blue skirt, Abby's skirt. "Its' all right, Michael. Mother's gone for the doctor."

Raymond Fletcher and Officer Hannay arrived. Raymond treated Michael for his head injuries on the spot. There was no evidence of serious injury. Michael told Hannay about his altercation with Corrigan after the first altercation witnessed by certain attendees at the banquet. Raymond, Abby, Maggie, and Hannay helped Michael to the carriage and accompanied him home, guarding him like a group of soldiers shielding one of their own who had been wounded on the front.

At the Kramer house, Giny Kramer reacted to Michael's bandaged forehead. Before Hannay had a chance to explain to Giny what had happened, Michael lied and said that he fell and hit his head coming back from the banquet. Everyone just stood there waiting for to see if Giny believed him or not. Maggie also went inside the home and nodded to Giny, who respectfully nodded back. The group knew Michael was sparing his mother from any unnecessary worry or stress. Raymond assured her that he was fine but to make sure he would recommend that Michael stop by for a checkup in the morning.

"He'll be there," Giny said.

"Where's Eric?" Michael asked.

"Probably with that girl," Giny replied. "Why are all these people here?" she said.

"They brought me home, Momma," Michael said.

Giny expressed her gratitude to everybody, and they left bewildered.

Michael's head began to ache. He took one of the headache powders in a glass of water. "Why can't we get a gun, Momma?" he asked.

"If you had a gun and shot Henry, you'd be in jail, Son," Giny said, getting up to take a bath. "I'll hear no more talk of guns."

William Corrigan paced back and forth in the living room. Henry sat on the sofa. His mother Henrietta sat alongside him with mournful pitying eyes that despite their life on a grand spiral staircase there was also the occasional broken glass and splinters to be avoided, which is why she turned to drink.

"I can't stand to have you near me!" William shouted to his son and then to his wife, he said, "This boy has been a problem ever since we were summoned by the school principal because he was beating up on the smaller kids! It doesn't stop there. Oh no! He was rude to the teachers, and they threatened to expel him if he didn't change! The only thing you and I share is the embarrassment of having this loafer for a son!"

"Henry, the people in the town won't even speak to us," his mother explained.

"It's gotten so that if I greet someone in the market, they give me the most insincere smile and turn away. I'm so used to the rejection that I rarely speak to anyone anymore."

"You can't blame me for that," Henry said in his defense. "A lot of the people resent Dad for being rich, and they take it out on the rest of us."

"Our standing in the community isn't the reason people hate us. It's you! Now you make a fool of yourself at the banquet, picking a fight over my secretary." He turned toward Henrietta and said, "You remember what that duty sergeant said years ago about his violent outbursts? He said he'd kill someone one day. He needs a psychiatrist, that's what!"

"Your father and I have always tried to provide you with the best of everything to make you happy to grow as a person," Henrietta said.

"A wasted effort, you spoiled him!" his father shouted back.

Henry knew this. But as he grew into his own instead of learning how to make friends and influence people, he grew accustomed to the indifference of others who avoided him like a contagious disease. To be free of committing sin was far from his mind. He knew he would have to say many rosaries, but he wasn't really into doing that either. This could also be said of his father and his philandering ways. But Henry lacked the courage to tell his mother and save her from a life of lies and deceit.

"You're a bad seed," his father said. "I'd like nothing better than to relocate to a place where no one knows me, and I can start all over again." But he knew this was the place he would remain for the rest of his life and that his son's actions were now bent toward violence.

"Why did you attack Abby?" he demanded the truth.

"I didn't touch her. I took the music box from her and threw it on the ground."

"And you crushed it with your foot several times, right?"

"I was angry that he gave it to her."

"Then you fought Michael Kramer in the church and then another fight in the woods?"

"The church was empty, and yes we did fight."

"It's very fortunate for you that he wasn't seriously injured or you'd be in jail right now," Corrigan said.

William Corrigan knew his obligation to Abby must be protected, and he was not going to be made a fool of again. He knew he did not have the commanding presence of other fathers and as a result was not respected as he felt he should be in his own home. He had the God-given right to act as head of the household. The two had his undivided attention. He knew apologies were in order. It would begin with a visit to see Maggie at her home during the day when Abby was working in the office followed by a visit to see Michael Kramer next door and to call Dr. Fletcher to personally guarantee that he would pay Michael's medical bill.

"Tomorrow, you will apologize to Abby in the office and then clean out your desk. I don't want you working at the company anymore."

"Fine."

"And you will accompany me to see Michael Kramer and Maggie Whitman to apologize to them as well."

"Forget that, old man. I won't speak to that guy at all."

"You will do what I say or you leave this house!"

He knew lecturing Henry fell on deaf ears so this final utterance would certainly rouse him up and perhaps get him to take some responsibility. Henry looked into his father's hateful eyes and knew he meant business.

Then Henry made the mistake of his life when he lunged at his father, but the father surprised him with a left hook that sent Henry flying into the stand-alone mirror, shattering glass all over the floor. Henrietta screamed.

Henry got up and felt his mouth for any loosened teeth. He never knew his father's strength as he was never spanked. Henrietta did not permit spanking in the house. Henry walked over to the family collection of framed photographs, which included pictures of William's mother and father, and he swung his long arm to completely knock the pictures off the table onto the ground adding to the broken glass from the destroyed mirror.

A family destroyed as the pieces of glass on the floor. The governance of the family was no longer in the father's hands as there was no longer a family to govern. William took Henry by the shoulders and pulled him away from the littered floor and kicked him in the side. Henry groveled and cursed both of them. He vowed to leave.

"That's fine with me. Get out!"

"William, you can't do this," Henrietta said.

"It's done! When you clear out your desk, stop by the accounting department and pick up your final wages. And that's all the money you'll ever get from me!"

Chapter 16

Henry went to visit the accountant and chatted with him as they were schoolmates and knew each other enough to discuss the most personal and painful events in their lives. The accountant couldn't believe that Henry's father fired his son and threw him out of the house. Henry said he was glad about it. He had no use for typewriters and was bored by and frustrated at having to go out to peddle the merchandise. It wasn't for him. Abby and the accountant were the only people he would surely miss. The accountant asked Henry where he would go to live. Henry wasn't sure nor was he sure what type of work he would do. He said goodbye to his friend the accountant and walked into his father's office to tell him what he really thought about him before leaving. His father wasn't in the office so he went to the desk to write him a note, when looking for a blank piece of paper he discovered a bill from Pennsylvania Hospital.

The bill was dated March 8, 1910. In large bold script, on top of the invoice was the name Abigail Whitman and underneath in much smaller script was in c/o William Corrigan. Invoice No. 76193. Henry read the typed itemized list of charges for the room, the operating room, X-rays, medicines, and the operating procedure—removal of cancerous lymph nodes (right side). At the very bottom also in script it read, "We would appreciate your check as a/c is past due."

He handled the bill delicately with his fingers as if it were a brittle old document of value that would turn to dust if he didn't respect its fragility. It added another element to crowd his tortured brain. Henry saw Abby through the window coming into the office. He quickly folded the invoice and put it under a folder.

"Henry, your father is out at a meeting, and he instructed me to tell you to please pack up your desk as soon as possible."

It wasn't much to conquer cleaning out his desk. A messy desk had been a sign of creativity and imagination, but the truth was that Henry had neither and was just lazy about organizing his papers. The clutter buried in his desk was minuscule compared to what was buried deep in his mind that Abby was seriously ill and his father was paying her medical bills. The fact that he was paying the bills didn't bother Henry at all. But it was that he knew about her illness and kept it from him. He went into his desk with full ferocity, and while normally he would have resented the eyes of people staring at him as he removed his papers, he simply willed himself to banish everyone in the office from encroaching on his consciousness.

Abby said to him that his father wanted him to leave immediately. Henry looked up from his desk and saw Abby from very different eyes. He was not the arrogant misfit who caused her so much distress. She still saw him that way. But she didn't know that he knew her secret. He got up and composed himself. Abby didn't even want to look at him.

As she prepared to leave the office, he said, "Abby, please accept my apologies for my behavior at the banquet. I was drunk. It wasn't me."

"Oh, but it was you, Henry," she said. "It's always you. It was you who left a dead rat in Mr. Kramer's syrup vat. It was you who tried to look up Mrs. Haversham's skirt. It was you who urinated on old man Finklemeyer's lunch and then said that he did it himself."

"Abby, that's not fair. That was years ago."

"You have never been able to stay out of trouble. You've left an incredible legacy. I pity your parents, the heartache you give them."

"There's no need to feel sorry for my family. My father's thrown me out. Did he tell you?"

"No. But I can't say I'm surprised. You've made a life of poisoning everything good that comes your way."

Henry held up the severance pay he collected to show Abby. "You see, these are my last wages. I'll be living on this for a while until I make my own way."

He pulled out a ten-dollar bill and handed it to her for the cost of the music box.

"You keep it," she said. "You'll need it more than I do."

Abby turned her back and left the office. Henry finally saw the stuff she was made of. He made up his mind to be strengthened by her from a distance even if he never saw her again. He hoped that one day she would realize he wasn't such a bad sort. But that would not be today.

The mother dove was in a state of sheer panic. She looked down from the nest and saw that her son had fallen to the ground. He screamed for help.

"What can we do?" cried the mother dove, helpless to save her son from the crows and other predators that lurked about waiting for an opportunity. She called to him, and he said he hurt his leg. He was unable to fly yet so essentially he was trapped and clearly visible to overhead predators. The robins stayed with their young in the nest while the two finches and two of the starlings flew down from the tree as well. Four big pigeons joined the others on the ground, to protect the little fellow. They knew they would not have a chance should a pack of crows show up.

Abby was in the kitchen and heard the abnormally loud chirping, and she came out of the house to investigate what all the commotion was about.

"Where's that damn cat?" asked one of the finches.

"He's not here today. Here she comes. Let's go," cried one of the starlings upon seeing Abby emerge from the house.

The pigeons were not quick to fly away as much as walk in the opposite direction from Abby's presence to maintain their vigilance over the injured squab. The mother watched Abby's every move, while reassuring her son that the woman was a good person and that he was not in danger.

As Abby got closer, she could hear the peeping sounds from the ground get louder and louder. She bent down and gently took the squab in her hand.

"Where did you come from, little one?"

Abby saw the blood from his leg on her hand. It was not much blood, but she had to get the bird home or it would surely bleed to death. She looked up into the tree and saw the mourning dove calling from the nest. She knew it was her young that had fallen from the tree.

"I promise to return him or her to you once his leg gets better," she said, holding the bird gently to her face to hear it peep.

The dove followed Abby while the other birds guarded her daughter in the nest. From outside the kitchen window, the dove saw Abby retrieve a large mixing bowl and line it with a cloth towel. She placed the squab inside the bowl. This would be his home for at least a week. Abby boiled an egg and mixed it with cereal and water to make a paste. She spooned a tiny amount and placed it in front of the bird to see if it would spark anything. There was a little blood on the towel. She feared it may die if something wasn't done, but she didn't know what to do. So she decided to call Raymond to ask his advice. Raymond advised her to keep the bird in a warm place away from drafts and to try a little water and salt on the leg. The bird should be calm and not disturbed too much to reduce stress.

Perhaps it may eat after it gets comfortable in its new surroundings. Abby bought a small cage from Mrs. Clark's store. And as the days passed and when she saw the bird was getting better, she put him in the cage.

During the evenings, Abby noticed the mother dove at the kitchen window. The squab kept peeping so Abby figured mother and offspring must be conversing.

"She's wondering when you'll return her baby to her," Maggie said.

"I wonder if it's a he or a she."

"Who can say," Maggie replied.

Abby decided it was a he. She didn't know it, but she was right.

"You've made those birds your pets," Maggie said.

"What of it?"

"You see how they gather at the tree waiting for you to feed them. They're used to you." Abby's illness made her more observant of God's creatures in her own backyard.

The dove flew back to the nest, and she was unsettled about her squab in the house. The female robin told her that she and her brother were abandoned by their parents at infancy. And were it not for the kindhearted nature of an elderly couple who fed and sheltered them, they would not have survived.

"You just have to have faith. Not everyone is all bad."

This advice was contrary to what her mate told her on the day he was killed.

After a while, the little squab's leg got better, and Abby got used to having him around. She knew it wasn't going to be easy to return him to the nest and his mother. The squab was growing attached to Abby. When she approached the cage with some food, he got closer to her rather than escape to the other side of the cage. He was turning into a regular eating-and-pooping machine, and he was growing rapidly and fully feathered in two weeks.

She saw he was quite active and hopping about in the cage, grasping the side of the cage with his legs and dangling his weight at an angle. It was time for him to start exercising his tiny muscles. She opened the cage door, and she placed her hand inside and he jumped on to her hand. She took the squab out of the cage, and he roamed around the kitchen table and then jumped on her forearm and soon she was able to put him on her shoulder. He attempted to fly by jumping from the countertop to the floor, but he stumbled and Abby was afraid he would hurt himself all over again.

The time had come. She picked him up and took him outside to the oak tree where she knew his mother was probably watching.

"He's bringing your son over, look," said the robin to the dove.

The dove spoke with her son and asked if he was all right. Abby heard the squab peep loudly. She wasn't sure if he was communicating with his mother and the other birds that were all chattering away or if he was truly frightened and wanted to go back to the safety of the cage. Abby debated with herself on this point. Was it selfish of her to take him back into the house after the mother and everybody else in the tree were calling to him?

Considering all she had done for him in his fledging stage, she knew what she had to do. She left the dove on the ground for a moment while she went into the kitchen to retrieve a ladder. When she returned, she saw his mother and a robin, two starlings and two finches by him on the ground, chattering. When the birds saw Abby approach, they flew into the lowest branches possible to see what was happening. Abby placed the ladder against the massive trunk, picked up her beloved young dove that in just three weeks was now an adolescent, and climbed the ladder and returned him to the cramped nest, where he was reacquainted with his mother and sister.

The gathering of all the birds plus others from outside the tree made for a celebratory occasion on his safe return home. The young dove expressed shame for not being able to fly as his sister could. He knew his place as head of the family would happen soon enough. The other birds cheered him on and many questions would be asked as to how he was treated by the woman in the house next door.

"Thank you for taking such good care of my son," said the dove to Abby who went into the house and closed the kitchen door behind her. As the widowed dove who vowed not to forget her mate's killer, she also vowed not to forget the kindness of the woman who saved the life of her son.

"Tomorrow," she told her son, "you will learn to fly."

Chapter 17

Mrs. Haversham who caught the mocking eye of Henry Corrigan's pretentious desires years earlier was retired from teaching and lived alone in her house.

One of the worst mistakes she ever made was hiring a lazy undeserving housekeeper who was not doing her job.

The night of Eric and Ella's joint burglary adventure had come. They walked around to choose the house they would break into. They passed by the Haversham house and heard some commotion. They went around to the kitchen window to see Mrs. Haversham standing in her robe shaking a plate of chicken-fried steak and mashed potatoes with peas at the housekeeper.

"I told you no goddam salt!" she shouted.

"It's my way, Mrs. H," the housekeeper said in a tone suggesting nothing bothered her.

"I don't give a damn! Dr. Fletcher says it's bad for my blood pressure! You know that! If you want salt, then put it on your portion, don't saturate the whole damn meal with it! You're not cooking just for yourself!"

It was surprising for Eric to see Mrs. Haversham curse. She was always so proper in front of the class.

"Why do you leave the dishes accumulate in the sink? That's why we get bugs!"

"This is my house and you will do as you are told, not what you want to do!"

The housekeeper grabbed the dish from Mrs. Haversham and smashed it in the sink breaking some other dishes.

"Get your things and leave immediately!" Mrs. Haversham shouted, "I've had it with you!"

"You have to pay me two weeks' severance pay," the housekeeper said, turning her back to her and taking her hat and coat that hung on the kitchen door.

"I'm deducting the cost of those broken dishes plus the dress you burned! I shouldn't pay you anything at all. You have been nothing but trouble ever since you came here!"

"The feeling is mutual, you repressed hag!" the housekeeper shouted back and slammed the kitchen door behind her.

The kids ran behind bushes when they saw the housekeeper come out. What they didn't see was a tranquil peace that came over her. It was a personal satisfaction for having rubbed Mrs. Haversham the wrong way again. The housekeeper was out of sight. They returned to peek in the kitchen window again. Mrs. Haversham wasn't there. The broken dishes were still in the sink. The two kids went back to the safety of the bushes before somebody caught them spying.

"We gotta do something to help Mrs. Haversham out," Eric said. "She can't be left to take care of that big house by herself."

"Who is she to you?" asked Ella.

"Mrs. Haversham was our teacher for many years. Nice lady. She taught my brother and me and just about everyone else's kid in town. Never asked anything for herself."

"What can we do?"

"How about we wait till she gets to bed and we clean up the kitchen?"

This wasn't what Ella had in mind at all. She protested. She said the purpose of breaking in was never to disturb anything but to accomplish the task. Now by a strange turn of events, they were to break into this house to do chores without a reward. She got enough of that at home. Eric pressed on that Mrs. Haversham was a rare breed. She dedicated the best years of her life selflessly to the education of the children of the town for over thirty years and many of her students had grown into fine young men and women. In his eyes, this victimization of Mrs. Haversham needed a remedy.

They waited until they saw the bedroom light on the second floor go out. It was not a long wait. About 8:00 p.m., she was in bed. The kids crawled through the ice box door and were in the kitchen in no time. They kept the kitchen lights off, and Eric lit two candles so he could see. Ella's main interest was to see the living rooms of the homes she broke into. She wanted to see what material possessions they had, and in her mind, she was justified in taking one item that would allow her to taste a sample of life that had eluded her. She spotted a most attractive wooden handcarved alligator nutcracker. It was quite heavy, about eight inches long with a tail and the mouth opened for placing the nuts. She loved it, for her grandfather who still had all his teeth and loved to crack walnuts with them. With that nutcracker, he wouldn't have to crack nuts with his teeth anymore.

Eric began to remove the broken dishes from the sink and placed them in the trash can. He pumped water into the sink and put some washing soda on top of the dirty dishes. Ella came into the kitchen and wrapped the nutcracker in a dirty towel and put it to the side so she would not forget it. Eric was too busy cleaning to notice right away.

"Too much suds," she said, while a gooey mass of soap formed in the sink.

"We're supposed to help clean up not make a new mess here," she said, playfully taking a healthy wad of soapy goo and slapped Eric's face with it. He did the same to her. They kissed and laughed while quietly washing the remaining plates and glasses in the sink.

Eric uncovered the cloth and saw the nutcracker. Ella quickly grabbed it away from him.

"It's mine!" she said firmly, forgetting they were housebreakers.

"Shush," Eric said, "don't make so much noise." He was getting nervous about Ella's outburst. "Where did you get that?" he asked. She told him where.

"But you said you wouldn't steal," he said.

"It's for my grandfather," she said.

"If we're caught, they'll be hell to pay. Put it back," he demanded. Ella would not do it.

Mrs. Haversham heard voices. She rose to look out the side and front bedroom windows. There was no movement outside from what she could see below in the dark. She listened again. The noise was coming from downstairs. The burglars would eventually make their way up to her bedroom, she feared.

From her night table, she opened the drawer and produced her revolver. She opened her bedroom door. Barefoot, noiseless, walking on air, she walked through the dark foyer to the top of the steps. She thought how ironic that she was made to feel frightened in her own home. Anger built up, and she had a gun afterall. There was something happening downstairs. She heard plates clicking. She went down the stairs. Her footsteps stopped and started again. She stood unseen by the kitchen door and looked through the crack. She exhaled a quiet release at the bewildering sight of her home invaders, two children cleaning her kitchen by candlelight.

The smell of soap and mildew mingled under her nose. She had forgotten she was still holding her gun. It would be the proper thing to go into her own kitchen and reprimand these housebreakers, but she didn't. She recognized Eric, but the young girl by way of memory, was a mystery. In no time, they had the dishes on the drainer and cleaned the countertop bone dry.

Mrs. Haversham gathered her thoughts together. Should she call the police? It would be trouble for young Eric. Why were they here washing dishes? Had they broken in before? Would they break in again? They would make it a habit and start stealing. She couldn't allow that to continue.

First thing she had to do was to replace that backdoor so there would be no ice box opening to crawl through. Eric looked about the cabinets to store the dishes. The upper cabinet above was the only place not taken up with pots and pans.

"Hold on. Lemme get something," he said. He opened the broom closet and removed a bucket. He turned it over and stood on it while Ella handed him the cleaned dishes.

Mrs. Haversham was humbled. This was both outrageous and comforting. The kids left and Ella did take the nutcracker, which Mrs. Haversham did not see. Outside the house, Eric said, "Mrs. H is sure to see that it's gone, she'll think the maid did it."

"Maybe she'll get a new maid," Ella said.

"You're a troublemaker," he said. Eric held the stolen nutcracker for her, and they parted company at his house.

Mrs. Haversham was up all night wondering what the hell was going on.

When Ella arrived at home, she hid the nutcracker way back in the drawer of her night table. She wouldn't give it to her grandfather until she could think of a good lie how she came to get it.

The next morning, the maid returned back to apologize to Mrs. Haversham and to get her job back. Mrs. Haversham let her into the kitchen and to the maid's surprise, her eyes met a spotless kitchen gleaming white with the morning sun. She was speechless—not a stain or misplaced dish as if the kitchen had never been used before that very morning.

"Don't expect me to forgive you so quickly. I went to bed very upset last night because of you. I want my breakfast," Mrs. Haversham said. She went upstairs with a sense of gratitude she hadn't felt for a long time. How the kitchen got so clean was never discussed between the two women.

The maid went to work and prepared two poached eggs, one biscuit, jam and butter, and a pot of hot coffee. Her arrogance was never unleashed in that house again.

Ella presented Zachariah with the nutcracker. He admired the quality without knowing what the thing was.

Ella demonstrated its efficiency by taking a walnut and crushing one in the alligator's mouth for him to marvel and while he chewed, he asked where she obtained it.

"I found it in a trash heap in town. Just saw it there and picked it up."

Zachariah examined the nutcracker and found that it was too handsome to have been discarded in a pile of rubble.

"Now you don't have to use your teeth to crack the walnuts," she said.

"Are you certain you found this in the garbage?"

"Yes, sir."

"What were you doing looking for garbage?"

He had her where he wanted her. She couldn't respond.

"How many times have I told you not to tell lies? You'll grow up wretched and alone like me. Is that what you want?"

"No, sir."

He was old and afraid for her if something was to happen to him. There were no other relatives to look after her.

"If you stole this from someone," he told her frankly, "I won't ask you who, but you must return it. If you don't, you will feel the end of my strap and be on a path to destruction." He laid down the law and told her to get supper ready. Meanwhile, he went to his chair in the living room and practiced cracking walnuts until he fell asleep.

Chapter 18

"Grounded?" Eric shouted, his eyes resting on his mother's tired face, Mrs. Haversham and that Officer Hannay sitting in the living room in judgment over him. Eric explained to everyone that his meeting up with Ella at Mrs. Haversham's house was purely by accident with no malicious intent.

"We heard shouting, and we peeked in the kitchen window and saw you fighting with your maid." Mrs. Haversham was embarrassed at having personal matters spilled out in the open.

"We cleaned up your kitchen, that's all," Eric said.

"I don't know who the young girl was, Virginia, but if she put Eric up to this, it's best he stays away from her," Mrs. Haversham said.

"Of course, she put him up to it," replied an agitated Giny, over police trouble in her house once again with Eric.

"It wasn't her idea. It was mine," Eric said.

"Oh, c'mon, Eric!" shouted Giny. "I know she's the troublemaker, and you're the fool for protecting her! I knew she was no good that day she came over here!"

"You have my personal guarantee he won't set foot in your house again." Giny said to Mrs. Haversham.

"What have you to say for yourself?" asked Mrs. Haversham.

"I apologize for entering your home. It won't happen again."

Mrs. Haversham and Hannay left.

Eric was now the designated scrubber of any area that required scrubbing, which was most of the house from the kitchen to the living room and bathroom, for a month. It would give Giny a rest anyway.

The conversation between Eric and his mother turned to Ella.

"What the devil has gotten into you hanging around that girl? She could be sick or diseased."

"She's not sick, and I won't stop seeing her."

"I forbid it! And while you live in this house, you'll do as I say!"

"How will you stop me? You can't lock me up in my room forever."

"Son, consider what people will think. You associating with that . . ."

"You know nothing about Ella or her grandfather," retorted Eric.

"Nobody knows them, because they live in the woods like animals."

"She's my friend, and I'll see her when I feel like it." And with that, he went up to his room and slammed the door. He was asserting himself. He was growing up.

In the solitude of her bedroom, Henrietta Corrigan lamented that the scotch was all gone. She held the bottle upside down to lap up the last of it. While William and Henry were at work, she was dependent on her scotch to get her through the day. Her mind was now troubled about Henry's future, and the scotch became an essential element to deaden the pain and her self-consciousness.

She got up out of bed. The room bent, blew, groaned, and shone of blue and green colors that spread itself over the furniture. She managed to go downstairs to the trash bin outside and squatted by the pile of empty bottles looking to see what if any liquid was left. She smelled some of them and let the bottles drop, clanking and breaking apart. She got up and propped herself against the porch railing for dear life unless she wanted to wind up a battered broken mess with the bottles.

Although her mind swam in the torrent, she had the ache to call back the time of yesterday when, as a much younger woman, she had married a virile, handsome, somewhat brash young man named William Corrigan who single-handedly created a company and lavished on her all the wonderful riches that success can bestow. Added to that, the anticipation of the birth of their child granted the most joy when in the throes of youth it was the looking forward to that was the most fun.

There wasn't much to celebrate now which is why she needed to drink. She returned to her bedroom and not long after she thought she heard William's footsteps coming up the stairs. It was only midafternoon—too early for him to be home. She grabbed the empty bottles of scotch she had just finished, and as the door opened, she opened the window and chucked the empty bottles out the window. The crashing noise made the poor squirrels dash like mad, leaving their acorns behind. Henrietta hopped into bed like a brat child trying to hide some trivial secret from the adults. And she had a longing for coffee as there was the smell of coffee coming from somewhere. The bedroom door opened.

"Henry. I thought it was your father," Henrietta said.

"Here, drink this." Henry had made his mother coffee as he knew what she had been up to without saying anything. Henrietta sipped it slowly, and it dawned on her that in all probability, this would be the last time her son would be in the house.

"Henry, will you reconsider leaving home?"

"Only if he will, which he won't."

"Stubbornness runs in the family," she said.

"Stubbornness, lying, cheating, loathing, what more can you expect from a family that hates each other?"

"We don't hate you."

"He cheats on you, and you just let him get away with it."

"And what would you suggest I do about it? Divorce him?"

"Make him respect you. Stand up for yourself!"

"I can't change him, and I really don't have the desire to try."

"You mean, you don't care about the marriage."

"Not in the least. If I left, then what? He's alone, I'm alone, and you're alone."

"I hate having this conversation. I don't believe anything in his house anymore."

"Don't worry about it, Henry. We're not a family anymore. We haven't been for a long time. Where will you go, Son?"

"I'll be taking the four o'clock train to Philadelphia."

"How will you live?"

"I'll get a job."

"Where will you live?"

"Who knows?"

William Corrigan came home as he had a thousand lifetimes ago. He placed his coat on the coatrack and his briefcase on the floor. He saw Henry's suitcase there as well and knew he was home. He called out to Henrietta.

"I'm upstairs," she said.

He entered the bedroom and found his wife in bed half-drunk, not surprisingly, and he saw Henry sitting in the guest chair. The sight of his "family" turned his stomach. He hated them and the fact that he had wasted his life on such people. That was the honest truth that he never spoke.

Henry got up from the chair and approached his father. "I went to your office to see you, and I discovered a hospital bill addressed to you."

Henrietta sat up alert to this bit of news. Corrigan couldn't believe how he could have left the invoice for anyone to see.

"You were rummaging through my desk?"

"It says that Abby has cancer and that you paid for the operation."

"I asked you if you went through my desk!"

"I looked for some paper to leave you a note, which I never wrote. Does she have a cancer?" Henry asked.

Corrigan had no choice but to answer and to break his promise to Maggie about keeping their secret. "It's true," he admitted reluctantly.

"How sick is she?" Henry asked.

"She had an operation to remove some cancer under her arm. She's under Dr. Fletcher's care now."

"Bill, why did you agree to pay for the operation?" Henrietta asked.

"When the mother told me how serious Abby's illness was, I offered to help them. She didn't ask me to do it. I volunteered, and I don't regret it."

"Does Abby know you paid for it?" asked Henry.

"Of course not, and don't you tell her either. She doesn't want anyone to know that she's sick."

"No matter what you think of me, I won't betray Abby," Henry said.

"Sure you will." Corrigan turned to his wife. "What a family I have," he said. "Look at her, will ya? My wife, who wastes her time drinking, and you, a worthless piece of garbage, who doesn't deserve any consideration at all."

"I'm surprised you don't blame me for Momma's drinking," Henry said.

"I hope you mind what I'm telling you, and don't harm that girl any more than you've already done by telling everyone that she's ill."

"I'm leaving home and going to a place where no one knows me," Henry said. "Who could I tell?"

"Well. I'm off to Philly. With the little money this guy gave me, I can't afford to go out of state."

"You're lucky I gave you anything at all," Corrigan responded and left the room without saying good-bye.

Chapter 19

William Corrigan stood on a wooden board that elevated him slightly, puffing on his Havana cigar as Raymond fitted him with his new electric belt that was guaranteed to reduce back pain.

"William, put out that cigar," Raymond insisted, pointing to the "No Smoking" sign on the wall. "I'm not going to tell you that you made a wise investment."

"I'm the one who insisted on buying it, Doc, so I'll take my chances and try it out."

The belt was a chainlike contraption with silver buttons, and the electrodes were on the opposite side and covered with a clothlike material. It was worn and adjusted like a regular belt.

Raymond showed him how it worked. "You can adjust the electric current by this lever here, see, it can reduce or increase the current depending on the severity of the pain you have. You can wear it over your long johns or wear it during the day for a couple of hours or in bed all night if necessary."

"In bed? I'm sure my wife will be thrilled with that idea."

"The fastener is in front."

Corrigan looked around to make certain there were no women within earshot. "It's not going to burn off my balls, is it?" he joked.

"It comes with instructions," Raymond said, ignoring the caustic humor.

"How much?"

"Ten dollars."

"Have you been taking the tranquilizers I prescribed for you?"

"I have, and I am feeling much more relaxed. Thank you for asking. I take it that my debts have been paid in full."

"With the exception of this belt," Raymond said.

Corrigan removed his wallet from his breastpocket. "It wasn't that I didn't want to pay you," Corrigan said, referring to the outstanding bills from his wife's visits. "We all have our priorities." Corrigan took out a twenty-dollar bill.

Raymond only had five dollars change.

"Never mind, Doc. Keep the change, and put the extra ten toward my next visit. I trust you."

"William, now no one can ever accuse you of being a deadbeat."

"Sure, they can. I go through it every day. It's easy for those without to attack those who are more successful. It's all jealousy anyway."

There now came the moment when even the most powerful have their head down with vulnerability and are compelled to seek the advice of someone they respect, for Corrigan had promised Maggie not to divulge Abby's secret. He had broken that promise. The only hope was that his wife and son would not tell anyone. He couldn't trust them, and he knew that he would have a hard time explaining to Abby and Maggie in the event they found out, in what was the most important issue in their lives to which he had committed himself not just monetarily, but also morally to protect, and in that, he had failed.

"Raymond, have you thought of what life is supposed to mean?"

"At least every other minute. Why?"

"I've always made it a point to grab as much money as possible and have thought of nothing else. I know someone who is very ill."

"What's the illness?"

"Cancer."

"You see, Doc, I took it upon myself to help finance the operation she had, and I promised her mother I wouldn't breathe a word about this to anyone. Without my knowledge, word got out about my involvement and that she is ill."

In an instant Raymond knew that Corrigan was aware of Abby's illness.

"Are you concerned about how they will react when they find out?" Raymond asked.

"It will be a terrible blow."

"The best thing to do is tell them outright. That way they will hear it from you and not from someone else. Also tell them that you had no control over it."

"But that's not true. I authorized the hospital to send the invoice to me at the office, and I distinctly remember placing it underneath my pile of letters. My son discovered it and well . . ."

"Then it wasn't your fault, William. You took precautions. It just happened, that's all."

Raymond was pleased to hear that Corrigan had paid for Abby's operation. At least the financial burden was lessened. Corrigan prepared to leave.

Raymond did not know what to think as Corrigan's reputation had led him to suspect he would use the gesture to harm or coerce Abby or Maggie into doing something that was not right. Maybe he was letting his imagination get the better of him. Was it possible that people could change that much? And that William Corrigan did it out of compassion?

"If you're not able to get rid of that backache with this belt, come and see me."

"I will, Doc. Thanks."

Corrigan took his new electric belt and walked out of the doctor's office with much to consider. He got into his car and started the motor. Difficult choices were an everyday occurrence for a man in his position. He concentrated best when driving, so off he went. Instead of going his usual route, he decided to take the left path of the divided road: one that he had never taken before so he could keep driving and not get home so soon.

If he didn't say anything to either Abby or Maggie about not being able to keep the secret, and they found out that others knew, it would surely diminish his reputation as that of an unreliable, untrustworthy sort who couldn't keep his big mouth shut when it came to a private matter, no matter what he said in his own defense.

If he took Raymond's advice and came clean about it, he might be taken into their good graces once again with an honest explanation of what happened. But as he drove, he remembered that Maggie did not want Abby to know of his involvement. So he finally decided to tell only Maggie in the hope that his admission would be kept between them and prevent friction between mother and daughter.

This is the route he chose to go as a feeling of liberation tore through his frozen heart, and for the first time in many years, a golden moment of pure passion that didn't involve making money found its way. He turned a corner and upon recognizing a familiar street, took it home. Now all he had to do was arrange a meeting with Maggie and pray that she accepted what he told her.

Abby sat in the camp director's office with folded hands slightly clenched on her lap, waiting for the camp director to interview her. She rationalized why on earth she should be so nervous. She recalled having the same tension-filled moments the first time she met William Corrigan for a job. It was the doubt about the outcome of the interview as much as being judged by a total stranger that she was uneasy about. But if this is what one had to go through to get experience, so be it. Her delicate health contributed to her strong will. No one forced her to reply to the advert, and no one had forced her to sit in that office. Abby had wanted to be there, and on that basis, there was no reason to worry. There were photographs hanging on the wall of happy boys and girls sitting around a campfire toasting marshmallows. Another picture showed young scouts raising the American flag and a group shot of girls in their cabin each holding up a small sign with their names written in crayon. It all seemed delightfully pleasant.

The camp director emerged with a pot of coffee in one hand and a plate of biscuits in the other and with words of apology for keeping Abby waiting in quick breaths as she focused on getting behind her desk. Abby's confidence was given a slight boost when she saw the director was a woman and not much older than she. Abby would know soon enough if being there was a mistake or a blessing.

"It's been hectic around here," she said and offered Abby a biscuit. As tempting as the smell of freshly baked biscuits in the morning, and they appeared done to perfection, Abby declined, too nervous to eat.

The camp director sat behind her desk, organized the resumes, and placed Abby's on top. She poured a cup for coffee for herself.

"We're still planning the schedule for the summer," she said. "Now that we're very close, we're under the gun to get everything ready. So, you're interested in working as a counselor?"

"I'd love to be considered for a position."

The director had foregone her professionalism and gave in to hunger. She took a quick bite of a biscuit and washed it down with a couple of sips of coffee.

"You're currently employed as a secretary at Corrigan Typewriters?"

"Yes. I'm Mr. Corrigan's personal secretary," Abby said somewhat ashamed at her unabashed self-promotion.

"He must be quite a boss to allow you time off to join a campsite."

"Yes, he is." Her confidence rose up until it was shot down.

"I don't see any related experience in your resume. We usually contact previous staff members about open positions first before we advertise that we're looking. Our counselors are responsible for maintaining the campers on schedule with their activities, you see. At the very least, we prefer any potential candidates to have some previous experience."

"I have excellent organizational skills," Abby offered. She had to remember to respond to the director's statements positively without seeming to only give the answers she wanted to hear.

"How are you at settling arguments? There will be plenty of them, believe me."

"I think I'm intelligent enough to understand that whether it's in an office or outdoors, not everybody is as understanding and tolerant of the other. I have no problem being a mediator."

"But you need experience in dealing with a large group of kids. Have you ever tried to pry two boys apart during a fight?"

"Yes, I have," Abby fibbed proudly, recalling Michael and Henry's scuffle at the Easter banquet, although she didn't physically try and breakup the fight.

"Have you ever camped outdoors?"

"Yes, when I was younger."

"So you're familiar in dealing with mosquitoes and other insects?"

"Yes, ma'am."

The camp director sensed something beneath Abby's carefully prepared answers. She looked into Abby's eyes for a few seconds without saying anything, and Abby turned away, noticeably uncomfortable. There was some secret that this interviewee would not divulge unless it was extracted slowly with tact and understanding. Abby felt she should be asking some questions to communicate her interest in the position.

"Can you please tell me about the camp itself?"

"Certainly. There are two neighboring campsites, one for boys and one for girls. This summer, we have members of the local Boy Scouts to use the site for their training. Some of our girl campers will be from foreign countries. It should be interesting to say the least. Both camps utilize the main hall for dining and indoor recreation. Since each camp has its own activities schedule, we coordinate the time to allow the kids in both camps to meet and get to know each other. We do have a healthy supply of kids that come from varied backgrounds of well-to-do parents and through sponsors who pay for them and others who are not so fortunate. We have hiking, nature study groups, fishing, and wilderness survival excursions that have left some campers lost in the woods, and we've had to send out a rescue team to track them down," she said and smiled.

"The most popular activity is swimming, diving, and canoeing. Do you swim?"

"Yes."

"It's not all pie and cake," the camp director said. "Although we take pride in the fact that the physical and social environment we offer will help in the child's development, some of them come here for the first time and the idea of living outdoors with a group of strangers is an inconvenience and in some cases a terror for them. We do our best to make this outing a happy one. It's not just teaching them how to catch a fish or sail a boat. We need to guide them through the tasks and instill a sense of self-reliance as they work in a group to appreciate the value of what they are doing, individually and as a team. Since you have no experience working at camp, we do have entry-level positions where you can get to do a variety of different things. I am in need of an assistant. Would you be interested in working with me in the office?"

Abby reflected negatively on this offer as her smile vanished.

"Not interested in being cooped up in an office?"

"No."

"I take it you're a healthy woman. Is there anything that would physically prevent you from the responsibilities of the job?"

"Not at all," Abby said. The courage to battle a dreaded disease influenced her reasoning that no one had to know about her illness. If she got the job, it would only be for three weeks. She could handle the three weeks.

"Does the idea of helping young people matter more to you beyond the position you will receive which may not be the one you had in mind?"

"Yes, indeed."

"I can tell from speaking with you that you are a responsible person, and I know you will treat the position with the same respect that you would an office job. I can only tell you that I will check with the counselors that will be hired for the summer, and if any of them require the assistance of an able, sincere, hardworking person like yourself, I will be in touch with you."

Chapter 20

Raymond paid a visit to the Whitman residence to give Abby her usual shot.

"Your presence has drawn attention, Doctor," Maggie said, quite accepting of the regularity of his visits. "Michael Kramer was here asking why your car was always parked outside our home."

"You told him I was OK?" Abby asked.

"Of course I did," Maggie replied.

"If you feel more comfortable, Abby, I'd be happy to administer the dosage at my place, and I would make sure you arrived safely home before the effects kicked it. You would need to come after hours."

She didn't have to think twice about Raymond's offer.

"That's very generous of you. I'd like that," Abby said. "Yes, that's fine with me."

Maggie politely but firmly insisted that they discuss the matter after dinner. Abby responded that it wasn't necessary to discuss the subject as she had made up her mind, and the matter was closed.

"Would you like to stay for dinner, Raymond?" Abby asked. "We're having chicken."

"If it's all right with your mother." He looked up at Maggie before answering, and she went from a straight face to a forced smile right before his eyes. It didn't matter that Maggie was not thrilled at the idea; it was Abby's invitation.

During dinner, the chair the doctor was sitting on gave way, and he fell down on the floor. Both Abby and Maggie helped him to his feet. They tried not to laugh for the longest time, but it couldn't be helped. Raymond picked up the busted chair and its detached, broken leg.

"Don't worry about it, Raymond," Maggie said, still laughing. "I'll take it to Michael next door, and he'll make it as good as new. He's great at repairing things."

After dinner was over, Raymond did not overstay his welcome. He thanked both women, injected Abby, and left.

"Have you lost all your senses? The last thing you need is to start having an affair with your doctor. My god!"

"Who said anything about an affair?"

"I'm just worried. Besides you have nothing in common with him."

"He likes music. You know, I never had someone call on me before."

"That's not so. What about Michael?"

"Michael is perhaps the best friend a person could have."

"Yes. He comes calling for you."

"To see how I am, sure. I'm the one people feel sorry for."

"Abby, you don't know how beautiful you are. You don't take time to notice. But let me tell you, others do. Michael Kramer has always liked you. Even Henry Corrigan, that bastard. He attacked Michael because of you. Oh, and don't forget the birds outside. They like you too."

Abby looked right at her mother, and they both cracked up. For the first time in years, the laughter sustained in their souls rose so dear.

"Why am I so popular?" Abby asked.

"Maybe it's your long hair."

Abby sensed that the mood had lightened enough to make the request.

"Do you think you have time to make me a dress from some of that purple material?"

"Why do you need a new dress to call on him?"

"I just do," she said.

"I can't remember the last time you asked me for a new dress. And when you do, it's just to go and see . . ."

"I just want to look nice when I go there, that's all!"

Maggie had no desire to upset her daughter. If she wanted a dress, she'd have one.

That evening, Raymond sat in the bathtub, thinking that each day he left Abby's house, he longed not to leave. After he bathed, he put the cake of soap back on the edge of the tub and sat there. His mind opened to retracing the times spent with Abby and the good fortune that there would be more to come. The level of familiarity was about to become more pronounced with each visit. He knew it, and there was no doubt as he rose to dry himself that she knew it also.

But he also had to remember that as surely as the day grew dark and the sunshine turned to thunder and the thunder turned into pouring rain, he had joined the ranks of a selfless army and had to march to its sometimes very unhappy tune, and not to deviate from the cause of his life's work. The moon and the stars might very well be his only nighttime companions for the rest of his life.

Abby arrived at Raymond's home. Her dress was a darling, quaint, cunningly simple thing of purple velvet very fashionably old-fashioned. She hoped that he wasn't going to inject her right away and send her off. If that was his intent, she would have to find a way to stall. She didn't get all dressed up for nothing.

She was greeted by the doctor who looked every bit the man out of his medical attire in a shiny brown host's robe. He carried a plate of some disgusting mush, and he admired her in the dress but chose to say nothing as it might be inappropriate.

"I was just going to feed Stanley," he said.

"Let me feed him," she said. Raymond was surprised but obliging.

"If you want to, OK," he said, whatever made her feel at home was fine with him.

He gave her the plate, and he directed her to the kitchen where Stanley usually had his meals. In the kitchen, which was quite small but had a cozy table in the middle, Abby looked for the spot to feed the dog. She watched Stanley walk over to his water bowl by the corner, and she knew to put his food there. She sat at the table and watched him eat while Raymond poured two ice-filled glasses of fruit punch. She saw that his countertop needed a good cleaning with a sponge. He placed the glasses on a tray and asked her to join him out on the back porch while Stanley ate.

The late afternoon smelled of early summer when the mind planned for things to do in the coming months. Abby sipped her punch and asked the doctor when he thought the treatment might end.

"We'll continue for another couple of weeks, and then I will send you to the hospital for another set of X-rays."

"Good. I'm getting tired of it."

"I know it's hard, but this treatment can't be rushed. It must be done in stages and repeatedly."

"Do you think I'll get well?"

"If you believe it, you will. I know I believe it," he said, exerting his influence in Abby's healing process through words of encouragement as he propelled her through self-improvement both physically and mentally.

The telephone rang in his office. Raymond excused himself to answer it, thinking it was a patient.

"It's your mother. You can take it in my office."

Abby wasn't surprised by the interruption. She wondered if she would ever have children and annoy them as much.

While she went into the office, Raymond selected a record to play on his Victrola in the parlor. Abby recognized the opening from Tchaikovsky's Piano Concerto no. 1. Abby abruptly ended her mother's meddling and hung up on her so she could enjoy the music outside the confines of Raymond's office. She followed the music down the hall, passing an impressive collection of seashells adorning a bookcase. She picked up the largest shell and held it to her ear. On the wall was a collection of paintings depicting great ships at sea with towering masts battling storms others in calm seas.

Raymond went to see what was keeping her. He noticed her with the seashell, and doubt swiftly overshadowed his personal satisfaction. Was he doing more harm than good in diverting the attention from Abby's illness to these extraneous objects like seashells, fruit punch, and music playing in the parlor? Should he spend time discussing current events in the newspaper, the latest novel he was reading? He was not making light of her illness, on the contrary. He tempered his medical experience with discretion, and his manner was always that of a gentleman. Conscious of his power over his patients, he mastered his profession, but this was something completely different. He waited for Abby out on the porch.

"I'm sorry about that," she said, obviously embarrassed. She saw that he had freshened her punch. "Mother wanted to know when I would be going home. What time is the next car due?"

"Six o'clock."

"That gives us some time," she said, noticeably less shy and more comfortable as she sat down and sipped her drink while the second movement began.

"I was admiring your collection of seashells. I hope you don't mind."

"Not at all. You're welcome here anytime."

"My mother thinks it's not good for me to be out."

"She's concerned about your being here with me?" he asked.

"That's mother-love," she said.

"You're lucky to have a family who cares."

"You've never spoken of your family."

"He's my family." She saw how Stanley rested at his feet. There was a strong bond there. "This old dog's been with me for almost fifteen years. He's never disappointed me or hurt me."

"Are your parents still living?"

"Yes, they live in Lancaster," he said reluctantly. He didn't want to spend the time talking about his parents, certainly not about his father.

"Any brothers or sisters?"

"I had a brother. He died years ago."

"You and I have something in common," Abby said. "I have no brothers or sisters. We've spent most of our lives without siblings." She wondered what it was like to have a large family at the dinner table sharing their individual daily experiences and strengthening the fragile unity of family that can so easily be broken. She knew this all too well. Abby noticed a closed, handsome cigarette case by his table.

"You smoke?"

"Yes. I do. I hope you're not going to ask me for a cigarette?"

"No," she said jokingly. "Maybe later."

"Raymond. Can I ask you a rather personal question?"

"Absolutely."

"We've been living in the same town for years, and we've never seen you at church services."

"Oh, that's easy. I don't go to church."

Abby nodded slightly and did not press the subject.

"It's not a problem, is it?"

"No. Momma mentioned it to me, and I picked up on it."

Raymond knew this to mean that Abby looked for him at church, and when he wasn't there, she was disappointed. He enjoyed the subtlety of his occasionally self-absorbed imagination.

"I guess I put such an emphasis on my abilities as a doctor and the reality of dealing with life and death every day that the subject of God hasn't made much of an impression on me." Abby listened and said nothing.

"I'm sorry if I sound cold. I don't mean to." He knew he had no use for the preaching of God or anything pertaining to religion.

"Well. I think it's time we get started on your medication and send you home before your mother thinks I've abducted you."

Raymond went to get the medication, and Abby rose to bring the glasses into the kitchen.

At her request, they sat outside on the porch again. As the needle went in, Abby asked him what he valued most in life—not something related to his work, she emphasized. He was never asked such a question before. So he thought about an answer until he finished administering the medication. Everything had its value: the old pump, the well, the valley, the trees, even his grumbling father, certainly his mother who had nursed him and his brother through sickness, Stanley when he barked, when he was sick and had to be looked after like a child. But what he answered was that he valued true friendship more than anything since it was the most difficult to obtain and the most difficult to sustain without hard effort.

Abby rested for a minute before he took her hand and escorted her outside. Raymond gave her a card on which he had written his office hours should she ever need to refer to it.

"Ring me day or night if there's a problem," he said.

He opened the front door. She did not want to leave.

Abby gazed at a handsome, white, horse-drawn carriage with white wheels parked in front of the doctor's place. It looked like it had come off the pages of some fairy tale storybook. Even the horses were white.

"You didn't think I was going to let you go home in a streetcar after an injection. It's too risky. You could faint."

"You're sending me home in that?" she asked with a sense of unworthiness.

"Is anything wrong?"

"Raymond. How much did you pay to rent it?"

"It doesn't matter. You need to get home now before the effects kick in."

The coachman, an elderly man with a tall hat and tails, approached to escort her into the carriage.

"Do you feel like a princess?" the coachman asked as he took her by the hand.

She smiled and looked back to Raymond. "Go ahead, enjoy the ride," he said. "I'll phone your mother and tell her you're on your way."

She waved back to Raymond as he went back into his house. She felt like royalty on her way to an important event. If there was one thing that would have made it complete, she would have enjoyed Raymond's company in the carriage going home.

Chapter 21

Several more visits occurred both at Abby's home and Raymond's home. At Raymond's home, he carefully selected from his record collection which records to play first and last. For their listening pleasure, it began with Beethoven's Fifth Symphony. Abby sat on the couch with Stanley, resting his head on her lap. Raymond sat in his arm chair next to her.

Hearing the first movement made Abby think of being on one of those ships in Raymond's paintings in the midst of a raging storm in the dead of night as colossal whitecapped swells mercilessly rocked the ship back and forth threatening to capsize the ship and the crew well aware that certain death being plunged into the murky depths of an angry black sea might be only moments away.

They sipped a robust red wine since Raymond had promised Abby there would be no injections on that visit so she was free to indulge.

The next record was the Chopin Sonata no. 3. Listening to another pianist's interpretation offered Abby the opportunity to hear what was possible with a piece whose structured notes were played with tonality and disarmingly natural phrasing. The recording seemed to capture moments that she was unable to notice in her own playing of the piece.

Raymond wanted to begin sharing the joys of a household with Abby but in a subtle way that would not interfere with their bond; he was in her life to relieve her pain and to offer comfort when the stream of unease and sorrow worsened.

"The music's made me hungry," she said. "Do you have any eggs?"

"Yes, I do."

"Well, how about an omelet? May I?"

He accompanied her into the kitchen where she retrieved four large eggs, some butter, a plump tomato, an onion, and a pepper—a perfect supper for two casual acquaintances.

"We have the makings of a Spanish omelet," she said with excitement. As she melted the butter, Raymond, for his part, found a record of Mozart's Piano Concerto no. 21 and played it while Abby cooked to her heart's delight as the rising melodies uplifted her spirits. She always enjoyed the element of theatrical surprise in Mozart's concertos as musical characters come out of nowhere and have something to say that is different and challenging both to play and to listen to.

Abby was extremely pleased about her visit. Maybe it was the wine. He was pleasantly surprised about her desire to prepare a meal for the two of them since it meant she would be staying for a while.

After supper, they sat out on the porch with coffee, and the last music composition of Franz Schubert played. Listening to the String Quintet in C major made for an easy digestion, but during the second movement, it altered the mood considerably. Raymond felt the weight of the piece as too sublime and not fitting for their time together, but he did not stop the Victrola until the end of that painful second movement, after which Abby preferred not to listen to anymore music. He hated himself for the bad choice.

At what point do I stop believing that I will live a long life, she thought as the last of the sunset slipped slowly away.

Her torment at the unfairness of it all was eased as long as she embraced this special time which most likely would not be repeated. Too bad! She would have liked him there at all hours, but life and the demands it imposed would not allow such a delusion to be fulfilled except in her mind. Content for now, thoughts about tomorrow or next week or next month had to be put on hold as the anguish would return just as surely as the cancer within her devoured everything in its path until it reached her at her most vulnerable; then it would be the end of the line—isolated, detached, and alone with darkness. That was the reality that no amount of music or any other self-entitlement could obliterate. She thought of what it was like after death when she closed her eyes forever. Would she know anything at all? Would she know what her soul was like? Was it hidden somewhere inside the realm of her being, kept out of reach, placed in a silver chalice to be released upon her death? Was her soul something tangible? This she thought about as she noticed the doctor had fallen asleep in his chair as had Stanley next to her.

Time went by. Raymond awoke to find himself alone on the porch. He panicked slightly at the thought that Abby would've left due to his inconsiderateness. He called to her. She answered. Relieved, he found her with Stanley sitting at the small table brushing her long hair. Captivated, it was the first time Raymond had seen her hair undone and so long that it reached the floor. He couldn't decide what was more precious: her smile or her hair.

"I'm sorry I fell asleep."

"It's understandable. You've had a long day."

He looked at the clock. It was after midnight. Was she planning on staying all night? If so, how would he handle it? Was it right for him to take advantage of her just to fulfill his desires? Was she interested in him that way? There are circumstances which always exist between physician and patient, sometimes secretive in nature as those hinted at and are without censure. Whatever happened was no one's business but theirs.

"Sit down for a minute. I need to tell you something," she said. "I will be going away for three weeks this summer to work as a camp counselor."

"That's wonderful. It'll do you good to spend time outdoors."

"I want to know your thoughts about stopping the treatment for the three weeks that I will be away."

Raymond's tongue was fixed to the roof of his mouth. Why was she saying this? Had she lost faith in his abilities as her life rested upon his honesty and quick decision?

"I don't like it. I think it's a terrible idea. The latest X-rays show the cancer is slowly dissipating. You've been making progress. Why would you want to stop?"

"Because the effects make me very sick, and at the very least, during my time at the camp, I want to feel energetic, not sick as a dog."

Raymond's primary objection was that she would refuse to continue the treatment if she stopped for any length of time. It was only natural that she would want it to become a distant memory and not be reminded.

"How about a compromise?" he suggested. "We can lessen the dosage, and I'll make arrangements with the camp nurse to administer the medication privately, so you have my guarantee no one will find out."

Abby declined. What was important to her was to be selfish and concentrate her energies while she still had them to remain emotionally and physically fit for the three weeks of this exercise. Raymond understood, and he knew he was also there to lighten the burdens of his patients whenever possible. Easing up on the medication for a while served that very purpose that Abby wanted for herself.

"What does your mother think about your plans?"

"She's OK with it. She knows me well enough not to interfere when I've made up my mind."

He couldn't argue against her side of it. But in his own defense as her physician, he was willingly allowing his patient to dictate terms to him and thereby make reductions to please her. As a result, Raymond knew he was doing himself grave harm professionally. Nevertheless, he decided to let her have her way.

Abby did spend the night in the guest room, sharing her bed with Stanley, the dog.

Chapter 22

This place had Abby's heart: first, last, and always. The campgrounds were open meadows and forests full of summer character. A lake flowed at the edge of the camp. Hummingbird moths hovered over sweet violets, sipping the nectar. There was a main building which included a large recreation hall. Innumerable little shacks rested along a rocky, wooded hillside. These shacks would serve as the primary residences for everyone at the camp. Abby was so taken by the surroundings that she started believing her problems and indeed the problems of the world to be a mere trifle. She visited her shack. It was sparsely furnished, with only the barest amenities: a bunk bed, a dresser, a couple of chairs, a large table, some oars mounted on the unplastered walls, and a fireplace. The outhouses were behind the shacks.

Abby unpacked and went into the main building where she was greeted by the other two female counselors as well as two male counselors and the camp director who had gained her confidence during the interview well enough to have hired her.

The Boy Scouts and the girl campers were due to arrive the next day, so there was no time to waste. The counselors went into the dining room where they enjoyed coffee and donuts and went over the daily activities schedule. The careful preparation of the program was the essential element to maintain the campers' interest. They went over the menus, met with the head cook, and checked all medical supplies with the camp nurse. Afterward, they had a proper tour of the entire campsite, which included a small nature museum.

Evening: Abby found it an adventure going to dinner, which was served in the dining hall in the main building. It was necessary to carry a lantern for the trip down the hill. Little swarms of flies circulated merrily in midair.

Around midnight, when all were asleep, she went into the recreation room where she discovered an upright piano. She was alone so naturally she couldn't resist trying it out. She played a bit of *Mozart's Turkish March* as it was so much fun to play. The piano needed a tune-up.

Sunrise. Abby awoke to the sound of bluebirds arguing with cardinals. She stepped outside her shack. A morning mist rested above the lake, radiant with color, drifting and spreading itself in silence. The sun began to cut an ideal orange hue over much of the most beautiful maidenhair that covered the surrounding hillside. Abby watched the mist dance with the sun and silently moved away from the ground.

She couldn't resist a private dip in the lake before her responsibilities were to officially begin with the arrival of the campers that day. She found herself in the company of a flock of robins that settled in a nearby tree, chirping loudly. She thought they were feeding on berries and were perhaps arguing about who gets what. But when she looked on the ground, she saw a line of red soldier ants marching from the grass over to a dead robin. The ants were huge about a half inch and great in numbers as they aggressively swarmed upon and devoured the poor bird. Abby knew this was what the robins were upset about. She was very careful to step over the ant line as she didn't want to be on the menu. Once safely away from the carnage, she went to the lake and saw there was no one around.

She disrobed and entered the lake. It was cold, but she devoted herself to the mood of the lake, and it was now a part of her nakedness for a while. The water lilies in the distance gleamed in the early morning sun. Abby vowed before her time at the camp ended that she would rent a boat and row out by herself to the lily pads and pick one lily for herself. Blackbirds passed overhead with such murmurings that soothed Abby's sense of hearing. When they left as quickly as they came, she strained to hear for more. When she had her fill of the lake, she went out and put her robe back on. Her solitude of bliss was invaded without her knowing it when a pair of youthful eyes watched her from the camouflage of thick shrubs. She was still for a moment as if something had forced her to stop breathing. She listened to the sound of twigs breaking and leaves rustling. A young Boy Scout emerged from the bushes. Dressed in traditional scout breeches, a neckerchief and hat, the tall scout walked over to Abby. In his hand was a dead garter snake.

"Have you been spying on me?" she asked, annoyed at the intrusion.

"No," he said, lying to her face. "I was surveying the terrain when I came across this snake." He held up the small, two footer decapitated snake for her to see he was telling the truth at least partly.

"Why did you kill it?" she asked, changing the subject as she knew boys will always be boys.

"I thought we could dissect it for the scouts as an exercise," he replied. He noticed her dismay.

"Don't be alarmed. It's a harmless garter snake," he said. "I'm sorry. I didn't introduce myself, John Barton, Scoutmaster. I hope I didn't scare you."

He wiped his hand before extending it. Abby saw that he was sincere and shook his hand.

"Abby Whitman, I'm one of the counselors. I don't like snakes much."

He tossed the snake deep into the bushes where the red ants would surely have a welcomed meal.

"You didn't have to do that," she said.

"I thought you should know, Abby, we plan to have an exhibition of snakes in the museum."

"I know," she said. "We spoke about it at the meeting yesterday. I understand two Cornell professors are due to arrive to talk about the snakes."

"Among other things, yes, I'm just on my way to the main building to check on the supplies when they come in," he said.

Abby noticed a slight scar on his eyebrow, where no hair grew.

"Will you walk with me as far as your cabin?" he asked.

The trail was perfumed with jasmine, and Abby walked slowly so she could get to know a little about him.

"Tell me. What does a scoutmaster do?"

"Much the same as you will be doing, actually. We both share the responsibility of keeping the campers entertained and making sure they obey the rules of the place."

"A lot of responsibility for someone so young," she said. Looking closer at his youthful exterior, he hadn't yet experienced the wind, hail, and fire of living as an adult.

"I'm twenty-one," he said proudly, also adding that he rose in the ranks due to his dedication. He was looking forward to help mold the character of his troops while they toughed it out together as a team.

"How many boys are coming?"

"I think about fifteen. All different ages."

"How long will you be here?" he asked.

"Three weeks," she said.

"The same here," he added.

When they reached Abby's cabin, he stopped to show her his embroidered Badge of Rank on his left front pocket.

"Graduated with honors after five years of training," he said. "Well, Abby, I look forward to seeing you around."

"Likewise, John."

The scoutmaster met the supply truck at the main building and surveyed the unloading of the essential equipment that included: two sleeping tents, one scoutmaster's tent, blankets, garbage pails, water pails, frying pans, tin dish pans, bread pans, salt and pepper shakers, pot covers, first aid kits, two bicycles for rapid transport, two life preservers, two fire extinguishers, one snakebite and permanganate outfit, two large axes, one shovel, two lanterns, one American flag, twenty rolls of toilet paper, two hundred paper napkins, scouring soap, and all the canned beans and canned soups the scouts could eat. Everything else including knives, forks, spoons, cups, table, and chairs would be provided by the camp staff.

Abby had a headache, so she went back to bed for about an hour to sleep it off so she would be right as rain to act her part intelligently as an assistant counselor.

Things moved so fast at the camp that there wasn't time to breathe. Forty girls arrived as well as the Boy Scouts. Later that afternoon, Abby and some of the nature-loving guests walked to the nature museum to observe and appreciate the two Cornell professors' vivid instructional knowledge of a small but impressive collection of flowers, live and stuffed birds, insects and reptiles including a lizard, one venomous foot long centipede, and a variety of snakes including a grass snake, a coach whip snake, several rattlers, a few little copperheads, and one huge Texas bull snake.

Abby and Scoutmaster Barton traded silly smiles of satisfaction when the collection included yet another garter snake. The snakes were all in separate ventilated glass cases to prevent the larger snakes from eating the smaller ones. The professors said they were perfectly harmless. The girls chuckled and wanted a demonstration to prove that they were harmless and how to handle a snake.

Suddenly, one of the assistant patrol leaders, eager to prove himself, volunteered. Scoutmaster Barton knew the boy's skills and gave his approval as the professors dubiously looked on. The boy took a poker, and with the greatest ease, hooked a rattler out of its cage and held him in his hand as one might hold a little puppy. The Boy Scout was proud of his expertise.—showing off his bravery as well—as he opened the rattler's mouth with a lollipop stick. The girls saw where the rattler kept his fangs. They were soft almost tender looking teeth that curved at the end, like eye teeth in position and claws in appearance. The Boy Scout took hold of the snake's head and pressed against the upper part which released the glistening venom from the poison sacs, and it ran slowly down one of the fangs. It was remarkable to Abby how some of the "she's" in the group were so keen about caring for pet snakes if only to make conversation with the boys. But they were just kids, and she wasn't. She had to get on with the job. Abby had no such enthusiasm for snakes, but as counselor she carefully concealed that fact.

Abby couldn't sleep. She walked awhile, and just when she decided to go back to bed to try to sleep, she heard the sound of the piano coming from the main building. She followed the music as a voice calling to her becoming a voice of promise down the stairs to the recreational hall where a change, an awakening, and above all a renewal came across the darkened recreation hall as the pianist, a young woman with long, red hair played the forbidding opening chords of the Rachmaninoff Prelude in C-sharp minor. Abby had never attempted to play the piece herself as it was too challenging and a little too bleak for her tastes. Abby stood at the back of the hall unnoticed and listened to the propulsive second part of the piece that passionately burst through the space that separated her from the talented pianist, finally closing with the third part that silently drew the piece to a quiet end. After just four minutes, it was over. The silence demanded applause. Abby's hand clapping startled the young woman.

"It was beautiful!" Abby shouted across the hall.

Surprised at being discovered by one of the counselors, the girl closed the piano lid, folded the sheet music, and turned to face her audience of one.

"Thank you. I know I shouldn't be playing at this hour."

"That's quite all right."

"Do you know Rachmaninoff?"

"I do," Abby said proudly, and she walked across the hall to speak with her. "I'm sorry if I scared you."

"Think nothing of it. I was just practicing a little. It's not the best piano."

Abby saw that she was very young with bright green eyes, dressed in her pajamas; her bare feet were on the pedals.

"Do you play?" she asked.

"Yes," Abby said. "I prefer the classics, Bach, Beethoven, Chopin, Mozart."

"I agree. They are the best. If the world had never known any other composers besides those four, we wouldn't be any less rich for it."

"What about Liszt?" Abby asked, enjoying the interaction.

"The Liebestraum is my favorite. I would definitely include that one. And don't forget Tchaikovsky and Mendelssohn." Abby noticed and recognized the other sheet music on top of the piano—the Bach fugue in B-flat minor, the Beethoven Sonata Pathétique and the Chopin Scherzo no. 3.

"You have a gift. How old are you?"

"Thirteen. What is your name?" the young girl asked.

"I'm Abby."

"Madison."

"I'm going to turn in now. It's been a long day. Let's do this again sometime," Madison said. "Good night."

That was rather abrupt, Abby thought. They were having such a nice chat, and she didn't want it to end so quickly. Perhaps she had intruded on Madison before she had a chance to practice the other music. She couldn't help but be impressed with such playing at such a young age.

"Don't forget your sheet music," she said.

"Oh, that's all right," Madison said. "You practice with it."

Abby preferred the Beethoven Pathétique Sonata as it was one of his easier sonatas. She began the first movement with its slow introduction, suggestive of being imprisoned and gradually evoking a worthiness of respect and devotion and a longing to be freed. Then as the tempo changed into a vigorous allegro, Abby felt an inward escape from all she was enduring. She thought of giving up the treatment altogether and just letting nature take its course. Then as the piece repeated the introductory section again, and the dark hall filled with music, Abby felt a mixture of pity and admiration for the composer who lost the one sense that should have been perfected in him more than anyone else. He had a rather brusque and often uncontrolled manner when it became apparent that he was losing his hearing rapidly. His friends from the noble sect were captivated by his talent, kindliness, innate friendliness, and charm.

Abby had brought with her a penciled drawing of Beethoven in a wooden frame. The drawing was a stocky older man with broad shoulders, short neck, a large head, and a round nose. The piercing eyes that saw a determination in him would rival the greatest of military commanders. Had Abby known him personally, she probably would have loved him as devotedly as many of the women of his own time. She wondered why he never married. Perhaps it was his worsening deafness that prevented him from letting anyone close to his heart. She would have liked to know from where he derived his inward strength to combat the disease. Just as his career blossomed to its full richness, then came the greatest of misfortunes, at the early age of thirty and worsened until he could not hear a single note. At his father's insistence that he practice for hours at a time, it's surprising that Beethoven wasn't driven to hate all things musical. In spite of this or perhaps as a result of it, he created his greatest works.

Abby wrote to her mother that she felt "splendid." That was the only word to describe the feeling. She wrote that she was drinking "gallons" of milk and that she had an appetite like an ostrich. "I shant get fat for I am exercising a great deal, but I'll be hard as nails by the time I get home. Tomorrow, I will lead my children to the Promised Land on a nature hike."

The next day, Abby and the group enjoyed the day in the woods. Abby took a break and sat on a moss-draped rock by herself surrounded by hemlock, red cedar, and blue spruce trees. She desired nothing more than to reflect. The hills seemed unearthly and carried some kind of inspiration to impart for those who sought it. She removed her shoes, and the cool earth caressed her feet.

The light was changing into late afternoon. Her welcomed solitude of the lake and the hills passed into hours as she had fallen into a deep sleep. While she slept, the changing light progressed over the lake and marked shadows on the headlands where among the hemlocks, the bluebird, and the goldfinch would soon end foraging for food and sing for the approaching night.

Abby felt as if ascending into the sky and again she was made aware that the beauty and harsh reality of this paradise was not without its peril. The star-shaped mountain laurel bloomed in a charming, clustered array of white and pink flowers that embodied a calmness and equally ferocious existence as a poisonous flower. Abby was suddenly thrust into reality when Madison and another girl woke her up and urged to come at once to a disturbing development. Wasps were abundant about the camp. They enlarged holes in trees to deposit their eggs and had wasp guards that hovered about the tree, never wavering from their position unless the threat of an intruder to the tree was imminent. Abby ran with the girls to discover that one of the girls had sat under the tree and had been stung several times.

"Mud. Mud," Abby said calmly and with authority, thinking of little Michael Kramer when her mother rescued him from a bee attack. One of the girls made a paste of water from a jug and some dirt. The first aid kit was produced, and after the fire of the sting had gone, the girl was bandaged, and everyone went back to the camp.

The next day, the foreign girls arrived and treated everyone to a sort of "International Night" program representing France, Hungary, Japan, Norway, Sweden, Armenia, and Italy. The two Armenian girls sang a love song in their language and their national anthem. A melancholic strain ran through the songs. The Japanese girl was the star performer. She drew characters and explained what words they represented in English. Abby asked about Japan, Japanese clothes, and nursery rhymes in Oriental music. Two little Italian girls danced a graceful Tarantella. The Norwegian girl, Gerta, was fourteen and big with a big voice. When she sang, her voice was like liquid velvet. Given half a chance, she would flirt with anything wearing breeches. Scoutmaster Barton asked Abby to keep an eye on the girls, and he would do likewise with the boys.

That evening, the group of girls and the Boy Scouts sat on the grass in a circle—a plate and fork in everyone's lap and a high expectancy for chicken, a much-anticipated event which the preparation was kept something of a mystery around the camp.

A homesick twelve-year-old scout, a tenderfoot named Eddie, sat next to Gerta, and he became excited as her perfumed scent overcame him, and he tried to hide what was causing his excitement by placing his plate between his legs while the soft whoosh of freshly disturbed earth added to the suspense as a work boy and the camp director dug some soil with a large shovel and uncovered a large square of canvas.

The canvas was carefully removed and a steamy mass of sweet fern came out. The young scout could not totally savor just the aroma of Gerta's perfume alone. No perfume could be as enticing as the aroma of what lay under the sweet fern, the most aromatic dinner of roasted chicken, potatoes, and carrots. The whole thing had cooked in a stone-lined pit all day. What a lark—to cook a meal that way!

It was campfire time. It was a cool night, so they would need more wood. Abby sent three girls to the midst of the tall timber to collect some firewood. The girls went shrieking and plunged through the bushes, and in about fifteen minutes, they had a royal heap of wood.

"Do tell us a ghost story, Ms. Whitman?" came next.

Abby was now challenged in a way she had never been. It was weird one. The first story she had ever embellished, made up—out of whole cloth—on the spur of the moment. During the recital of this chilling rendition of a man who stalks in his spare time, she pictured Henry Corrigan as the principal character, a personal private joke rendered as a piece of invented storytelling for the amusement of her girls.

It was after midnight, and Abby paid a visit to Madison who was at the piano playing the Chopin Scherzo no. 3. This time Abby did not startle Madison, but quietly approached her and did not interrupt the piece. What Abby was waiting for was the second theme—an almost instant serenity of waves of soft, falling notes like trickling water. When it was over, Madison asked if she was familiar with the piece. Abby said it had been a long time since she played it.

"I have an idea. Why don't we play it together?" Madison suggested.

"How?" Abby asked, not sure about how to go about it.

"I'll sit on the left side and play the first theme, and you sit on my right and play the softer second theme."

Abby thought about the challenge, and she gladly accepted. She watched Madison tackle the dramatic opening with its rapid scales that thundered off the keys. She was fearless in her playing. When Madison began the prelude to the second theme, Abby, so taken by Madison's playing, nearly missed her cue, but she began the downward spiral of notes, striking an occasional wrong note, but, overall, it was satisfying. An excitement and enthusiasm came over Abby that she hadn't known before. The elements in the piece were all there, and it didn't matter if she made a mistake or not. Madison didn't mind. After they finished the piece, they savored the moment.

"Can I tell you something?" Madison asked.

"Sure."

"I've always harbored a secret wish to become a classical pianist. To have people applaud me like you did the first night we met."

"Why does it have to be a secret wish? You have the talent."

"You think so?"

"Of course!"

"My mother wants me to study at the Institute of Musical Art in New York."

"What's stopping you?" Abby asked.

Madison paused, looked down at the keys as if searching for something. "A number of things, it's in New York, so naturally it's expensive."

"With a talent like yours, I wouldn't be surprised if they gave you a scholarship," Abby said, excited for her new friend's dream.

"Stay focused, and one day, you'll be on a stage better than this one, and I'll be right in the first row, shouting bravo."

"That would be a nice moment," Madison said, getting up from the bench. She asked Abby if she would like to meet regularly at the piano during the late evenings, if she wasn't too tired. Abby gave a definite yes. Madison said she was tired and needed to rest. This was the second time Madison cut their meetings short. Abby gave a parting suggestion. "Perhaps you might want to play for the other campers. I mean, if you feel comfortable."

Madison wasn't sure about that. "That sounds like something to think about. And I will."

❧☙

The next evening, they decided that Chopin was the composer of preference. Madison played the Chopin Waltz no. 2, and Abby attempted the Polonaise in A-flat-major. She managed the introduction just fine with its fast ascending notes, but when it came to the famous dance-like theme, she missed the virtuosity of the pounding octaves required of the left hand by hitting the wrong keys, and she gave up. Madison asked when she had last played the Polonaise. Abby couldn't remember exactly. She said it was at least three times before.

They finished the evening with Abby playing the Chopin Etude in E-major no. 3. Abby immersed herself in the slow romantic ambiance of its melody. Raymond Fletcher came to her mind, and she dismissed such expressive sentiments and concentrated on the complex middle passage that required a technical capacity to play its jagged rhythms to its successful conclusion followed by a fusion of the first theme to its end. Abby was granted an enthusiastic applause from Madison, and that made her day.

❧☙

Swimming in the lake was the favorite activity at the camp. The water was as cold as the day was warm. The girls swam toward a diving float in the middle of the narrow lake, taking turns diving from it. Madison was not among the group of swimmers. She chose to remain by the pond. Abby took note of this and asked the camp director who informed Abby that Madison could not swim, and she refused anyone to teach her.

The girls were all excellent swimmers and generous with helping Abby practice some of the basic stunts they knew. She was amazed at the courage of these young girls. Abby wore a bright red bathing suit which was her heart's delight.

Early one morning, Abby went for a dip before her 'tribelets,' as she called the girl campers, woke up. Madison was standing at the dock taking in the air and watching Abby swim and dive. Abby noticed this unusual almost pet-like routine for a couple of days and found it odd. Abby asked her to come in, and when Madison refused, Abby came out of the water dressed in her red bathing suit as the first encounter with John Barton was very fresh in her mind. She would avoid the temptation of skinny dipping for now.

"I can teach you," Abby offered. "It doesn't take long to learn."

Madison shook her head. She was embarrassed at not being able to swim in of all places, a summer camp.

"It's nothing at all. Why don't you just come in, stay in the shallow, and dunk your head. Believe me you'll feel the better for it."

Madison trusted Abby, and she went into the water slowly.

"That's it. Keep walking until the water reaches your hips." Abby swam over to Madison.

"Now bend down slowly, and hold your nose while your head goes under the water."

Madison followed Abby's directions, and she was OK with it. Then she tried holding her head below the water and blowing bubbles through her nose. She gasped and felt like she was drowning. Abby calmed her down. After a minute, Abby told her to lay flat in the water and float.

"Don't worry. I won't let you drown," Abby assured Madison. They remained in the water until they heard the morning bugle from the scout camp signal; it was time to start the day's activities.

The Boy Scouts embarked on an exploration hike in the woods. If it were said that man was naturally associated to the tree as to the soil, this would not be truer as during a hike, where the purpose was to keep the scouts mentally and physically in top form. Scoutmaster Barton led the hike with a compass. They passed by a dairy farm where every cow had a cowbell and scraped noses from trying to eat even the grass between the rocks and boulders. The scouts set up camp headquarters on a clearing that was still mysteriously shrouded by hemlock trees for privacy. Many more unsuspected points of beauty and interest were to be found if the scouts separated into groups of two.

Barton instructed the boys to choose their hiking partner and cautioned them not to stray too far. They were to return at noon for lunch. Eddie, the tenderfoot among others, would remain at camp for the morning, much to his disappointment as he had to pass fire lighting and cooking requirements. Lunch, that day, consisted of canned salmon, beans, bread, milk, and apples. Eddie wished he was back at home.

Evening came. Abby, Scoutmaster Barton, and the camp director together with two of the older Boy Scouts hiked seven miles to the village for Sunday Vespers. Fortunately they did not have to hike back after services. Two boys from the village in a wheezy car picked them up and drove them back to camp or they might very well have taken most of the night to get back.

That night, after counsel fire, about eight girls begged Abby to sleep outside as they were from the city and had never slept out in the open except on a fire escape in the summer. Abby was pleased and excited to accompany them as they scattered to assemble their possessions, and at ten o'clock, they went up the steep rocky path and encamped at the top of a hill high above the camp and settled along the soft side of a huge flat rock. They made the blankets into woodsman like sleeping bags that wouldn't be too hot yet provide the comfort they needed against bugs. They sang some silly songs until it was time for sleep. They downed the lanterns, and every camper crawled away into their sleeping bag and slept under the deep blue inverted bowl of sky. Abby stared into the star laden dome that seemed to be within reach. It rested its edge on the surrounding hills, while the arc above looked infinitely high but within reach even at such a great distance.

Madison chose not to go to sleep just yet. She made a small, private campfire and invited Abby to join her to watch the fire die out. The genial, crackling voice of the fire triggered thoughts of home, of destiny, and the wasp, and red army ant, and any other creeping thing that consumed whatever it inhabited. The two lay together on a blanket beside the fire with their faces toward the stars.

"We should be safe up here," Abby said, not entirely sure herself.

"Do you have the first aid kit, just in case somebody gets bitten?"

"I do."

"Who taught you to play the piano?" Abby asked.

"My mother taught me. She took classes when she was young, and she passed it on to me. I never studied professionally. I just kept at it."

"I envy you that. Have you ever played in front of an audience before?"

"Never. You think I should?"

"I think it would be a waste if you didn't. I used to play for my neighbors, but that was years ago," Abby said, with some regret for allowing the past to slip through her fingers.

"Have you given any thought to my suggestion of playing for the campers?" Abby asked. "I think they would get a big kick out of it." Madison was moved by Abby's suggestion, but she wasn't ready for it yet. Abby would not press her.

"Sometimes, I wish there would be someone back home besides my mom who could appreciate music as much as you do, to play for them and share the experience."

"Where do you live?" Abby asked.

"Connecticut."

"We have a lot in common," Abby said. "I've gotten used to playing mostly for myself for the same reasons."

"I have no doubt you will be a concert pianist," Abby said.

Madison glanced at the stars just listening and thinking to herself.

"How do you know that?" she asked.

"You have a fine ear, and you can read music which helps when trying to interpret the piece, so it becomes yours. You're not merely replaying what you've heard before. And you have passion when you play. I can hear it in the playing whether or not the pianist loves music. You have the one thing that will be to your advantage more than anything. You are young."

"Sometimes it's not enough," Madison said.

"What do you mean?" Abby asked.

Madison didn't respond to Abby's question. Instead she said, "I know I'm not old enough to give you some advice but here goes."

"Start playing for other people even if you have to travel by train and play in a pub, because you can't find any place close. You'll get more honest feedback from strangers than your friends anyway."

"I get nervous playing for others," Abby said.

"You'll be surprised how quickly you get over the fear and just concentrate on the music. There will always be critics. Just do your best and forget they exist. Remember when you're on that stage, no one exists but you. Why else would a thousand eyes be looking at you? Only you."

Abby made a mental note of everything Madison was saying, but she was confused why this talented young girl would say such things to her as she was much older and past her prime in the music world.

"And don't forget you're never too good to get a teacher."

"I used to teach piano, but that was very brief. I can't find anyone who's interested," Abby said.

"Never make excuses. Get away from anything or anyone that will hinder your playing and find some sacred time to practice."

"Madison, this is great advice, but it's not for me to take. It's for you to take advantage of your gifts and blossom. You have the time to do what you want."

Abby found a glow worm. In the darkness, it looked like a tiny fairy of pale jade. A hop toad, apparently with thoughts of suicide, tried to jump into the dying fire and landed on a hot stone and unfortunately burned his little paddies and his tummy. He looked dreadfully ill and discouraged when Abby rescued him from the fire and carried him to the safety of the tall grass. The toad died nevertheless. Abby and Madison buried the toad under a small bush and joined the other sleeping girls snuggled in their wooly blankets while the stars grew paler and the fire faded to a dream.

The scouts went on a field trip to a military academy so they could get a real sense of discipline and leadership by observing the cadets and walking the grounds. Scoutmaster Barton asked Abby if she and some of the girls wanted to come along. They went to the church where the sexton let the scouts in with a key the size of a rolling pin. It was a majestic site. Even the chattering group of twenty girls was silent in a few minutes. The stained glass windows were memorial windows given by each graduating class portraying a scene from the Bible. The nave was lined on both sides with battle worn flags. Looking far up to the dim front of the church, a golden crucifix gleamed from the gloom.

Later they were treated to a dress parade of the cadets. The girls were thrilled to see the young men, in white trousers and blue coats, drill with the accurate motions of a great, well-oiled machine, uniformed and with great precision. After the parade, some of the cadets made a big hit with the girls. Each girl would have loved to take one home for a souvenir.

Making the rounds at night, Abby heard a smothered shrieking sound accompanied by a giggle just as she closed the door to one of the shacks. She turned and flashed her big light in the direction of the noise. To her surprise, through the window she saw one of the girls prancing up and down like a bronco on the buckling bed and another girl on all fours. Abby entered the shack and surprised them. Abby very sternly ordered them back to bed and privately, once she clumped along the road back to her shack, she got hysterical and laughed until she was positively weak and slept good that night.

Abby and her girls were awakened by another shrieking sound this time like a panicky bird being devoured by a snake. In the air was the smell of rubber overshoes burning. Abby bounced out of bed, grabbed her lantern, and looked out of the wide open side of the shack to see two skunks rolling about on the ground: kicking, biting, and squeaking. It was a little battleground for a while. They were a handsome sight with their glossy black coats and white decorative stripes. Their plumy tails waved high. Finally, one of the girls sneezed, and the skunks in all alertness were driven away. Everyone laughed all the way back to their beds as the two skunks delivered their crackly retreat through the underbrush up the hillside. The argument between the skunks was apparently about a yellow jacket's nest. A skunk dug into the nest like a terrier. As the girls slept soundly, he whiffed, swore, sneezed, and appreciated. At intervals, the victor stopped to crunch and chew on a few bees.

In the morning, Abby rose early before anyone else and stepped outside and walked in the direction where the previous evening's commotion had entertained them all. All that was left of the escapade was a whiff of skunk scent, a freshly dug hole big as the crown of a large hat, and a half dozen very resentful yellow jackets buzzing around their desecrated home. Abby had a hunch the skunks were young ones, for the scent was not the normal scent. If it were, the camp authorities would have set fire to their shacks and the whole of the surrounding landscape. All in all, everyone escaped unscathed, excepting the targeted yellow jackets. All she saw and heard were the awakening sounds of birds—the lake and even the hills seemed to sound without pretense—only their beauty as a most satisfactory companion. The sounds of the Chipping Sparrow and the whistle of the Black-capped Chickadee were among so many intonations.

Abby also had an interesting bug conversation with one of the men from the museum staff. He came over to her little group and gave an informal lecture on handling spiders and many other loathsome bugs that he had a sample of. Although Abby appreciated the effort made, she complimented him on what could be learned under the influence of camp sportsmanship; she was not looking to remain in his presence all day.

The next day, Abby walked over to the boat docks and chose a small paddle boat, broad and scow like, but slightly upcurved, both fore and aft. A heavy thing! It would take at least half a dozen persons on one side to tip it. She had never been on a boat before, so she rowed away her troubled self to where the lily pads were and as true to her promise to herself, she picked up one lily pad from the water and rowed to an undiscovered place up the lake beyond two little islands.

Abby got out of the boat and walked onto a flat, soft, grey rock on the side of the lake that was opposite the camp. She could see the girls and a couple of scouts chatting away. A steep hillside rose almost immediately from the edge of the lake. Huge piled-up rocks with ferns and evergreen trees growing in the crevices formed the mountainside. When one wanted to rest and be absolutely lazy, Abby found regular cradles between some of the boulders and a deep mattress of soft pine needles embroidered with ferns. Abby nestled there, and she was lulled into oblivion by the breeze whispering through the boughs above. Abby wished she could live on a lake like this one. If she did, she would have her own canoe. She anguished only just the briefest possible moment from her present to devote herself to the moods of the lake in the hope that someday she could interpret that dreamlike spirit which was felt whenever hemlocks cast their shade by a lake. Maybe someday she would spend a summer in her own little cottage by the lake—if the fates were willing.

Eddie and Gerta, with their minds set on each other, leisurely approached a clearing surrounded by pinewoods and overlooking a swamp to which there was access to a steep slope. This little clearing was enclosed as to be entirely concealed from view. It made for the perfect place for them to get to know each other, but they were not alone. They spotted a solitary, pointed-eared coyote, not seventy yards away; surprised by the couple, the animal slowly made a retreat. Eddie looked to have some fun with the coyote and impress Gerta. He began to chase the coyote. The coyote broke into a run at such speed that it left Eddie way behind, and the boy marveled at the coyote's sustained and powerful flight, until it sailed away over the pines and disappeared into the swamp.

Their natural tendencies to explore were encouraged by the environment around them. But what influenced their eager inquisitiveness also lent a certain disregard for the cardinal rule of camp life not only to learn from, but to also respect every natural thing by leaving it exactly as it was.

They discovered a number of birds' eggs and a nest on the ground. They picked up the eggs that were not cracked and put them back in the nest. Exquisite to revel over but not sure of what to do, they pondered.

Fond of the challenge of watching the eggs hatch, they brought the eggs back to camp. It wasn't as easy as that when the scoutmaster asked the young scout where he and the girl went and what they brought with them.

"We were about to search for you two," he said, displeased with Eddie's lack of discipline by running off and shirking his responsibilities.

"We found a bird's nest. It fell from a tree," Gerta said.

The scoutmaster snatched the nest from Eddie and slapped his face in front of Gerta.

"Get back to camp! I'll deal with you later!" he shouted. Eddie said good-bye to Gerta and walked head bowed back to camp.

"That was a beastly thing to do!" Gerta said in total anger over her friend's unprovoked humiliation.

"I'd like to see you try that with me," she challenged the scoutmaster, who looked upon her as an annoyance. He ignored her and walked away realizing he was going to be reprimanded for striking a scout.

He walked back to camp, and the camp director asked to see him in her office. He gave the nest to Abby.

"Can you take care of this?" he asked. "Put it in a tree somewhere. I'm going to a meeting."

"Sure. Is everything all right?"

"Not sure yet."

In the camp director's office, the scoutmaster found Eddie and Gerta waiting to send him to the gallows. Eddie mentioned wanting to go back home.

"I've been a camp director for many years, but I've never heard of anything like this. It's difficult enough to deal with bullying among the kids, but to have a respected scoutmaster physically assault another scout is unacceptable."

"It was a just a slap, not an assault, and I have never bullied anyone," John Barton said in his defense. "I made a mistake, and it won't happen again."

"You have no idea how right you are," said the camp director. "You're supposed to be teaching the value of respect and tolerance of others, to educate these kids on how to act like adults, and here you are striking another scout like a brat who hasn't gotten his way."

"He left the camp and disturbed a bird's nest with eggs in it," Barton said.

"As I understand it, they found the eggs on the ground and brought them back to seek advice on what to do with them. There is no harm in that."

"You were very mean to my friend, and you should go to hell!" screamed Gerta.

The camp director calmed her down and told the scoutmaster that he must apologize to the scout who was sitting across from him, and she recommended that it would be best if he left the camp and went back home.

"I feel that after this incident, your presence here is counterproductive to the camp."

"How so?"

"You displayed violent behavior toward a member of the camp, and that more than anything is grounds for dismissal. My mind is made up. I won't argue about it."

The scoutmaster accepted the camp director's decision and apologized to the scout and to the girl. He left with a shattered ego and his reputation blemished.

The moon's yellow light made a path to Abby's eyes as she swam naked through the black water. When she finished her swim, she went to the main hall to see if Madison was doing their thing at the piano. She wasn't there. Perhaps she was too tired to be up. Abby missed her company. She sat at the piano and thought what more appropriate piece to play than Beethoven's Moonlight Sonata before retiring.

The first movement, the lamentation spoke to Abby's heart at not being able to share the moment with her friend Madison. The second movement professed the hope that was possible if she only allowed it to. She closed the piano lid, and she left the storm laden third movement for another time when she could enjoy its unbridled emotionality with Madison. She walked back to her shack fending off the ferocious mosquitoes—the worst experienced this season.

The next day, Abby found it odd that Madison was not at breakfast. She couldn't find her anywhere. She went to Madison's shack, and the one girl who was there told her that Madison had gone home early. Abby felt like someone had cut off a limb. She couldn't believe it. She asked why. The girl didn't know. Abby went to see the camp director.

"Madison was taken ill, and the nurse advised her she should go home."

The camp director saw the unhappy look on Abby's face and placed a little folded bit of paper into her hands.

"She left this for you. I'm sorry."

That night the girls cooked pancakes outdoors before going to bed. Abby kept reading Madison's letter over and over.

Everyone gathered for the last brekky. Coffee was served, first and last. Eddie didn't want to get up out of bed. The smell of frying bacon, which he relished and had grown so accustomed to, enticed him. He realized it was the last day. He tossed back and forth the splendid moments both happy and not so happy and stretched his legs and wiggled his toes under the blanket, while he pretended Gerta laid next him in his mind, although she was nearby outside waiting for him to come out. He managed to get up. He took his time dressing in his travel clothes, and it wasn't long before he and

Gerta were enjoying their last breakfast together, in a secluded area away from the crowd, without worrying that they would be punished for having strayed too far.

The group read some poetry and engaged in some kind of ceremony for the camp counselors as their time was ending. Abby and some of the girls became teary eyed. She would never forget the hilltop scenes she stored away in her memory.

Abby prepared to leave Shallow Lake. She had her belongings in tow with the help of Eddie who seemed to be taller than she remembered. They walked to the coach that would take them to the train station. On the way to the station, Abby pulled out Madison's letter to read again.

"I wrote this last night after campfire, for you," she said. "I am going home in the morning, and I want you to always keep this letter in memory of one of the most precious friendships I ever made. Please don't be upset at my leaving without saying good-bye. Some things are best left unsaid. Never forget the purity of music is in its character. Its significance only matters when we as artists are willing to sacrifice to bring to fruition the incredible power that music provides us to think and feel as part of our own existence. I do hope you will continue your piano lessons at home. And the next time you sit at the piano, always remember our time together as I will never forget the inspiration and compassion you have given me."

What followed was a prayer, written in light blue ink in very tiny but readable handwriting.

"God our Father, Great Shepherd, King of all creation, bless this gift of Thine—our love for each other. Through it, may we have a glimpse of thyself and thy love, which is our life. Raise and honor this love of ours until we come nearer a realization of Thyself and of Thy power.

"God, our Father, we so love these hills of Thine—the work of Thy Hands. We love them for all they inspire in us. Keep us always, we pray thee, in the simple trust and fearless faith that we have in Thee, even now, in time of great peril. Draw us close to thy great heart, so we may come closer to each other and know in some measure the unity of Thy love and life."

It suddenly occurred to Abby, in the most profound way as if she was hit by some inanimate object, that she didn't know Madison's address or phone number, not even her last name.

Chapter 23

As dusk approached, Eric marveled at the rifle Zachariah had once owned, and now through the old man's generosity, Eric owned. He grasped the barrel with one hand and the stock with the other. It was a handsome piece of craftsmanship of walnut stock and glimmering steel. He clicked on the safety button and pushed the locking lever to disengage the barrel. There were two cartridges in the chamber. As Zachariah always said, the rifle was useless unless it was always loaded. It was an impressive clicking sound when he opened and closed the chamber. He felt empowered by the heft to it. He took out the two cartridges, fondled them in the hands, a cool and somewhat unsettling feel to them and put them back in their chamber.

Later, Abby drew near the deafening sounds of crows, in countless numbers roosting in the oak tree, releasing an unsettling menacing element in the air and all the surrounding areas including her roof, the Kramer's roof and on the wire fence that protected her chicken coop; their silhouettes were against the still bright sky filling every branch of the oak tree interacting with each other on an individual basis, giving the landscape an indication of their powerful existence.

Abby wondered about the mourning doves and the other birds. Were they OK? Were they forced to abandon their nests against the invasion by the overwhelming mass? Many of the crows in the roost were young and unmated without their own territory. Many had been foraging together for food all day and roosted together at night like a wild party.

As Abby drew closer, she made out the remains of what looked like two dead birds on the ground. She was struck by the red clumps of flesh and feather being devoured piece by piece by some of the crows. There was no way to tell what type of birds they were, or if one of them was her beloved mourning dove or her son that she nursed back to health. She prayed they left the nest and were safe somewhere. She didn't want to look at it, yet she was gripped at the nature of the crows' feeding habits. There were a few crows lined up and encircling the kill, challenging anyone to try and take it away. Each crow waited to get its share when the opportunity came as others stepped aside once they were done feeding. At various intervals, a crow perched above, lured by the meal below would swoop down to get a morsel and fly back up before being chased by the others on the ground who claimed the kill as belonging to them.

Maggie came out with a broom and headed toward the chicken coop to chase the crows away. Eric darted out of his house with his rifle and a young man's exhilaration to try it out on something more challenging than empty liquor bottles and tree trunks. What better way to leave his shameful innocence behind and act with a semblance of courage like Ella and kill a pesky crow. Michael stood by his side to make sure he aimed properly. Even Giny came out of the house in the excitement. The boys shouted their greetings to Abby and Maggie to make sure they were heard in all the noise.

Eric aimed and fired twice into the oak tree. The loud rifleshot shattered through the tree, and the flock of crows rose up and out—a surreal thickening swell that moved gracefully into the night and out of sight—leaving an absence of the unintentional vulgarity they took with them as they were no match when man's hand intervened to make things right again.

One of the crows was hit and sent reeling as the bullet ricocheted in his chest and through his ribs and hurling back through his chest again. The crow attempted to escape with the flock but fell short and crashed into a dried-up water fountain that birds were using as a food depository. Among the carcasses were a couple of rats, a dead mouse, an old fish, and some worms. The crow lost the feeling in his legs, yet he still felt like he was flying, only backward. Breathing pained him like a knife, stabbing him repeatedly in the chest. The crow didn't know where he was. His eyes lost their focus, and he went in and out of consciousness.

Then he heard the muted sound of a creature of some mystery, another bird perhaps. He opened his eyes and felt the dawn slip quietly above. He recognized at first a blur then he closed his eyes and opened them again to the flesh and blood image of the mourning dove that contained in herself the dignified virtue of forgiveness without reservation upon the crow that killed her mate and now lay dying in a pile of garbage.

"I am the one whose mate you and your friends killed for having unknowingly encroached in your territory," she said.

"I'm sorry I don't remember you. I have killed so many."

Whereas the sight of her in the flesh produced no discernable trace of familiarity on the crow's part, he had no misgivings as to the purity and inherent goodness of this bird and whatever he did; he was paying the price now.

The dove recalled for the dying crow the tragic sequence of events, of his arrogant and shameless manner on conferring his territorial superiority over the undesirable doves before the male dove was slaughtered for feeding in their turf. The crow finally remembered her and knew shame and regret for the first and last time.

"I am not worthy of being in your presence, not even for one more minute," said the crow.

"The birds killed on the ground by the oak tree, what kind were they?" she asked.

"A robin and a finch, I think," he replied.

The dove felt a part of her own float away on hearing this unfortunate news.

"Were they living in the tree when you found them?" she asked.

"Yes."

She was commiserating with the crow in his suffering, but she had to get back to the oak tree to find out if the dead birds were her neighbors.

The crow knew his death was only moments away, and he asked the dove if she would pray for him. The dove was puzzled by this request.

"Why do you ask me this? Praying only offers absolution for humans. We have no spirit that lives after we die."

The crow responded by saying, "It is not so. Since I have killed so many in my life and have not given a thought to either them or their families I have destroyed, it is possible to redeem myself now so that those that I have killed will be reunited with their family, both animal and human in that perfect place called heaven. I myself will cease to exist forever."

The dove was intrigued by the notion that through the crow's salvation she would be reunited with her mate and her children at the end of time.

The dove sought not only to lift the pain of the loss of her mate, but also to secure the possibility that her young would be rewarded and perhaps she as well for being cared for by the beloved woman who lived in the house by the tree.

The dove noticed an angry woman emerge from the house shouting at her husband. She was upset over the mess that the birds were making in the fountain and demanded that he remove all the trash from the fountain and get a tarpaulin from the garage to cover up the fountain until it was able to be fixed. The man said nothing as the wife retreated back into the house, and he saw for himself the collection of scraps, a dead crow, and one live mourning dove. He clapped his hands to shoo the dove away. When the dove saw him going into the garage, and it was safe, she flew back to comfort the crow in his last moments.

"I haven't left," she said. "That man will be back soon."

"I ask your forgiveness for what I did, and as I die before you, I seek absolution from you for I will exist no more."

The truth of the situation involved no room for emotion as there was no need for it nor much time before the man came out to collect the trash. It was an opportunity to get closure through understanding, and she knew there was no obligation on her part to do this.

"I forgive you and hope you will find peace," she said and remained with the crow until he closed his eyes. Mischu, Ella's cat turned up, and the dove greeted him, and she was not afraid.

The man returned with a sack and a tarpaulin and began to collect the rubbish from the fountain including the dead crow while the dove flew back to the oak tree.

The mourning dove reached the oak tree. The crows had left and thankfully the tree was still her home. In flight, she looked below and saw sorrow in the form of the gathering of the residents of the tree on the ground surrounding a small patch of bloodsoaked earth. One of the starlings landed with some grass in its beak and placed it on the ground with the other twigs and blades of grass as a wreath. From this, the dove knew that tragedy had struck. She landed in the midst of her neighbors and inquired what had happened as they had all fled when the invasion began.

The male robin was there as were his two children but not his mate, and when the dove made eye contact with him, even before speaking she knew her best friend, the female robin, was gone as was one of the finches.

"She refused to leave when they attacked her," said the robin. "We all flew away, but she did not. I am so ashamed."

"Don't be ashamed, my father," said his son.

"Where are they?" asked the dove.

"They're buried here," said one of the starlings. "The woman in the house," referring to Abby, "buried them where they died."

Mischu, the cat, stood by the back entrance to the Kramer house maintaining his own vigil for the fallen birds.

"Look who's here," said the finch, suspiciously.

"Don't worry about him. He will not harm us or any bird," said the dove, well aware of the understanding that in nature, cat and bird were enemies and even more aware that the predatory instincts of the cat did not apply to Mischu.

"He has befriended me," said the dove. Surprised by this revelation, the birds asked her to explain.

"I too was afraid when I first saw him on that rainy day when I came to live amongst you. When I saw him again, after the birth of my squabs, he told me how his life was saved from drowning by the girl who lived with her grandfather in the woods, and whenever there is an impending death, he will seek the dying to show compassion and comfort in his own way."

"Tell us how he came to have this gift?" asked the starling.

"He just has the ability to sense when a human or animal close by is going to die soon."

"If this is true then why didn't he save my mate?" asked the robin.

"He cannot save any more than we can," the dove replied.

"The cat was with me a few moments ago when I faced the crow that killed my mate, and I watched him die before me."

"You sat with him until he died? Why did you do that?" asked the robin, feeling betrayed that his mate was killed, and the dove was not there sooner.

"I assure you, my friend, I did not plan to meet him. The crow asked me to forgive him in the hope that he might be redeemed."

"Ridiculous!" shouted the robin. "There was no point in him asking your forgiveness! He was condemned. It wouldn't have made any difference for him."

"Ultimately we're all condemned in this life," said the dove. "The crow told me that in seeking my forgiveness, it was possible that when I die, I would be reunited with my mate and my children and possibly the woman in the house who has cared for us so lovingly and once saved the life of my injured son. This would be his one and only act of kindness ever in his life."

"Who had the power to make such things possible?" asked the finch.

The dove did not know the answer.

The dove's two children landed. They had heard about the invasion and came to see what they could do.

"My dear," said the starling. "You have been fooled by that vicious beast who, even in his last moments, conjured up in his evil mind something to give you false hope."

The dove did not agree. "He was sincere," she said strongly.

"So be it. I hope for your sake that it is true," said the grieving robin, no longer able to contain his sorrow. "I have decided to leave the tree," he said.

The birds tried to convince him otherwise. He listened to what they had to say but not earnestly. He would leave once he found another place. His heart was dead, and he would not consider anyone else's opinion. His children were now of age, to be on their own, and there was no point in remaining in a place that brought him unhappiness. The birds understood this.

The birds stood vigil for a few more minutes, and one by one they paid their respects to the robin and his children and flew from the graves to search for food before they returned to the oak tree.

Chapter 24

A package arrived for Abby, and Maggie brought it to her in the kitchen. Abby looked at the return address and saw the name Diana Hendricks, a name she did not recognize. It was from Stamford Connecticut. She remembered that Madison had told her that she lived in Connecticut. Abby went upstairs to her bedroom and locked the door. Anything that came from Madison was regarded as very personal, and not even her mother was allowed to penetrate the sanctity of her bedroom while she opened Madison's package. She wondered how Madison had obtained her address. It didn't matter. What was important was that now, she had her friend's address to write back.

She opened the package tearing at it to undo the seal. Inside was sheet music for the Rachmaninoff Piano Concerto no. 2. A letter was also enclosed. Abby got in bed, placed the sheet music by her side, and read the letter. The handwriting did not resemble Madison's handwriting in her letter from camp. This was in very fine script indicating that perhaps an adult had written this and not a thirteen-year-old girl.

Dear Abby,

I am sorry to tell you that Madison recently passed away. She had been sick for sometime with leukemia. She was taken from us very quickly. The camp nurse telegrammed every day to let us know how she was doing. Madison was in remission for most of the year before the summer and she was doing very well.

She often spoke of your kindness at the camp and of your shared interest in music. I wanted to tell you how much I appreciate how you touched her life and made her so happy. When she returned from the camp, she was so alive and had so much energy. And I know that you were largely responsible for that. I thank you from the bottom of my heart for allowing our daughter to experience the joy of living again. I have enclosed the sheet music she wanted you to have. Please feel free to communicate with me anytime. My address is on the package. Please give my regards to your mother.

Regards,
Diana Hendricks.

It would have made sense for Abby to cry until all her tears dried up, but she wasn't one to express her sorrow in that way. She went downstairs and spent some time with her mother to talk about the letter she received. Now she knew why Madison had left their sessions together so quickly when Abby would have liked to spend more time with her.

That night Abby didn't sleep but felt the quiet of the unseen force that shaped the very existence of her life and of all life and upon the will of that entity it was decided with judgment when a life was to end. It was the same for her as well. She knew her time would come as surely and unexpectedly as it was for Madison who was robbed of her right to fulfill her destiny.

The next day, Abby met with Raymond over coffee, to talk about Madison and her time at the camp, and to inform him in a manner that was unequivocally clear what he feared most, that she would no longer continue the treatment.

Chapter 25

Henry Corrigan arrived in the city of Philadelphia lost as a wandering stray dog. The brisk fall wind made it difficult to wander on foot for very long. He had eaten a ham sandwich for lunch the previous day and nothing since. He remembered the taste of the toasted bread and the slight salty ham with a pickle on the side and the hot cup of coffee he drank. His legs and feet were sore. He thought of the comforts of home and quickly dismissed them. No matter what happened he would not go back.

Henry's sorrows were many, but even he had a right to bury them for a few hours while the sandman did his work. The day gave in to the night. He had never slept outdoors before. He found a spot under a stone arch bridge, put his suitcase next to him, and used some of his clean shirts to roll up as a pillow. He kept his jacket on as protection from the cold and slept soundly all night.

When he got up the next morning, his greatest challenges were ahead.

His hunger was all too present. If he wanted to avoid sleeping outdoors in the future, he had to find a job and a place to stay soon. When he raised his head, he felt his neck ache terribly. He got up, and he saw that the shirts he used for a pillow and suitcase were gone.

He looked around all over in a panic, but whoever took them clearly had a talent for it and was long gone. He looked around for a street sign and pulled out of his pocket his Mendenhall's Guide and Road Map of Philadelphia. Something else was wrong. He reached inside his jacket and his wallet, with the money his father gave him, was also gone. Henry's alertness never failed to come up with a solution to his own problems. But this time, he was at a loss of the worst kind. He checked all his pockets, and he didn't have a dime. The thief really cleaned him out but good. He used to like to sleep. It was the only time his troubles were suppressed. Now he was concerned about what would happen if he fell asleep again.

This was the first time he felt truly helpless, and his heart beat faster as he feared he would not be able to find a haven in such a heartless world. He passed by an automat, looking through the window to see people enjoying their breakfast. He passed by a telegraph office when the idea of sending his father a telegram for more money came to him. But he vowed to remain steadfast besides the fifty cents required put that idea out of his mind. So he continued looking on the ground as he walked to see if there were any coins.

He arrived at a park where an elderly woman sat alone on one of the benches, bundled in a dark coat, reading a newspaper. Her coat was heavily caked with soil. Henry knew the woman had seen better days. Yet, despite his own misfortunes, he remained true to his inherent character and deemed her unsuitable and walked to another bench further down. He couldn't help but glance over at her and wondered if it was his destiny to share the same fate as an idle displaced person with no money and nothing to look forward to but the relief of death. From behind her newspaper, she turned her head and their eyes met. Henry immediately looked the other way. The woman folded her paper, got up, and walked over to him. He pretended not to notice her.

"Pardon, young man," she said, standing close to him and extending her bony hand. "Could you spare any change?" An elevated train roared by on a curl of tracks drowning out the sound of the birds.

"I haven't anything to spare," Henry said, in a voice that he thought was loud enough for her to hear.

"What? I can't hear you?"

Henry waited for the sound of the train to fade away, and he repeated that he didn't have any money. He saw through her wrinkled features, and her doubt became apparent. He wasn't sure why, but something within him made him want to prove to her that he wasn't lying.

He opened his pockets, turning them inside out. He even removed his shoes.

"You see," he said, thinking how amusing the situation was, "nothing. Not even five cents to get a Coke." It wasn't so amusing.

The woman was convinced and apologized for bothering him. Henry raised his hand dismissing the subject and asked her if she knew of a place to live.

"I need to get a room somewhere," he said.

"You're not likely to find anyone who will give you a room if you haven't any money to pay for it," she said flatly.

He knew this more than anything. He had to get some money and fast. He wasn't the type to beg.

"Can I offer you this peach?" She held out a ripe peach for him, but he declined and thanked her for her generosity.

"Are you going to South Street?" she asked.

"I don't know. Where is it?"

"That way."

"OK sure, if you'll lead the way."

They walked, and Henry was rekindled by that rare momentary spark that comes when two people meet who have nothing in common but actually have everything in common. He began to pay attention to others who, like himself, were on their own shaky foundation.

South Street was alive with the music of horse-drawn wagons, cars, crates crashing, and people. There were wagons and carts crowding both sides of the street, making it difficult to get to the sidewalk.

"You might try over there." She pointed to a run-down apartment building with a sign, "Low Rent."

"First I have to get a job," he said.

Henry and the woman were lured in the direction of the bakery by the aroma of fresh-baked bread. There was a brother and sister, aged seven and six, standing at the entrance to the bakery, dressed in what were once kids' clothing but had been put through the ravages of being worn endlessly. They had a wheel cart full of newspapers to sell and a little border terrier sleeping on top of the stack of papers. There was so much produce, Henry considered taking an orange. He looked around to see if he could take one without being caught, but there were too many people around. He turned to say something to the woman, but she was suddenly gone, disappeared into thin air. All that was left to remind him of her existence was the peach she had offered on the ground. *It must have fallen out of her pocket,* he thought. He quickly picked it up before somebody stepped on it, dusted off the dirt, bit into it, and let the juices flow down to his chin. It was the sweetest peach he had ever eaten.

There were many taverns around and several places to eat, including one diner that advertised they were looking for a busboy. Henry, refreshed and taken aback by his own eagerness at the prospect of getting this lousy job, entered Clingman's Diner. A bell over the front door announced his arrival to the handful of people in the place, who by the slightest turn of their heads, acknowledged Henry and resumed their meals.

A waitress approached. "Is the manager here?" Henry asked.

The manager came out from the kitchen where he oversaw the short-order cook. He wiped his hands on his apron and greeted Henry.

"I'm Clingman."

"Henry Corrigan." Henry shook the man's hand.

He was in his early fifties and a man of few words. As an unsuccessful salesman for his father, Henry did possess a talent for judging people on sight. Clingman was having a bad day and was not in the mood to waste time. Henry got to the point.

"Is the busboy job still available?"

"It is," said Clingman, who took it upon himself to tell Henry that he owned as well as managed the diner.

"I need someone to wash the dishes, mop the floor, and bus the tables."

"I can handle that," Henry said, for the first time expressing an honest desire to work.

"For how long?" asked a skeptical Clingman. "I need someone who can stay in the job more than a couple of days. It gets busy during the breakfast rush and also lunchtime, and I want to make sure you're not going to run off because of the pressure."

"I won't do that. You can trust me."

"Don't say that word," Clingman said.

"What word, trust?"

Clingman had had his fill of disappointments with people who worked for him and customers who never came back to repay what they owed for a meal after they stuffed themselves and didn't have enough money.

Clingman sensed an educated young man who belonged in an office instead of doing menial work.

"I won't bother to ask if you have any experience working in a diner," he said. "What I want to know is *why* you want to work here?" he asked.

"I need the money. I'm new in town, and I haven't got a cent to my name."

Clingman knew the truth when he heard it. "The job pays eight dollars a week. Interested?"

Henry felt the constraint that was partially self-imposed on his life, ease up a bit. At this point, any job would do as long as money came with it. He realized what it meant to see things from a weak perspective. And now the tide was turning in a new direction, and he could now resume a life with an awakened interest.

"I'll take it. When do I start?" he asked.

"Right now."

The manager of the apartment building was not keen on renting a room to someone who didn't have any money. Henry noticed a Corrigan typewriter on the table behind the sign in desk.

"Three dollars by the day. How long do you plan on staying here?"

"I'm not sure. I see you have one of my father's typewriters," Henry said. The manager didn't understand what Henry was talking about.

"I'm Henry Corrigan." He wished he had one of the company cards. They were in his stolen wallet. Henry wished for the thief to receive all of hell's tortures and more.

"Your father is William Corrigan?"

"Yes."

"I don't have one of my business cards on me. You see my wallet was stolen last night."

"Sir, it's not my business."

"Before you say no, I can tell you that I have a job."

"Where?"

"I work at Clingman's Diner."

"It's very strange that a person like you, who comes from a rich family, wants to stay here."

"I won't ask my father for money."

"I would, if I were you."

"A person in your position wouldn't give up that security unless you were forced to."

"You're right about that," Henry said.

"Can you ask your boss for an advance? That's the only way. I'll hold a room for you if I can get the first three days' payment first."

Henry wasn't up to looking for another place, and the price was dirt cheap.

"I'll ask him."

After one month, Henry was a productive and respected if no longer a rich man of society. He got to know the regulars who came into the diner. Clingman took note of his work ethic, and Henry began to help out in the food preparation and taking orders when one of the waitresses was sick. It got to be pretty routine, until one day, the woman who had befriended Henry in the park showed up at the diner. She wore the same dark coat which was clean this time. Henry recognized her immediately like an old friend. She wanted a cup of coffee and a roll. Henry was only too happy to oblige.

Clingman didn't particularly care for street people entering his establishment. He saw Henry was spending an unusual amount of time talking to that woman.

He went over to Henry and asked to speak to him in the kitchen.

"Do you know her?"

"Yes. I met her the first day I arrived here."

"Let me guess. You met her either in the park or on the street."

"It was in the park."

"Henry, I would appreciate if you would tend to some of the customers and not spend so much time talking with her. Just give her the check and have her leave."

"What's wrong with her?"

"People get nervous when they see street people come into the place. Sometimes they don't bathe, and it puts people off their food. They create problems when you try to get them to leave and they're asleep at the table."

"She's not like that." Henry couldn't put his finger on it, but she was different.

Henry took care of the customers, who needed refills on their coffee, and he sat at the counter with the woman, and they talked about how everything changed for him after they met that very day; he got the job at the diner, and he was staying at the apartment building she recommended. He hated the room. It was dingy, and the paint was peeling off the walls. His companions were roaches, and a mouse he named Fred who lived in a hole in the wall and who poked his head out when Henry brought something home to eat.

He asked how she was. She said she was the same, still living in the streets.

"Have you thought about going to a shelter?" he asked.

"Oh, I detest those places. They treat you like garbage, and they make you feel like you're an imposition. I'll never go to another one. I prefer the outdoors."

"Where do you go in the winter?"

"Coffee shops and libraries," she smiled, and Henry smiled along with her.

She finished her roll and drank the last bit of coffee, and she stared at the empty cup.

"I'll get you more coffee," he said.

"No thank you, dear." She looked disturbed about something. Henry noticed she was troubled.

"What is it?" he asked.

The woman knew she had to break free of her unwillingness to tell him, but there was no alternative.

"I'm afraid I don't have the money to pay for the breakfast."

"I didn't think you did," Henry said.

"I didn't mean to take advantage of your good nature. I promise you I didn't."

"I'll take care of it this time. But next time you'll have to have the money, OK?"

He felt bad having to lecture her, but this was his job, and he had a responsibility to Clingman, who overheard the conversation and came out to set things straight.

"All right, you get out!" Clingman shouted to the woman.

"It's all right, Mr. Clingman."

"If you want to be taken for a fool, that's your business," Clingman told Henry. "I won't have her come in here and eat my food and then try and skip without paying."

"Thank you," she said to Henry and left the diner.

"Henry, you're an intelligent man, and you know it doesn't pay to do something nice for anybody in this world. They'll just take advantage of you, and you'll hate yourself for it later. Believe me, I speak from experience."

Chapter 26

The afternoon: Early fall storm clouds rumbled above the distant hills surrounding the ranch where Ivanhoe Miller made his home. The waking winds' prelude slowly spread a harmonious gathering of soft sound, churning itself with all speed.

As the day progressed into evening, the storm pushed away the remaining low clouds to unleash its fury.

Ivan's cabin was dark and cold. Thunder and wind roared about the darkness whipping and whirling. Huge boulders of rain and hail drummed down against the arched ceiling above Ivan's bed, where he lay naked, silent, with a gun in his hand. The cotton blanket his mother wove for him was in a heap by the foot of the bed. He remembered his father telling him to breathe deeply when the weather was cold. "Cold air in the lungs is a reminder that you are alive," his father said. Ivan didn't feel alive. He hated rainstorms at night. The sound of rain furthered Ivan's melancholic state, and he felt lost as a solitary, grazing cow. He hated the name Ivanhoe—it sounded like something out of a Shakespearean play. He had nothing against Shakespeare, but Ivanhoe sounded like a medieval name from old England. He preferred those who knew him to call him Ivan. He was twenty-seven and delivered ice in the neighborhood.

Ivan knew while it poured outside, no one would come to harm him. The storm's grand ferocity would prove significant enough to disrupt their plans for him. They would wait until the weather cleared before they gathered themselves together for their cause, to make sure he hanged.

As he lay there clutching the gun's cold steel, Ivan shut his eyes to the loud bang of a lightning bolt that took him to a distant summer when he used to help his father deliver ice. Customers who wanted ice delivered placed a red and blue company ice card, in their window. The card displayed four different pound designations in each cross section, and the customer would check off the pounds of ice they wanted.

Each day, Ivan's father drove slowly down the street in a flatbed truck looking for the card assuming it was placed in the proper position, in the window or on the mailbox with the number of pounds checked off. This would save a lot of backtracking trips up and down flights of stairs.

Ivan admired his father's impressive physique gained through twelve years in the business, and he wanted to be just as big as he was. His father never went to school, but when Ivan saw how his father could cut a block of the required size with an ice pick, attach tongs to the block, and with a mighty swing hoist the block onto his shoulder, he gained even more stature in Ivan's mind, because he thought his father was so clever.

Now Ivan had grown into a man with his own powerful attributes. He was a testament to his father as he took over the reins of his father's legacy. Like his father before him, Ivan knew the total amount of ice needed by his customers before he entered their houses. Year round, many customers wanted their iceboxes filled as full as possible. Sometimes, the housewife forgot to remove the ice card from the window if she didn't want any ice. For those customers who lived in multifloored apartments, it made for a difficult climb only to be told that they didn't need any ice. This caused many a block of ice to be thrown from porches of those buildings. When Ivan had these outbursts, his actions always made the kids happy getting a free hunk of cold, refreshing natural ice from the iceman in the summer.

The ice was chipped with chisels to fit the compartment of the icebox. Ivan would carry an average of fifty to one hundred fifty pounds of ice from the wagon to the icebox at each stop.

Mrs. Haversham was a regular customer, and when she wasn't at home, her maid received Ivan as an old friend when trust came first and foremost in those days. When Ivan entered the kitchen, he found Mrs. Haversham and the maid disturbed about something. Mrs. Haversham asked him if he remembered seeing her handcarved alligator nutcracker. Ivan didn't know what the hell she was talking about. He was tired and wanted to get on with his deliveries.

"I always keep it in the living room on top of the small side table near the bookcase."

He couldn't have cared less. "I've never been in your living room," he said.

"Please don't think we're accusing you," she said in a patronizing way. "My maid and I have looked for it everywhere, and we're trying to figure it out where it could be."

It didn't occur to either Mrs. Haversham or the maid that it was Ella who had stolen the nutcracker since the break-in happened months before, and Mrs. Haversham rarely spent time at her library, so she never noticed that it was missing until recently.

Mrs. Haversham regretted mentioning the nutcracker to Ivan. "We know you are busy, so we won't keep you Ivan. Thank you."

Two boys up to mischief looking for something to entertain themselves spotted two women in the park. One of the women bragged at length about her beautiful red and gold broche that her husband had given to her for her birthday. She was wearing the broche pinned to her upper blouse. Since the boys had nothing else to engage their minds, they followed the two women, and one of the boys mimicked her behind her back with exaggerated mannerisms on how silly she was for feeling the way she did about her beloved broche.

Ivan had finished his work and parked his wagon by the park entrance to steal some time for himself and observe those who were not subject to the legal barriers that prohibited him from entering the park. Was it luck to occupy a position in life and hold on to it desperately only to be disconnected by impolite refusals just because it was the law? He looked on the ground and got off his wagon to find his stimulant for the evening in the form of a red and gold broche.

"It's terrible!" the woman screamed. Her broche was gone, vanished as if she only had the thing in a dream. "I just got the damn thing!" she shouted. The two women made it their priority to find it. So they retraced their steps back to the park. If she was so fortunate to find it, she vowed that she would never worry or complain about anything again.

Ivan admired the broche and pictured his mother wearing it. If only she had lived to be able to receive this glorious present from him! He imagined the look of passion on her face as she received it from him. It was not a normal occurrence for his mother to get presents. But that didn't mean she wasn't loved. They just never had the money. He imagined what life would be like if she and his father was still alive.

The woman spotted Ivan standing by his wagon with her broche in his large black hand. A sudden hope flashed through her mind as well as a bit of vengeance. If only Ivan had put the broche in his pocket and not taken it out until he got home instead of having the thing out in the open where the woman had just seen it, his life would not have ended so unnecessarily.

"Look!" she shouted. "That man has my broche!" She went to confront Ivan and demanded the return of her property. Ivan looked at the woman who indirectly would be responsible for his hanging, her face white as death; she lifted her head to face him, enlarged her nostrils, and whined. A mare if ever there was one.

Two men immediately rushed to her, and they all gazed at Ivan with hard-set eyes.

"I didn't steal it, ma'am. I found it right there on the ground," he explained and quickly returned the broche to the woman. It might have ended without further incident, but it wasn't enough for the men who wanted to display their power over the hulking Ivan and teach him a lesson. They closed in on him.

"Kill me if you can," Ivan said, raising his massive arms wide open. One of the men tried to grab Ivan's wrist and hold it down, but his hands were too small for the task. It was a brief struggle with not much passion as Ivan easily grabbed the man's neck, and with one hand, lifted him up into the air and smashed him to the ground leaving him stunned and panting on the pavement like a dying dog that had been carelessly run over. The other man was the larger of the two, and his confidence was foolish as Ivan, with a slight grin, shot his fist into the man's face and head with the force of a sledgehammer, not once but two more times until the man's face caved in, and he fell to the ground with his buddy. Ivan's hand was dripping wet with blood. He knew he was in big trouble as he hurried to his wagon and drove off to his home as the clouds grew dark and a crowd gathered behind him to see the carnage. It rained down on those twittering last hours when those caught in the downpour turned their faces to the dawn.

Ivan, in the midst of the storm that swept the catastrophe behind him, could only think of getting home. When he lay in bed that last night, he lived the events with fearful realism and knew he would not survive the coming day.

The rains stopped in the morning. There was an instant quiet, apart from the sound of droplets falling from leaf to leaf.

Ivan stood up and stared out into the sky. He walked outside and smelled the fresh daisies. He was at peace until a voice called his name, a faint voice, almost too faint to be heard properly. He looked around the area, for the presence he felt was there in his midst.

He looked to the east, down the splendor of forest and saw the crowd who walked to his property to take him as their prisoner. Ivan stood there and waited for them to come to him. He decided to submit without resistance and gave the arresting officer his gun.

"Son, one of the men you beat up died last night."

Ivan didn't have much longer to wait for the blessing of his last breath.

Chapter 27

Ivan was cursed, punched, and spat at while on his way to the place of his execution.

The crowd moved toward the large tree with a swinging rope. It was afternoon, and the crowd increased in numbers as people asked of each other in the excitement as to who was going to be hanged. Many of the crowd knew Ivan and his father and were shocked as they tried the get the best view. Ella was there holding Mischu in her arms. Sandwiched in the crowd, she observed and heard. Ivan stood before the crowd naked and silent, a blazing fierceness in his eyes. There were children propped up on the heads of fathers and some holding onto their mother's hand. The adults whispered to the children, "This is what happens to you when you break the law."

Another couple mentioned that they had attended a hanging the previous year. One of their children, picking flowers, caught a black man in relations with a white woman in the park. When the girl told her parents, word got around to the woman's father, and it turned out that the man worked for the father as a stablehand. When the father confronted her with this accusation, she admitted it to him. She found the man in the splendor of his own perfection of manhood with all the suppressed vitality of his youth ready to be unleashed. The father feared a scandal, and to protect his name, he encouraged his daughter to say that the man forced himself on her. She refused to lie. And he took steps to get rid of the man who he felt had violated his daughter. The father confronted the man and hate carried him too far as he produced a knife and lunged after the man, stabbing him in the leg. The stablehand was much larger and more powerful. He didn't mean to kill the father. But it happened, and it didn't take but a second for the man to know his fate if caught. The man's leg bled terribly. He half ran, half limped to a freight car where he took refuge. When he saw the police closing in, he decided to make his last stand and shot two policemen, mortally wounding one of them. It was the last time he would fire a gun. In a matter of seconds, a bottle of lighted kerosene was thrown into the tiny opened window from where the man had picked off his kill. The explosion engulfed the car in thick clouds of smoke and heat. The man forced out of the car, made a run for it but a wild roar of fury as the men pursued the assassin prevented his escape. He was bound and gagged and the same fate that took the life of the stablehand was about to be shared as a chain was placed around Ivan Miller's neck and looped around the tree limb. He recognized the face of Mrs. Haversham as she walked over to him.

The crowd hushed as she approached the condemned man. In silence, she was assisted by the hangman, and she stood next to Ivan. He looked long and patiently into the old tired eyes of this woman. And she kissed his face and kissed each iron shackle that cut through his wrists and feet leaving blood stains on her lips. She removed her shawl and wiped his sweaty forehead.

"I pray thee to find a better life in the next world," she said and left Ivan who did not reply, but in his eyes, he knew she was a woman of rare compassion.

"That is the teacher," said a woman in the crowd who stood in front of Ella. "She is such a good person to forgive him for what he did." The other woman who listened was confused.

"What did he do?" she asked.

"Oh, you didn't know? He stole something from her, some stupid nutcracker or something. I don't know what it was actually. But isn't it a shame to see a young man die for such a trivial reason."

"I don't believe it."

What Ella overheard the woman say was wrong, but she took it for the truth, and in her young mind she reasoned that she was responsible for the man being hanged.

The act of castration was dispensed with as there were children in the crowd. But there needed to be an example set as well as provide something in the form of entertainment so the folks had something to talk about. Vendors sold sandwiches and soda. One overzealous spectator threw a rock at Ivan and cut his head. The police quickly ordered the man to be arrested as he might incite others in the crowd to throw rocks and accidentally hit people who were standing close to Ivan. There was a sudden mad rush as word went out of the execution and people abandoned their wagons and cars to view the spectacle.

The two boys from the park began to build a pyre out of any kindling they had, newspapers, branches, and broken wooden posts. As a prelude to the main event, a man with a pair of shears arrived and began to slice off Ivan's ears and three men poured cans of kerosene on the pyre and all over Ivan as the crowd cheered. It dawned on Ella that he wasn't going to hang but be burned alive. Suddenly, Mischu became agitated and started scratching Ella trying to break free of her grasp. He was erratic, crazed with a panic that she had never seen in him before. She had no choice but to let him go. He sprung away from the scene and turned the corner. Ella didn't know if she would ever see him again.

"May you roast like the fucking pig that you are!" screamed one person.

"Cut him some more before you torch him!" screamed another, adding to the desires of the blood thirsty crowd. Many were snapping pictures; others saved their film for the burned corpse.

The fire consumed Ivan very quickly. He was no longer visible to the crowd as a wind blew the smoke into the crowd and filled their lungs with the burnt essence that was Ivanhoe Miller. They watched him crumple away in the light of the flames. Photographers had to wait for his burned body to cool before posing for pictures to make their postcards. Ella left the site and heard Mischu meowing in an alley. He had waited for her.

Ella went to an abandoned house that she came upon one day in her housebreaking adventures but never attempted to go into. She put Mischu on the untended grass that was over a foot long, and he seemed to enjoy getting lost in it. The windows were all boarded up. Whoever lived there left empty beer bottles in the crevice near the front entrance. The boards were heavy and could not be pried open so she walked around to the back of the house along a path where the weeds were yellow and where she knew someone many moons ago had walked.

There was a porch there, and along the edge of the roof were enormous amounts of weeds growing from the rain gutters. There were rafters along the underside of the porch roof. She looked in the crawlspace and found a long piece of rope coiled up and gone terribly hard; it was difficult to unravel. Ella had to once and for all settle the uncertainty of her dilemma. The death of Ivan was so odious by reason of her own selfish act—the only remedy was to pretend to hang herself and maybe, just maybe, she might pull it off. If she didn't, she was no great figure that anyone should miss, not even Eric, whose friendship was engraved in her heart for a lifetime, deserved to give her a second thought. The trick was to pretend to hang herself by not letting the noose slip too far down to cut off the airflow.

She needed to soften the rope to make it more flexible. She found an old well with a bucket and pulley. She looked down the well, but it was dry, so she walked around the property and found an outhouse that was not boarded up. She took the rope to the cesspool inside there, and what passed for water was the foulest smelling garbage she had ever seen. No water to be found. Not one to give up so easily, she unraveled the rope and inch by inch, she pulled and tugged letting the fibers stretch and centuries-old dirt and grit fall off, despite her hands getting raw, she kept at it until there was a loosening.

Mischu stared up at her curiously. She tossed him a stick, and he played with it while she took the rope up the steps and coiled one end of the rope around looping it several times to make the noose. She took the end of the rope that formed the coil and put it through the loop and held it in place with one hand while pulling on the loop with the other hand to close it. She flung the rope over the rafters and tied it. There wasn't anything to stand on, so she balanced herself on the frame and placed the noose around her neck pulling the noose until it was tight.

Ella looked at Mischu, who she had rescued from certain death, and now saw him fully grown. She embraced his wonderful mystique not knowing what it was about him that made him so special. He came up to her and put his front paws on the edge of the frame where she stood. She stroked his head, bid him farewell, and jumped.

Before reaching unconsciousness and allowing her body to surrender, her mind lingered in the deep of things, not sure where she was crossing to, and if it was a place where burden and misery no longer crowded her world. She didn't know if she was really dead. She didn't see any angels around, so maybe she was going to hell. She wandered within the nothingness—where there was no color, no light, and no darkness—where not even the most subtle things mattered as there was nothing that lived. She hoped to meet her dying fate and get away from this uncomfortable place. Would anyone cut her up and take bits of her flesh home with them as souvenirs—as was done to Ivan? She could still feel that she was not quite dead.

Mischu, the cat, ran to Eric who was with Zachariah savoring the afternoon sun. The cat meowed incessantly scratching at Eric's leg and arms.

"What's gotten into him?" Zachariah asked.

Eric rose from where he was sitting, and the cat immediately reacted by darting away and turning back to look at him. From this Eric understood that something was wrong. Eric told Zachariah that something had happened to Ella. They followed the cat and drew upon this creature's knowledge that he tried to impart to them.

Zachariah was now placed in the position of having to turn to someone other than his granddaughter for assistance. He had to trust. As his granddaughter had always been there for him, it was his turn to be there for her. And he sent Eric after Raymond Fletcher.

Raymond attended to Ella's bruised neck. He gave her some water. Zachariah and Eric were in the room. Zachariah asked her why she did what she did. She recounted for them the awful story of Ivanhoe Miller and the woman in the crowd who said he died for having stolen the alligator nutcracker from Mrs. Haversham, when in fact Ella lying in her bedroom finally admitted her guilt to the theft. There was an inexhaustible sadness in her voice. She sounded like she was speaking her last words as the images of Ivan's burned body—real and fixed—assumed a tangible almost obscene form of diabolical proportions that she did not want to live.

Zachariah told Ella that she was not to be blamed for Ivan's death. He opened the night table drawer and searched all the way in the back until he felt the smooth wood of the nutcracker. "I've had a good many nuts with this thing," he said. "And you were right my dear, it's a lot easier crackin' them things with this than with my chops, but I think it's about time we brought this back to the lady. I'll take care of it myself."

Eric explained to Ella that it was all a big misunderstanding. Ivan found some woman's broche that she had lost, and she accused him of stealing it. There was trouble, and he killed a man. Ella listened, and she sank into a deep sleep.

Zachariah returned the nutcracker to Mrs. Haversham and begged for forgiveness for his granddaughter's act. Mrs. Haversham was so pleased that it was returned that she invited Zachariah inside for coffee and conversation. The nutcracker matter was never mentioned again.

Chapter 28

The gathering menace to the town included those whom the laws had trampled on in the killing of their people without mercy and without trial. Although they knew they were weak individually, when they heard the cries of anguish for a brief moment from Ivanhoe Miller, they took the savagery of the lynchers and made it their own. Now it was time for retribution for the killing of an innocent man. The mob moved swiftly with a deliberate awareness of their collective power.

The Kramer household was awakened by a sudden unmistakable bang of gunfire and angry voices echoing from the street. Giny ran to the window where a mob of black men armed with guns, fuel filled bottles, and torches spread out indiscriminately beating up people, smashing windows with rocks and whatever else they had, and randomly shooting into homes.

Giny was in bed when a stray bullet shot across her bedroom and landed in the wall.

"It's a riot!" shouted Michael as he burst through the door and pulled Giny out and down the cellar. Eric got his rifle, and with eyes widened, resolved to defend the house. Michael quickly took the rifle from him, kissed him on the head, and ordered him down the cellar with his mother.

"Don't come out till I say so!" he commanded.

Someone threw a large rock at the living room window. Michael ran to see that their defenses were down. In the shattered window, Michael saw two black men with the flames of hell in their eyes, armed and determined to break into the house. One of the men tried to climb through the broken window; Michael cocked the rifle and fired. The man's head exploded into a fine mist. He landed with a hard crashing thud onto the porch. Brain matter and blood splattered all over the place.

The other man was stunned when he was hit in the face by his friend's brains. It stirred his blood to see a buddy killed, and vengeance darkened his heart. He went to light a fuel filled bottle when Michael shot him in the arm. That didn't stop the man from throwing the bottle through the window and bursting into flames. The man still wasn't satisfied. He aimed his gun at Michael and fired. The bullet collided with Michael's chest and exploded inside him. Michael's legs no longer supporting him were featherweight against a force sending him several feet into the air. An immense sheet of flame emerged from the chairs to the rug to the curtains and spread quickly. Eric came out of the cellar with Giny and saw Michael on the floor. The fire raged. The man outside aimed for one final blow to his injured brother. Eric leaped at the rifle and buried two bullets into the man sending him to join his buddy on the porch, both dead for sure.

Another bottle intended for the upstairs of the Kramer house missed its target and broke apart on the limbs of the great oak tree. The birds flew to the roof of the Whitman house as it was not on fire and therefore safer. The two starlings had mated and were planning a family of their own. They built their nest, and there were four eggs in it—pale blue in color and the size of a quarter. They watched as the flames quickly disintegrated the leaves of the tree.

"Our home is in flames!" cried the starling. "Our children!"

"Get a hold of yourself!" urged her mate. "We have to get the eggs out of the nest!"

"It's too dangerous," said the finch. The female starling was too petrified to go into the tree as the fire leapt, foamed, and rippled against the bark. The female mourning dove that stood by her, volunteered to help the starling's mate drop the eggs from the nest.

"Don't go!" cried the starling. "It's suicide!"

The starling flew into the water dish in the feeder and soaked himself thoroughly.

The mourning dove followed him into the water dish.

"It would please me greatly, my dear, if you didn't risk your life," said the male starling.

"Nonsense!" screamed the dove. "That's what neighbors are for. We're wasting time. Let's go before it's too late!"

The mourning dove and the starling flew into the dense smoke and were showered by flaming leaves and falling twigs. The heat was intolerable. One by one, with their beaks, they tossed the four eggs out of the tree and onto the grass below in the hope that at least one egg would not crack as it hit the ground.

The female starling flew down to her eggs and in a circular pattern flew around them, spinning and spinning hysterically. It rained, burning leaves and branches, so it was difficult to land. After the deed was done, the other birds flew around the dropped eggs in the same spinning fashion getting closer to the ground to inspect if any eggs could be saved.

Suddenly Mischu, the cat, noticed their plight and dashed toward the dropped eggs in an effort to help. He was singed by the burning leaves. The birds became crazed with fright.

"He's going to eat the eggs!" the birds screamed with anguish, thinking that all was lost after the rescue effort. The mourning dove assured them that the cat would not harm the eggs. Mischu saw that only one egg had not cracked, so he picked up the egg carefully in his mouth and dashed into the Kramer's shed where he sprinted up to the worktable and carefully dropped the egg in a wooden box Michael used for tool bits.

The Whitman home was being riddled with bullets. Maggie grabbed her handgun, and they went to the kitchen lured by the orange glow of fire outside.

"The chicken coop and the oak tree are burning! What can we do?" screamed Abby.

"There's nothing to do, they are everywhere! If we go out, they'll kill us!"

"No! I've got to free them!" Abby cried.

Maggie looked at the mayhem outside. Everybody was running wild. Abby pumped a bucketful of water and ran out of the kitchen with the speed of a deer to the burning coop; she opened the fence and splashed the water at the front door to the coop to open it and let the chickens out. She prayed the birds in the burning oak tree were all right. She got too close, and flames set her skirt on fire. Maggie came running after her daughter's screams and wrapped her child in blankets to smother the fire. They both rushed back into the house. Abby had some burns on her legs, but she was luckier than some. The chickens sprang loose through the door, and they wandered out of the fence and into the obscene roar of violence where no one knew a place of safety. The rows of houses were ablaze.

Black smoke billowed overhead. Eric had put out the fire carrying buckets from the kitchen pump. He wiped his forehead and listened to the faint cries of his neighbors as the violence moved out of his section into another. Giny gave the last echoes of prayer as her son lay mortally wounded on the ground where they found him. Eric came over and stood in silence.

Mischu suddenly appeared at the broken window and sniffed around before climbing into the black-coated living room.

"Go on! Get out of here!" shouted Giny.

"Let him be," Eric said. "I've called the police and Dr. Fletcher."

Mischu had burn marks on his body, and he went over to Michael and curled up beside him.

"You see, Momma, he is doing what he is meant to do," Eric spoke as the man of the house.

Mischu left the Kramer home in the night. He walked by the sheet-covered bodies that lay in the street. In the sadness and turmoil around him, it was time to move on. He had done his work. The pain of being was hopelessly engrained in his watching eyes. And he could no longer stay in a place where people killed each other so mercilessly. He would continue to hold vigil with and mourn the passing of those who he sensed needed to be comforted in their last hours. He would continue to meet the challenges of an unfriendly world with joy in the company of other strays, abandoned but not alone.

Chapter 29

The town had survived the uproar, and it was time to bury the dead. The police cleared all the double-parked carriages and cars in preparation for the funeral procession. Vast crowds crammed the sidewalks to remember the victims of the riot. Flags flew at half-mast. Everywhere there were people, people, people, sharing the grief, looking through shop windows from the inside when there was no room to stand in the street, poking their heads out of windows in buildings holding the American flag in their hands. The display was dazzling in its solemn splendor.

The church sounded its bells, but it was not the pleasant doubled toned chime that announced services would begin in fifteen minutes. It was the mournful toll of a funeral. Once the bells tolled, everything stopped. The tailor stopped cutting fabric; the cabinetmaker stopped hammering, went outside, and bowed their heads with the others at the same hour.

Two unmounted horses preceded each coffin followed by family members of the deceased walking behind. The sudden emotional poverty of their loss was so great for some mourners that they were escorted out of the procession to rest by the sidewalk until they recovered well enough to rejoin the funeral march or go home. Giny Kramer, Eric, and coworkers from the lumber company, where Michael worked, followed behind his softwood coffin, draped with the American flag.

There was no solemn music playing, no drums. A light rain fell on the crowd which came prepared with lighted candles and opened umbrellas. The only sound complementing the rainfall was the clicking of shoes and grinding against the pavement. A tragedy of this sort, any tragedy really, made for something to talk about at the dinner table.

As Giny walked behind her son's coffin, the immensity of the gathering failed to move her broken spirit, until she spotted Maggie in the crowd, and at once Giny broke from the procession that stopped as onlookers watched the two women embrace as the distant formality of Maggie's occasional presence in the mercantile store was a thing of the past.

Maggie raised her umbrella to shield Giny from the rain, but it wasn't large enough to accommodate the two women, so they got wet. They bent their heads together under the umbrella as if there was an essential connection after all the years of silence between them. Giny invited Maggie to join her, and the procession resumed amid applause from the crowd with the two women walking arm in arm.

"It's amazing how this neighborhood turns out to give you a pat on the back when they know you're down," Giny said. "Otherwise you'd never even know they exist. Isn't that right?"

"They're offering their condolences, just like me," Maggie said.

In the crowd were also William Corrigan and Henrietta. Corrigan saw Lydia Ramon in the crowd carrying her son, their son. She glanced in his direction and turned away. It was understood as part of the agreement between them that Corrigan would finance both her and their son for life as long as she never spoke that the child was his.

At the cemetery, the rain ended, and the clouds remained as patches of misty gray cotton balls hovering while the sun shone through speckled with memories of the crowd drifting up and away.

Abby looked up to a large, lone cypress tree that rested on a hill above the cemetery. The tree was split in the middle, and its branches twisted outward and spread itself offering a comfortable shade. She noticed the man standing below the tree looking down at the burial and turned to her mother.

"That's Henry Corrigan," she said.

After the ceremony was over, Henry took the train back to Philadelphia. He thought about the old woman and sought comfort in her presence. The diner was closed, so he was able to prepare a ham and cheese sandwich and a container of coffee to bring to her without any hassle from Clingman. He went to the park where they met. She wasn't there. Disappointed, he ate the sandwich, drank the coffee, and explored the barren wasteland of closed factories and rotting front entrances while remembering Michael Kramer. He knew this was a dangerous part of town at night. It was rumored that there were gangs who claimed certain vacant areas as a hangout.

He heard the sound of boys shouting from behind the skeletal remains of an old textile factory. It was loud and disturbing enough for Henry to ponder whether to ignore it and go home or see what was happening. *A gang fighting with knives, maybe guns,* he thought. He walked to the chipped light blue paint of the entrance door. With each step, the shouting grew. He wasn't more than just a couple of steps away when the door burst open and a boy shot through it. The boy was shirtless, sweaty, wearing dirty jeans, and he had a massive cut on his forehead. He stank of smoke and drink. Henry grabbed hold of him but the boy panting for breath pushed him away and ran into the night.

Henry went inside the abandoned building, where he saw three more teenage boys beating on a person. Henry picked up an empty bottle and threw it in their direction. The boys stopped their assault and produced knives to threaten him. Henry wouldn't succumb to fear in the presence of these hoodlums. He shouted for them to leave the building as the police were on their way. They didn't believe him until a police siren made them scatter like rats to Henry's relief. The boys rushed out to rusted bicycles that looked like they were dug out of a swamp. With defiant smiles at their accomplishment, one boy pulled out a packet of chewing tobacco and passed it to the other boys. One boy climbed behind him on the bike, and they quickly peddled away, separating as the night swallowed them.

Henry ran to the victim who lay motionless on the ground. It was a woman. He knelt down and slowly turned her over. It was the old woman, his friend, who he searched for but could not find, until now. She was unconscious, badly beaten about the face and head. He pulled out his handkerchief and wiped her face. The police arrived in the building and with them was the young boy who had run from the building before.

"Why did you attack this lady?" Henry shouted to the boy. "Are you so weak that you have to gang up on other people to feel strong?"

"I didn't!" the boy replied. "I tried to help when they got me on the head." Henry looked at him again. His right eye was swollen and nearly closed. Blood covered half his face.

"Considering the bruises on his face, sir, I believe the boy when he says he tried to help her," one of the cops said. "Unless you think he caused those bruises to himself?"

Henry didn't respond. He gave the boy his handkerchief that he used on the old woman. The woman was taken to the hospital. Henry was there in her room all night.

The doctor spoke with Henry in his consulting room. He told him that the woman had no identification on her. No one knew her name.

Henry was beside himself that he never asked her name.

"Did she mention any relatives?" asked the doctor.

"No," Henry replied.

"If there are any relatives, we can't locate them until we know who she is?"

"They beat her pretty bad," the doctor said. "I don't know if she's going to make it or not."

Henry went into her darkroom where a single light shone on her pale face. She was still unconscious. He watched the agonizing effort it took for her to inhale and exhale. He wondered if living had been as painful for her as it was for him and that perhaps death might be a welcomed release. He wondered if she had ever loved in her youth or even recently in her troubled state. He sat there stricken with the prospect that she would become a distant memory for him very soon.

Henry got up to go to the cafeteria to get a coffee and escape the depressing smell of disinfectant in the room and in the halls. When he returned, suddenly the woman knew he was there. She opened her eyes a little, and the slight smile on her face acknowledged that she was happy he was there. She managed to say his name very softly. Henry still didn't know hers. He went over to her bedside astonished and glad that she had awakened.

"I'm here," he said.

Her only response was that she wanted him to hold her hand for minute. As Henry took her frail hand in his, he watched her slowly go to sleep. He tried to figure out the best way he could save her in the future. Mulling the sparse options, the only thing suitable was for her to live with him. They both had one thing in common. They were isolated and alone. If they lived together, he could look after her, buy her some clothes, and get her to a doctor. This was a turning point for Henry Corrigan who while sitting in that darkroom holding the hand of his friend, did not know he would blossom into a very different person from then on. The continued practice of living for himself and not caring for anyone else whom he regarded as inferior was mercifully over. The old woman may have lost her luster years ago and no doubt the same would happen to him. He would wake up one morning and feel his limbs stiffen with pain, and he knew he would not be mellow about it but would curse the stars as he lamented his unfulfilled past. This he vowed as he caressed her hand would not happen to him while he still had time on his side.

The woman, whose name he did not know, was raised from her bed, floated through the hospital walls, and in the infinite horizon before her, she came to those who she knew in life and in spirit. They complimented her on her greatest achievement that she had transformed a spoiled young man who had it all and found himself living in the dumps and made him see he could no longer neglect the world around him. It was proof that sometimes people could be changed for the better. A job well done!

The two boys who followed the broche woman in the park had some time to kill, so they decided to go game hunting with their bow and arrow. They spotted a starling and a mourning dove together on a fence.

"Go ahead. It's a double kill," one boy whispered to his friend.

"I'm nervous."

"Don't overshoot."

They giggled at the prospect of their first kill. He took aim.

"Careful."

"Shut up."

"We must go!" cried the starling. "They're aiming at us!"

"They don't want to you," said the dove. "They want me. Go now."

"You'll just allow yourself to be killed."

"Go back to the tree and raise your young, and have as many babies as you can. When you see my children, tell them I love them. Go, my friend. We will see each other again."

The starling flew away and heard the silent snap of the arrow as it pierced the dove's heart and she fell. She was killed instantly. Her body lay in a crimson circle of blood and feathers defined in the green grass. She had scarcely ceased to breathe when her killers, screaming with crazed joy of their conquest, picked her up by the arrow deep inside her, dangled her lifeless body upside down to shake off more feathers, and marveled at the wound and the preciseness of the aim. Before dying, the dove remembered what the crow had said, that she would be rewarded for her forgiveness of his evil acts by seeing all of her loved ones in that perfect place called heaven.

Abby awoke to the sound of a mourning dove that landed on her windowsill calling out. It was not her beloved mourning dove. She was gone. Abby thought perhaps she had fled for good during the night of terror. She thought this to be one of her young, perhaps the one she nursed back to health, but it had been so long, and she wasn't sure. The dove walked along the windowsill for about ten minutes interacting with the woman who saved his life when he was a squab and about whom his mother had spoken so fondly. He flew back to the oak tree which was growing back its leaves, and soon its thrusting limbs would be back bending and twisting in all its lavishness. This was the place he called home. The dove rejoined his mate in the tree. His sister and her mate and the mated starlings had built their nests there and nursed their young in the spirit of their collective instinct for survival and in the spirit of the esteemed courageous mourning dove no longer visible to them in whose heart she knew when it was time to do battle and live and when it was time to die. These birds infected with the breath of life would continue to soar high up into the sky doing cartwheels until the day turned into night.

Chapter 30

New York 1930, Carnegie Hall

Abigail Whitman was invited to play at Carnegie Hall for the first time. Twenty years earlier, it never would have dawned on her that she would even be alive at this point. By choice she had decided to discontinue the experimental cancer treatment that the late Raymond Fletcher had recommended. She realized that it might prove fatal for her to do so, but it was her life, and the choice was hers. She decided to use whatever time she had to follow the advice of her friend Madison Hendricks, to make music her life and to practice and grow with it.

The representatives of the hall had asked Abby what she would like to play. Abby told them without hesitation that she wanted to play the Rachmaninoff Piano Concerto no. 2. It was the music that Madison had wanted her to play. This concert would be a benefit concert to raise funds for the Madison Hendricks School of Musical Studies. This was to be Abby's honor to Madison.

On the night of the concert, Abby walked alone through the artists' entrance backstage. She looked through the door that led to the stage and saw the Steinway piano sitting there all alone, beckoning to be played. The audience sat and waited, anticipating, longing for Abby to express something that was valid in their lives.

In the audience were Maggie, Eric Kramer and his wife Ella, who ran their own general store in Philadelphia where trade was brisk. His mother Giny was also there. Zachariah lived to walk his granddaughter down the aisle when she and Eric married. That was the happiest moment in his long life. Shortly afterward, he died. Henry Corrigan was also there. He had done well in his own right as a restaurant owner in New York. After the concert, he was throwing a party for Abby, and they were all invited to celebrate the evening at his restaurant in midtown. Madison's mother, Diana, was also there in her daughter's memory. It was the happiest moment of her life.

The whole thing promoted more nerves for Abby. She thought how on earth she could face anyone again if she failed that night! She remembered what Madison said, "Forget about the critics. Some will like you, some will not." It didn't matter. What mattered was that the music spoke to Abby, and through her talent, she passed its beauty onto the audience. She hoped to be worthy of the privilege of playing for them. Playing for the pleasure of moving others as Beethoven said, "From the heart to the heart."

Abby did not eat anything since breakfast, and she felt some hunger pangs. She asked one of the staff for a drink of water. She breathed slowly and deeply, and she was calm until the time came for her to go onstage and play for the world. The world was in that auditorium.

At the end of the performance, Sergei Rachmaninoff himself walked on stage to greet Abby and to thank her for an inspirational rendering of his composition. She was without words and thought embarrassingly she would faint. It was probably just as well that she didn't know he was present before the recital, otherwise her nerves would have gotten the best of her, and she would have cracked under the strain of his presence. This was the man in her dreams on the day she told her mother about her cancer. She never forgot the image of his face.

As Abby left to join her family and friends, she was swarmed by fans, and she graciously signed programs and received compliment after compliment on her performance. Henry pushed his way through the crowd and said if she wasn't out in five minutes, they were leaving without her. She smiled back and kept on signing. Abby said she would be there soon. He blew her a kiss and went outside to the cars to take them to his restaurant. When the crowd thinned out a bit, Abby received another program to sign from a man in his eighties somewhat thin and frosty like in his gaze but appreciative of the opportunity to meet her. Abby looked at the man and asked if they had met before. The man said no and thanked her for a lovely evening. Abby signed the program for the man and returned the thanks and went to the waiting cars. A lady came up to the man and commented on how fine a pianist Abigail Whitman was. The man agreed wholeheartedly.

"That's my daughter."

Edwards Brothers,Inc!
Thorofare, NJ 08086
07 October, 2010
BA2010281